Time out of Mind

Time out of Mind

by

GRAHAM LORD

HAMISH HAMILTON

London

First published in Great Britain 1986
by Hamish Hamilton Ltd
Garden House 57–59 Long Acre London WC2E 9JZ

Copyright © 1986 by Graham Lord

British Library Cataloguing in Publication Data

Lord, Graham
    Time out of mind.
    I. Title
    823'.914[F]   PR6062.072
    ISBN 0–241–11876–X

Typeset at The Spartan Press Ltd, Lymington, Hants
Printed in Great Britain by
St Edmundsbury Press, Bury St Edmunds, Suffolk

For Mandy

'Each age is a dream that is dying,
Or one that is coming to birth.'

Arthur O'Shaughnessy, *Ode*

I

There comes a time for all of us when we start to think too much about death. So I killed myself.

I had been having too many dreams about corpses. I would wake in the night with my heart thundering, and the green luminous numbers on the digital alarm clock beside the bed seemed a grim omen: it was always 2.22 or 3.33 or 4.44. Sometimes I would be gasping for breath; sometimes I woke with an inexplicable terror and clutched my wife, as though the sleeping warmth of her flesh alone could keep me alive.

The doctor could find nothing wrong. Physically I was in good health, and there was nothing much amiss with my mind. I suspected that I was suffering a disease of the soul because I felt I had nothing much to live for any more. It was my soul, not my body, that was dying. It had run out of dreams worth dreaming, and had nothing left but nightmares.

I knew that the answer was to change my life. What had once been just a mildly boring rut had become a ditch and was threatening to deepen into a chasm. My marriage had been happy enough, my children quite fun, my career reasonably successful, my hobbies and lifestyle not unsatisfying. But they had all become so humdrum. There seemed to be no challenges left, and I rebelled against the possibility that this dull, predictable existence was all I could expect, for year after year, until the nightmare of death finally came true.

It happens to many men of about my age. Most of them grind their teeth and live through it, forcing themselves to believe that they can live without dreams and accepting the passing years and the inevitability of their small failures. Some of them change their jobs, as though a different form of slavery will make some difference. Some of them run off with new women, as though different lips and arms and legs will somehow change their own. Some, in despair, commit suicide or punish themselves with

I

drink. None of these alternatives appealed to me. I decided to change everything, even my name. For the good of my soul I decided to be born again.

If you've read *The Day of the Jackal* by Frederick Forsyth you'll know how easy it is to take on a new identity. You just steal the name of a dead stranger who was born about the same year as you were. It's simple after that to buy a copy of the dead man's birth certificate, and that will allow you to apply for a new passport and probably even for social security. And then you merely disappear, and start again as whoever you choose to be, unburdened by your past or by your future.

Why don't more of us do it? The answer is fear, and superstition: fear of the unknown, of the loss of everything so familiar to us; and superstition that to give up your identity is to give up something of the essence of yourself. I overcame my own fear and went ahead and did it. I took the name of a dead stranger, and changed my life, and was born again. But I never conquered the superstition. Knowing what I do now, I suspect that when you take the name of a dead man you also steal his soul.

Of course I felt guilty about abandoning my wife. She had tried so hard to make me happy, and she had been a good mother. But the children were almost adults and I no longer felt, as once I had, that she and I were one flesh. I had often idly considered leaving her, but I had never been selfish enough to make the children fatherless when they were small. And to be honest I had also been afraid of the loneliness you see in the eyes of middle-aged men without women, and I had dreaded the prospect of paying alimony and living in a bedsitter. At least my wife still warmed my bed and drained my lust.

'Don't you ever think of anything but sex?' she had asked.

'Not when I'm with you,' I had said, and she had taken it as a compliment. But it wasn't. There was nothing else we had in common. Neither of us was especially to blame. It was not her fault that the brilliant green eyes I had loved so much had faded. A marriage has no villains: it has only heroes and heroines who defy logic and fate and sometimes succeed. Ironically many of our acquaintances considered us the ideal couple and failed to understand that this was an insult to each of us, since she and I both felt we deserved better. We were good together in public and called each other darling, but sometimes it seemed we did so only because we had forgotten each other's real names.

Don't get me wrong. It was not a bad marriage, and certainly no worse that millions of others. We were comfortable enough, successful enough, popular enough. We liked our children and they liked us. We were tolerant of each other's weaknesses and considerate enough to hide our occasional infidelities: she discovered only two of mine, I learned of only one of hers and never mentioned it. We were pretty civilised, and there was no violence, no great rows or sulks or hatred of each other. Perhaps that was part of the trouble. There was not much passion of any sort. I had always enjoyed books, but now I was reading far too much, anything at all, from Chandler to Pepys, to escape my everyday dullness. Reading is no substitute for life, and a marriage needs peaks and depths, reds and golds as well as pastels. Ours was an off-white marriage that slowly turned pale grey without any drama. She had stopped laughing at my jokes, and I had stopped bothering to make any. It was all so *ordinary*, and I wanted to be special. I needed to massage my numbed emotions back into life with surprises, risk, fear, exhilaration, maybe even hatred. It was not that we had nothing left to give each other: we had nothing left that we wanted to take.

'Do you ever wish you had married someone else?' she had asked.

'No,' I had said, and it was true, and again she took it as a compliment. But again she was wrong. I never wished I had married someone else because marriage to her had put me off the idea for life.

'It's funny,' she said, 'I always know when you're telling the truth. Your eyes go all liquid and soft and trusting, like a monkey's.'

'Charming.'

'And when you're annoyed they go hard and black.'

'What rubbish.'

'It's true. And when you're randy they're brown.'

'And when I'm lying?'

'You don't look at me at all. You haven't done that for a long time, not since that last stupid woman of yours.'

If I'd stopped even taking the trouble to lie to her any more, then the marriage was surely dead.

3

I spotted the stranger's tombstone in a suburban cemetery on a bleak autumn day. We were there for the funeral of an elderly relative, doing the decent thing although we had never been particularly close.

'Do we really have to go?' I said.

'It would look odd if we didn't. The rest of the family will be there.'

'Only out of guilt, or hoping to pick up a family heirloom afterwards.'

'Why are you always so cynical?' she said. 'You always expect people to have the very worst motives.'

'Only because they usually do. Within a couple of months they'll be squabbling over the will, and the ones left out will never speak again to the ones who've been left something. We haven't seen the old lady for years. We could never be bothered to visit her when she was alive.'

'That's different. She's dead now.'

I was never one of those husbands who complain that their wives don't understand them. Mine understood me only too well. It was I who didn't understand her.

At the graveside we stood back a little, as seemed fitting for the more distant relatives, and while the priest mumbled and a niece sobbed quietly I glanced away and noticed a startlingly vulgar grave covered with bright green gravel, as though the garish colour of summer could warm the corpse beneath. What unfortunate stranger had been consigned to so tasteless a resting place? The tombstone told me. There, engraved in stark capitals, was the name I was to take. But it was not the name, it was the dates of the stranger's birth and death that jolted me into the recognition that was to spur me finally, at last, to make the effort to change my life. For he had been born the same year as I, and already he was dead. Without knowing each other, the stranger and I must have shared so much: the same childhood crazes, the same school textbooks, the same teenage music, the same first fantasies of similar girls. And already he was dead.

Something slithered in my mind. If he could be dead already then so could I tomorrow, next week, next year. Yes, yes, we all have to die, of course, but we don't have to die bored. I knew then precisely what I was going to do.

My wife nudged me as we turned to leave the cemetery and

4

muttered, 'Stop grinning, for God's sake. This is meant to be a funeral.'

'Funerals always make me feel cheerful,' I said. 'They remind me of life.'

'There are times, darling, when you can be damned irritating. Just try and look miserable, will you?'

'It won't be easy,' I said, but it was. I thought of the stranger and imagined I might be him.

I bought a copy of the dead man's birth certificate and discovered that he had been born in this country. But there were two surprises that made me hesitate. The address of his mother was given as somewhere in the tropics, not far from the Equator. And the space for the name of his father was blank. My alter ego was a bastard.

I hesitated for only a moment, and then laughed. It seemed so appropriate, because I too was about to be a bastard: to my wife, the children, the insurance companies who would eventually pay out large amounts when they would be forced to accept that I was probably dead. Already the stranger and I had something in common, and already his life and death had begun to tease my imagination. Why should his mother have come so far from home to have her bastard baby? To hide the scandal from the gossips back at home? And who had paid for her trip and the hospital? The unknown father?

Curious, I bought a copy of his death certificate as well. That provided the third surprise. The stranger had committed suicide.

I confess I shuddered superstitiously, and briefly considered forgetting all about him and his name. There must be plenty of other men born in the same year and now dead of something less dramatic. Any of their identities would suit my purpose, any name. But then I pulled myself together and told myself not to be so ridiculous. What's in a death? That had nothing to do with me. And as for suicide, wasn't I about to commit it myself?

Should I tell you the name I took and the name I had? No, it's better not to. The insurance companies would realise they had been conned and would demand their money back, and my wife would be destitute. I didn't want that. And anyway, the names don't matter. It was my soul that mattered, not my name. Can a name affect your soul? I didn't think so then. Now I'm not so sure. When I signed the dead man's name for the first time I felt oddly confident. It was almost as though something was guiding my hand.

Thousands of men each year just disappear one day and never come home again. They shave and dress as usual, they grunt at their wives and children over breakfast, they leave the house at the normal time, and they never look back. They simply walk away. Perhaps they take off with another woman, perhaps they go to ground somewhere new, with a different name, and start again. But unforgivably they leave no clues, and they never get in touch. Their wives and families are left to wonder, to suffer nightmares of uncertainty, and are not even allowed the dignity of grief. Such silent men must have hated their wives very much indeed to torture them so coldly.

I didn't hate mine, and I couldn't treat her so brutally. After all these years together, and two children, she deserved at least the courtesy of a decent lie. Just walking out on her would have seemed to be monstrously callous, and merely to pretend that I had another woman seemed crass and unimaginative. Even nowadays, with divorce so common, the wounds of separation still cut deep. One of the cruellest things a husband can do to his wife is to make it plain that another woman is so much more desirable that the marriage can never recover. A marriage can survive adultery, because adultery is mainly about sex, but to leave your partner for another is a vicious denial of love, a rejection of everything you have shared together. It is a sort of slow murder.

Death is much kinder than divorce, and to pretend to be dead is at least polite. Every wife expects that one day she will be a widow. It's a simple matter of statistics, and the knowledge of this inevitability is probably built into the female genes – otherwise why do widows survive their husbands' deaths so much better than widowers do the deaths of their wives? Widowers go to pieces. Widows often blossom, and do their damnedest to prove that there is indeed life after death. At the time of a husband's death, of course, a widow may be stricken

6

with misery and fear. But death, unlike separation, marks a clean break from which it is possible to recover. It is so final it leaves no doubts, recriminations or feelings of rejection and betrayal. A husband's death need be only the long, cold winter before spring returns.

I knew my wife would weep, and I was sorry about that. But the tears would be cleansing and at least they would give her the consolation of bereavement. She would mourn for me, even pity me for dying too young, and my 'death' would allow her to remember only our good times together. It would brighten her happiest memories and fade the bad ones, and leave her thinking of me fondly. Before too long she too would begin to live again. She was still not too old to find another man. By liberating myself I was freeing her, too. I was doing us both a favour.

The children? Yes, they would grieve, but not for too long, and mainly for themselves rather than for me. Teenagers are selfish and resilient. Their world is too exciting and bewildering for them to wallow in sorrow. I had given them life, but that didn't mean they were entitled to claim the rest of mine. Above all, at least they could never blame me for dying. I would not be leaving them a legacy of bitterness.

In fact their legacy would be a generous one. I had always taken out far more insurance than was strictly necessary, perhaps to prove to myself that I really did care for the family, and although the insurance companies would howl with suspicion when no body was found, the sea offers a rare and private escape and the assessors could hardly insist on a body. They would probably refuse to pay up until seven years had passed and I was officially presumed dead, but they would have to pay up in the end, and pay up handsomely. Until then I knew that my fellow directors would be generous towards my wife and family. They would take care of their financial needs. They had always been good that way in the past, and like the deaths of other colleagues at work mine would be swiftly forgotten. Within a few weeks I would be worth no more than an anecdote or two, just now and then, when the whiskies had been poured a little too often. And the anecdotes would not always be affectionate, either. That too I knew from previous deaths. It is now quite the done thing to speak ill of the dead, as though to scorn our old superstitions and to deny our own terror of mortality. I rather wished I could return in disguise to overhear what my friends and colleagues really thought of me.

It didn't take long to arrange. We are meant to be riddled with cynicism these days but in fact many people are curiously trusting. It was easy to increase the mortgage on the house by several thousand to give my new self some spending money. I merely pretended I wanted to build an extension, and the cheque was in the post almost as soon as I had sent them the builders's estimate.

I paid the cheque into my normal account, withdrew it in cash a few days later, and paid that into a new account in my new name at a different bank. They swiftly gave me a cheque book, a banker's card, even a credit card. Money-lenders are the easiest touch in the world. It's their greed, I suppose. I was briefly tempted to fly to Hawaii and blow the lot in an orgy, but that would hardly have solved my problems.

The money sat in the bank, waiting. I left it for a week while I worked out what to do. I would treat myself to a quick escape, a plane trip towards the sun. I needed sun. My life had been overcast for too long. But to keep the cost down and make the money last as long as possible it would only be a short hop by plane and first I would spend a few days of blissful anonymity in a city, a big city where I could lose myself, where I'd never been before and ran little danger of bumping into anyone I knew. I would soak myself in freedom and aloneness. I would do everything and nothing. And after that, who knows? I would move on whenever I pleased, sometimes stopping for a day, sometimes stopping for a month. I might even take on the odd casual job if I felt like it. But I would make no firm plans. Firm plans were what had already suffocated me. For twenty years I had known precisely what I would be doing the next day, and I was not going to lock myself into any similar straitjacket again. Instead I would wake each morning with eager anticipation, not knowing what I might be doing two hours later nor where I might be next week. I deliberately made myself empty, and waited to be filled.

It was a long, slow week of anticipation. I was nervous, of course. What I was going to do was a criminal offence. Not only was I about to waste an immense amount of police time and public money as the coastguards and lifeboats searched for my non-

8

existent body: I was also about to defraud the insurance companies of hundreds of thousands. But there was also a heightened, dreamlike quality about that week. Time seemed suspended, and even the leafless winter trees were starkly beautiful. I found myself smiling at strangers, and curiously tender towards my wife. I watched her as she moved about the house, as though to fix her firmly in my memory. Her legs were still good, her body slim, her breasts girlish. For the first time in many years, oddly, I felt a powerful surge of lust for her. Is it true that when a man is hanged he has a final massive orgasm? I can well believe it. Knowing that your life is about to end at a specific time must be powerfully erotic, as though your genes like rats are desperate to escape the doomed vessel. Perhaps a condemned man deserves a final woman as well as a final meal. Until then our lovemaking had been rarely more than twice a fortnight, but three times that last week I ravished her, twice with a fierce longing. Already she seemed as exciting as a stranger, her body new again and unexplored. She never denied me. I certainly can't complain about that, and on the Friday I nearly changed my mind and decided to stay after all. Was this life really so bad? I had money, security, position, comfort, good food, wine, warmth, books and a woman to wrap her legs around me at night. My life would seem enviable to ninety per cent of all the men who have ever lived. But it still wasn't enough. I had to force myself to be resolute. It was not, after all, some sudden decision. I had dreamed of it for years.

Had she shown the slightest excitement that week I might well have faltered and postponed my disappearance, maybe for ever. But she went through the motions and groaned when she thought she ought to groan, and afterwards she yawned. She knew her duty as a wife, but that's all it remained – a duty. For her the urgency had long gone. It was not completely her fault. I was surely to blame as well. But I might have been no more than a whore's customer. She was merely servicing me, as she might oil a hinge: it made for a quieter life, and stopped me squeaking.

'Darling?' I said on our last night together, knowing I would never make love to her again.

'Mmmm,' she said afterwards, absentmindedly. We might have been sharing a bar of chocolate.

I had not hated her often, in all our years together, but I hated her then. She should have sensed that something was different and that tomorrow she would be a widow.

That night I dreamed of the green gravel grave and the faceless stranger, and I twitched in my sleep as though something had entered my soul.

I killed my old self on a wintry Saturday when the sea was as grey as my previous life.

From the moment I woke at home that morning for the last time I moved through the day like a zombie, as though I were no longer master of my actions but merely driven by some irresistible force.

Her sleeping face on the pillow seemed unfamiliar, the closed eyes sunk deeper than I remembered, the cheekbones gaunt, the flesh loose around the chin. She still smelled of me and yet I hardly knew her. My own face in the bathroom mirror looked lifelessly back at me, the eyes dead. My hand scraped at the stubble on my chin like an old man raking autumn leaves.

'Are you okay, Dad?' said one of the children. 'You look like a ghost.'

I stared at him, puzzled. Was he really my flesh? Had he really come from my body and from the corpse-like body of the strange woman lying upstairs? His voice echoed as though it came from another world.

'I'm fine,' I muttered. 'Just tired. I didn't sleep much.'

'You look terrible. You ought to go back to bed.'

No. Not that bed. Not ever again.

'I'm all right.'

I forced myself to eat some breakfast because they knew I was going fishing that day and I always ate a huge breakfast before I went fishing, to make up for a lunch of only bread and cheese. None of them ever came fishing with me. I had always been grateful for their lack of interest. Fishing had often helped me to kill at least a part of those interminable weekends.

I collected my tackle.

'I'm off, then,' I said.

My son was reading the paper. I felt a pang of love for him, for that bent head and gawky body that had once been so defenceless. But he didn't even reply. I hoped he would always remember that, and never forgive himself. Even as a zombie I needed someone else to share my guilt.

On the way to the coast I stopped in a town where I had never been before to buy a towel and a cheap old second-hand folding bicycle. Then I chose a rugged part of the coast where I didn't often go, a good 150 miles away, and drove to a deserted cove where I hid the bicycle and some dry clothes and shoes. So it was afternoon by the time I had hired a boat. I knew there were dangerous rocks not too far offshore, and treacherous tides, and the swell was enough for the boatman to warn me about the conditions and the weather.

'I've been in far worse than this,' I said. 'I've been sailing for twenty years.'

'So had the skipper of the *Titanic*,' he grunted.

I laughed. It sounded distant and tinny. 'I won't exactly be dancing below decks all night with the passengers,' I said, 'and I don't see any icebergs.'

'Nor did he.' He shrugged. 'It's your funeral,' he said, and my guts lurched. The sky was the colour of old weathered stone.

I insisted on paying for the hire of the boat by cheque, pretending I had little cash but really because I needed to make sure that there would be no doubt about my identity after my disappearance. Annoyed, he wrote my name and address and bank card number on the back of the cheque, and to clinch it I showed him my driving licence as proof. He would remember me, all right. I hoped his boat was fully insured, but it was too late to start feeling guilty about a complete stranger when I had already hardened my heart towards my wife and children.

It was only a small boat with an outboard motor. It would be easy to scuttle. I headed out towards the horizon, where already rainclouds were stacking up like dense smoke. It was too cold and gloomy for many trippers at this time of year, even on a Saturday. By dusk there would surely be no witnesses.

I spent an hour fishing and caught just enough to leave evidence in the boat that would suit my purpose. The swell and the silence calmed my nerves but the gathering gloom depressed me and the sea was cold and uninviting. My resolve faltered again. Did I really want to go through with all this? She would have lit a log-fire back at home, and there might already be something for dinner warming in the oven. If I headed back now I would be just in time to catch the early Saturday night crowd in my favourite bar. For a moment it seemed ridiculous to give up everything I knew and risk the uncertainty, the discomfort, maybe eventually arrest, prosecution and prison. But wasn't it risk I had craved for so long? My mind went into neutral and a voice in my head reminded me of all my regrets that I had taken so many years to reach this moment of decision. This was a final test of my strength of character. If my nerve failed now I would spend the rest of my life in self-pity and self-contempt.

Without my help the wind and the tide eased the boat's prow towards the shore, towards the cove where the folding bicycle and the dry clothes waited for me to prove myself. It was already almost dark. Nothing and no one stirred along the coat. I started the motor and headed towards the rocks, struggling out of my anorak and firmly zipping into one of its pockets my wallet and credit card, the small monstrosities of an unwanted life. Then I threw it overboard to be washed ashore later as evidence. My shoes followed.

At the last minute, a couple of hundred yards from the beach, I dived overboard. The icy water made me gasp, and the tide was stronger than I had hoped. The boat hit the rocks with a surprisingly quiet splintering sound and above the swell of a wave I saw her keel over and drift away with a hole ripped in her bottom. It didn't matter whether she floated or sank. Anyone aboard at the time would have been hurled into the water. I struck out for the shore, struggling against the tide and numb with the cold. For a moment in the darkness I panicked, completely disorientated, thinking I was heading out to sea, but then the dark shadow of the coast loomed ahead of me and I swam towards it steadily, my mind drained of all but the need to reach dry land.

Two hundred yards is a long swim in the dark and cold against the tide, and although I had always been a reasonable swimmer there were moments when, terrified, I thought I wouldn't make it. I swallowed water, went under six or seven times, and after two or three minutes I wondered briefly if it was worth it. Why not give up, and drift? They say that drowning is a relatively painless death. It would be easy just to let go. *Don't be so bloody stupid*, said the voice in my head, *it's not much fun being dead*. I forced myself to relax, to use the sea instead of fighting it, and after ten minutes I came ashore like flotsam, wet and tangled, exhausted and panting. But I dared not lie and rest even for a moment, not on a wintry night with the chill testing my wet bones. The clothes and bicycle were where I had hidden them. I towelled myself briskly, shaking with cold, fear and relief, my teeth clattering.

Then, when I was dry and warmer, I felt a gush of exhilaration. The stars were already sharp and bright by now and they gleamed like promises. *We've done it*! I heard my mind thinking. *We're free at last! Dead, but alive again.*

The boat was probably already half a mile out or at the bottom of the sea, but the anorak would come ashore one day to tell its lies.

Wearing gloves, I wheeled the bicycle towards the nearest road and pedalled into the future.

It was a long, tiring night. I rode twenty miles or so to the nearest town, cursing the bicycle's slipping chain and ramshackle creaking, and then stuffed my wet clothes and towel under some garbage in a convenient dustbin, and abandoned the bicycle near a rubbish dump. The bicycle was so old and decrepit no one would look at it twice: the refuse collectors would simply throw it on the dump with all the other junk. There would be no clues.

Eventually I caught a train to the airport and took the first plane that was heading towards the sun, booking a seat in the dead man's name, the stranger I had now become. I was so tired I didn't even buy a paperback for the flight. The man in the seat beside me was reading *Nineteen Eighty-Four*. A bit too late for that, I thought. I had read the damned thing three or four times myself. I'd done far too much reading: too much Chandler, too much Pepys, too much Shakespeare. But not any more. I was going to start living again.

As the plane surged into the air my heart was pounding and my breath was short, pain throbbing in my throat. I looked at my digital watch. The time was 20.20. I closed my eyes. For a moment I felt a grievous sense of loss, almost as though I had really died, and a vicious jab of affection for the children and a sudden shameful nostalgic lust for the body of my wife. Perhaps I did still love her in a way, but it was not enough. Perhaps dying is indeed something like this, at that final moment when you know it is all over, and how you have squandered it.

2

I hit town with all the finesse of a boxer's nose investigating the canvas. It left me bemused. What the hell was going on? One moment I was quietly gliding through the sky and the next I seemed to be on a different planet.

Sure, during the taxi ride in from the airport there were still automobiles everywhere, just like home, but they weren't the Chevvies and Pontiacs I was used to. Here there were weird, dinky little numbers that the cabbie said were called Minis and Volkswagens, the Minis so small that you could tuck them in a Pontiac's trunk like a peanut up an elephant. Something too had happened to the broads. It was a glorious spring evening and their skirts were as thin as a preacher's promise and short as a boozer's memory and perched on their fannies like lampshades. Their legs seemed endless, their hair was long and free, and the way they walked in the spring sunshine was enough to make a monk turn Muslim. The music on the taxi's wireless was a pounding rhythm that must have had old ladies bouncing in their wheelchairs: twanging guitars and thundering drums and some guy was singing through his nose and somebody else seemed to be doing something unpleasant to one of those Indian string instruments, which didn't seem to like it. I'd been down some mean streets in my time and I'd emerged neither tarnished nor afraid, but I don't mind admitting to a certain apprehension. Where the hell was I? *When* the hell was I? It was almost as though they'd managed to send some sucker to the moon, and that sucker was me, and they'd never warned me I might find more than green cheese.

'Been away long?' said the driver.

'It seems like twenty years,' I said.

'Business or pleasure?'

'Business,' I said, 'and yours is to drive and to mind yours.'

He didn't like that. They never do. At least the cabbies hadn't changed. He spat out of the window and sniffed as though I smelled bad. I began to feel more at home.

The sight of all those broads made me think I might find time to mix a little pleasure with the business. The business was to do with matching a body and a name, perhaps two bodies and two names, but I won't bore you with shop talk. You take bodies for granted in my line of work, and you get called a lot of names, but it pays for a drink or ten and some of the broads seem to think you're Humphrey Bogart, which is all right by me. You can even claim the cost of the broads as tax-deductible expenses. Let's hear it for the Internal Revenue Dept. Play it again, Uncle Sam.

It seemed to take hours to reach the hotel downtown. The sullen cabbie was probably treating me to the special roundabout scenic route. The fare on the meter was certainly something special. We kept stopping to see the sights at all the local beauty spots: traffic lights every block, bunched automobiles huddled together grumbling on either side and once a graveyard of dead cars parked six-high on a junk lot. Up there the sky was blue and the sun was bright; down here carbon monoxide was testing the windows like a sneak thief in the gloom. I passed the time rubbernecking the chicks on the sidewalk. Sometimes there's a lot to be said for bodies without names.

The hotel was about as homely as a hooker's hello. There was plastic everywhere and glass and chrome and concrete, and loudspeakers jabbering with what I guess was meant to be music. The desk clerk had long greasy hair and seemed to have found something valuable up his nose.

'Mitchum,' I said. 'I've booked a room.' I always travel incognito. It makes people notice you more. But you need to be careful about the details. It's not wise to call yourself Hamlet and then mention that your father is still alive and your mother and uncle are just good friends. People notice these things.

'Check,' said the clerk, wiping his finger daintily on his jacket.

'No, cash,' I said. The first rule of hotels is to make the staff feel inferior before they do it to you and you find yourself thanking them for accepting your tip.

'Prick,' he muttered.

'Pleased to meet you,' I said. I shook his hand. Soon he'd be eating out of mine. Then I remembered where his fingers had been. Desk clerks have this knack of getting the last laugh.

15

I waved the bellboy away and carried my bag to the elevator. Even here there was a tinny speaker that shuddered with the sound of some guys yelling a song about money, *that's all I want, just give me money, yeah, that's all I want.* It didn't seem tactful in a pricy hotel: I mean, whoever heard of an elevator demanding a tip? The raucous voices pursued me all the way up to the nineteenth floor, and along the corridor, and even in my room I could hear the loudspeaker outside yelling for a handout. In the old days at least they called you buddy and asked if you could spare no more than a dime.

The room was just a room. You know the sort: walls, floor, ceiling, bed, Gideon bible. Who the hell was Gideon anyway? I goosed the TV. It winked at me a couple of times in a bleary hangover way and then flickered with a film about some President getting shot in Dallas. These TV guys sure come up with some unlikely scenarios. They even had the killer hiding six floors up in a warehouse. Do they think we're simple? What about the FBI? Some people think we'll believe anything. I spend too much time with trash to have to watch it. I goosed the TV again. It flinched, and then offered a shot of two guys dressed up like Martians and apparently playing golf on the Moon. Next thing you know they'll be claiming you can send rockets to Mars and colonise the universe. I switched to another channel: a movie about the Second World War. At least it was true, but I knew the plot already. That's the trouble with history, you always know the ending: Errol Flynn strangles Hitler with his bare hands.

I tried a last channel. It gave me four guys yelling a song called 'Help!' I knew how they felt. I put them out of their misery and the TV sat there and glared at me with one bright little eye for a while. What the hell, I thought. The gentle spring night beckoned. I'd been behaving myself for too long. I decided to get laid.

Back home I would just have poked a cigarette in the corner of my mouth and the hat on the back of my head and narrowed my eyes some. That usually worked. But perhaps the dames round here expected more. So instead I ran my fingers through my hair and then poked a cigarette in the corner of my mouth and the hat on the back of my head. I narrowed my eyes and looked into the glass. Mean, maybe, but not afraid. Some broad was going to get lucky. I fingered the elevator button and went down.

She was sitting on a stool at the bar, all long blonde hair and long white legs and the tiniest skirt you ever saw stretched over the sort of ass that would have made a fairy come hollering down from the top of the Christmas tree. She knew I was coming before I spoke. I could see her checking me out in the mirror behind the bar. We both knew the score. So far it was 0–0.

'Hi, baby,' I said. I blew a thin jet of smoke and narrowed my eyes. 'What'll it be?'

She looked at me. Her eyes would have melted a bank manager at fifty paces. She had lips to launch a thousand sips. 'Beat it, creep,' they said.

1–0 to her.

'You don't have to be so ladylike,' I said.

'Okay,' she said. 'Piss off, then.'

2–0. These dames seemed different from the ones back home. They knew shorter words. Perhaps their tiny skirts had gone to their heads. She had nothing on under her blouse, either. Her chests pointed at me like cannon.

'I only want to buy you a drink,' I said.

'And then screw me afterwards.'

'Okay,' I shrugged. 'But only if you insist.'

I thought I saw her lips flicker. 'Christ, you've got a nerve,' she said. 'You could be my father.'

'It's possible. What was your mother's name?'

Her lips definitely twitched. 'I'm waiting for my boyfriend,' she sniffed.

'Fine. I'll buy him a drink too, but I'll draw the line there.'

'He's six foot two, and wide.'

'Then he'll probably need two drinks.'

She almost smiled.

'Now, what'll it be?' I said.

'An early night. Get lost, will you? You're wasting your time.'

'I've been doing it all my life. I can't change old habits now.'

'My boyfriend won't like it. There'll be trouble.'

'Trouble is my business.' I said. 'Now come on. What's yours?'

'Shit!'

'I don't think they serve it. Come on baby, live dangerously.'

She hesitated. I was leading about 6–2. I gave her my bewildered little-boy-lost look that worked pretty good in the old days.

'Oh, all right,' she said. 'Just one. But . . . . '

'That's all you're getting,' I said. 'I'll drink the doubles.'

She was shaking her head like she'd just walked into a tree.

'Way out, man,' she said. 'Oh, boy. Way out.'

I got them in, the drinks I mean, and lit a couple of cigarettes, and passed her one, and she took it and shook her head and said, 'Crazy, man, I don't believe this,' and crossed those endless legs. I narrowed my eyes and blew smoke.

'Do you make a habit of picking up chicks in bars?' she said. She used her lips like a dame in the orchestra about to blow the horn. They would have gone down well anywhere.

'Only pretty ones,' I said.

'You're a dirty old man.'

'I was a dirty young one, too.'

'This is weird. What am I doing?'

'You're having a quiet drink with a father-figure,' I said, and patted her knee nicely. It didn't feel like the sort of knee that spent a lot of time face down in a church.

'I just don't believe this,' she said.

'Have another,' I said. 'That'll help.'

'Well, just a small one. But don't think . . . .'

'I never do. Thinking complicates things.'

She had just the one, and then just another, and then just two or three more. She put them back like an oilman just home from a month on a deep-sea rig and she kept playing with her fingers, which seemed promising. A couple of times she said her boyfriend was coming and the way she used her mouth to say it I thought I might be too, but he never showed and I relaxed. She was just another dame looking for a good time and since there seemed to be no one better around it looked as if I was it. And she had that great talent in a woman: she never asked many questions, like was I married or what was my job or did I dress on the right. Pretty soon she got giggly, which seemed a bit early. The last thing you need is the dame passing out just as you're about to slip her a length and tell her of course you love her because of her mind. It was time I got something into her, so I took her to a restaurant.

'Don't think you're going to sleep with me,' she said, ''cos you're not.'

'It's the last thing I had in mind,' I said sincerely. Sleep had nothing to do with it.

We jumped into a cab and joined the jam of automobiles trying to edge through the tangled city but spending most of their time sitting cosily together, farting quietly. The automobiles in the streets were as crowded as crooks in politics.

'We should have walked,' I said. 'It would have been quicker.'

'Walked?' she giggled. 'Nobody ever *walks*.'

She was right. The roads were crammed, the sidewalks deserted. In a generation or two people would probably start to be born without any legs. I patted one of hers on the thigh. Its soft firm smoothness brought back memories. 'You're cute,' I said.

'You're pretty cool yourself,' she said, 'for an old guy.'

'This has got to stop,' I said. 'I'm in my prime. How old do you think I am?'

She giggled. 'Ancient. At least 35, maybe 40.'

'And you call that ancient?'

'It's geriatric.'

'Okay, then. How old are you?'

'Eighteen.'

Jesus. And they usually exaggerate at that age. She was probably even younger. 'You're right,' I said. 'I'm old enough to be your father.'

'Never mind,' she said, and she took my hand and leaned her head against my shoulder. 'You're kinda groovy, anyway.'

'Groovy?'

'Groovy, you know. Gear. Good vibes.'

'Gear? Vibes?'

'Where've you *been* the last few years?' she said.

'I wish I knew,' I said, and kissed her. She smelled great and her lips tasted good enough to make a dipsomaniac take the pledge, so I kissed her again.

'You might at least take your hat off,' she said.

'It hides the bald head, but at least I've still got all my teeth.'

She jabbed me in the ribs. 'You!' she said, and squeezed my hand. I hadn't been on such a certainty since Citation won the Kentucky Derby in 1948.

She knew an uptown club called the Maharishi's Armpit. It sounded hairy. It was. The joint was as dark as a witch's curse and up on the stage a guy in trousers as tight as a millionaire's wallet was trying to strangle his guitar while a couple of others were torturing theirs and yelling over the din and another guy with basin hair was beating his drums to a pulp. They made Sinatra look like a choirboy. The place was packed with more fairies than *A Midsummer Night's Dream* and most of them seemed to be in drag with frocks like tents and bead necklaces and flowers in their hair. I kept my back to the wall. A couple of them waved at her and shouted 'Cool, baby,' and 'Right on,' and 'No sweat, hey.' Perhaps we really had colonised the universe already and this was a different planet.

'Why are these guys all wearing frocks?' I asked.

She gurgled with mirth. '*Frocks*,' she said. 'What the hell are you talking about? They're caftans, from Carnaby Street.'

Where in God's name was Carnaby Street? They still looked like frocks to me.

She dragged me along to a corner table where a candle flickered inside a human skull, and we sat on stools that had been made to look like lavatory seats. Even the paper napkins were perforated. The ashtray on the table was designed to resemble a diseased lung, and the flower vase was in the shape of a miniature guillotine and inscribed with the message: 'These innocent flowers have been executed for your pleasure. Enjoy!' When they brought the drinks the glasses were labelled 'Cirrhosis' or 'Brain Damage' or 'Brewer's Droop,' and when the food arrived the rims of the plates were decorated with friezes of little lambs gambolling happily through a meadow and into an abattoir. The forks were like tridents, the knives shaped like butchers' cleavers. It was all about as tasteful as an orgy in a mortuary.

'Grotty, isn't it?' she yelled at me through the racket.

'What?' I shouted.

'Isn't it grotty?' she bellowed.

'Grotty?'

'Even you must know what grotty is.'

I had no idea. 'Oh, grotty,' I said. 'Sure.'

'But groovy, too,' she yelled. 'Fab. It's real cool. I dig it like crazy, man.'

'Yeah.' It was not the sort of dive for conversation, even in code, but I kind of liked the place. It was bizarre and pretentious but also young and alive with its vulgar excess and the darkness was kind enough to disguise the fact that I was probably the only customer older than twenty-five. I even felt younger myself and remembered girls and places that had also seemed vital and way-out in their time, and I thought of all those married suckers lying at home in bed with their wives and waiting for the big sleep.

There was a sickly odour drifting on the air. 'What's that smell?' I yelled.

'Pot,' she yelled.

'Pot?' I yelled.

'Snap out of it, Mitchum,' she yelled. 'Christ, it's pot. Hash.'

I didn't like to enquire why I should know what potash smells like or why it should be served in a restaurant. I didn't even know what potash was.

While the racket went on we ate something she'd recommended but I'd rather not remember, something red with lots of yellow rice and dark green bits in it, and we drank enough so that when she pulled me up to dance I didn't resist but she laughed when I tried to grip her in the nightclub clinch and press against her chest and she pushed away, giggling, and started to jump about and bop and twist and turn so I started jiggling too and there was nothing to it though it wasn't the same. What's the point of dancing if you can't have a feel? But the booze was beginning to do what booze should do and she was laughing happily at me with a silver smile like the new moon on a spring night and she was showing how much she could do with those lovely long legs and I started to enjoy myself and let the rhythm seep into my feet and jerk my limbs loose and she pointed at me and threw her head back with glee and there was magic there that night because it was spring again and years since I had felt so easy and filled with love and confidence. I felt like a recharged battery, I felt born again, and some of the kids started gathering round in a circle like you see in those Hollywood musicals but never believe and they started to clap in time and shake their beads, and bells seemed to be tinkling and there was lots of laughter. I knew then just how good it must feel to be a dung beetle in a heap of horse manure.

'Shake it, daddy,' cried one of the fairies, 'do your own thing,' and I shrugged and winked and white-faced girl in a shawl shouted 'Isn't he hip?' so I gave her a waggle of my waist and she cheered and clapped and yelled 'Isn't he great?' and some of the others joined in.

'Cool, daddy.'

'No sweat.'

'Isn't the old guy groovy?'

'Just grab his hat, just dig his baggy trousers and turn-ups.'

'Isn't he fab?'

And eventually no one else was dancing but just me and my beautiful teenage blonde with her long gold hair whipping soft in the gloom and the long white legs that I loved and the sparkling eyes and the kind of smile to make a preacher jump up and down on his sermon.

The band went mad and the guy who had been trying to strangle his guitar started yelling out the song I'd heard in the hotel, *just give me money, that's all I want, a lotta money, that's all I want*, and here it seemed right and not just a racket at all and the sounds penetrated my bones and I started yelling along with them *Yeah give me money, yeah, that's all I want, just give me money, yeah, that's all I want* until eventually the music ended and the kids yelled and clapped and my broad threw her arms around me and gave me a kiss as wet and deep as the Pacific and if I'd drowned right then it would have been worth it.

'Christ, Mitchum,' she panted, 'I could go for you. Right now.'

'Not here, baby,' I gasped. 'It might give the fairies ideas.'

'Let's go, then,' she panted. 'Now.'

I called for the check. Why hang around? I felt I could do anything, pull any dame in the place, win any race. I was breathing hard but so was she, and the sweat ran down my back like raindrops on a window pane, but I knew right then that if I backed the four kids up on the stage to become multi-millionaires and more famous than Jesus Christ, they would do it. I couldn't go wrong. I felt like a god myself.

As we left the joint they gave us a roll on the drums and when one of the fairies in drag tried to stop her and talk to her she pushed him away and pulled me up the steps and we hailed a cab and the driver had hardly taken her address before she was all over me in the back with kisses as wide as the Grand Canyon in a thunderstorm. Her hands were not where her teacher would have recommended. I reckoned there was more to be said for her sort of dancing than I'd guessed.

The cabbie was jealous. He dropped us at her place and she went ahead to open the door while I paid the fare. 'You should be ashamed of yourself,' he growled. 'A man your age.'

'You're right,' I said. 'I should have walked. I need the exercise.'

'She's young enough to be your daughter. What about her father?'

'I'm not too keen on sleeping with men,' I said.

'You're a shit,' he grunted.

'It takes an asshole to know one,' I said, and loped up the steps to her door two at a time. I hadn't felt so good since they nailed Al Capone for tax offences.

I don't believe in blow by blow descriptions. Let's just say I'd never known any dame like her. A few have been keen enough but none as keen as her. She didn't even wait for the bedroom. She didn't even take her clothes off. She jumped on me as I walked in the door. It was like being knocked over by a tornado and sucked down by a whirlpool at the same time. I began to understand what groovy meant. They didn't make them like that when I was eighteen. In those days we just held hands and licked ice cream sodas.

About a century later I was lying there comatose on the mat like a beaten wrestler after three submissions and her face was over me and her eyes had turned a dreamy green and her hair trailed over my cheek. Her perfume filled me. Her lips were soft and swollen, so I kissed them better. 'I take it all back,' she whispered. 'You're not nearly old enough to be my father.'

Fatherhood! Jesus! I sat up. 'Christ! I'm sorry,' I said. 'I didn't take . . . wasn't very . . . careful. Did you . . . are you . . . safe?'

Her eyes flashed. 'I'm not infectious,' she snapped, 'if that's what you mean. I haven't got anything.'

'No, no,' I said. 'I meant . . . well, I wouldn't like to get you pregnant.'

She looked at me like a kid seeing Santa.

'Mitchum?' she said. 'Are you real?'

I tested myself all over. 'I guess so. It all seems to be there.'

'I'm on the Pill, of course, stupid.'

'The Pill?'

She sat up, brushing her hair away from her face. She looked at me, worried. 'Surely you've heard of the Pill?'

'Sure,' I lied. It doesn't do to let eighteen-year-olds think they know more than you. It's not good for their souls.

'You don't, do you?' she said. 'You haven't a clue. Where the hell have you *been*, Mitchum?'

'Well, a moment ago I was . . . .'

'Stop fooling. I'm serious. You're freaking me out. You're like some creature from outer space, from a different time. It's the 1960s, but you're like something out of an old Hollywood B-movie.'

That stopped me. The 1960s? I think pretty quick as a rule, but my mind seized up then. Unless she was mad I'd lost years off my life. I didn't know what to say. I probably blamed the Russians.

'You breeze into my life like Humphrey Bogart with a baggy

suit and turn-ups on your trousers and a hat that nobody would be seen dead in these days and a fag in the corner of your mouth.'

'Hold it, baby. No fag's ever been anywhere near my mouth.'

'Shut up and listen. Fag, cigarette, what the hell.' She was standing up now, right over me. The view was terrific. I couldn't be nearly as old as I'd have to be if this was really some time in the 1960s, because already I was wondering how she would look without any clothes. If this really was the 1960s I should be tucked up in bed by now with a hot cup of cocoa.

'Let's go to bed,' I said. 'Then we can examine *all* the possibilities.'

'No way,' she said. She looked as worried as a snake that has just realised the rabbit it was after is really a mongoose. 'I'm going to get to the bottom of this as soon as possible.'

'Just what I had in mind,' I said.

She built us a couple of drinks, sat me on the couch, and looked earnestly into my eyes. I didn't mind at all, so I looked right back.

'You must tell me the complete truth, Mitchum,' she said. 'The pure and simple truth.'

'Truth is never pure and rarely simple,' I said. There was no need to mention that I'd stolen that from Oscar Wilde. She'd probably never heard of him. Growing older has its compensations.

'Be serious,' she said, showing me how, frowning. 'You're making me nervous. Spaced out. It's weird, like taking a trip.'

'A trip?'

She almost got angry. There were flecks of brown in her green eyes. 'There you go again. You don't even know what a trip is. Let me tell you, Mitchum. Let me bring you up to date. A trip is what happens when you take LSD.'

LSD? I examined my fingernails.

She raised a hand, like an optimistic traffic cop about to get run down at an intersection. 'Okay, okay,' she said. 'LSD is a drug. It makes you hallucinate. It sends you on a *trip*. It makes you see flowers breathing and you can hear the beginning of the universe.'

'Have they told the scientists yet? They'd be quite interested.'

'Shut up. Then there's the Pill. It's the sixties and you've never heard of the Pill. The Pill, Mitchum, is a small spherical object, made up of chemicals, that stops birds having babies.'

'And why should they want to do that?' I asked. 'All they need to do is to stop sitting on the eggs.'

She looked at me with awe. 'You don't even know what a bird is, either, do you?' she said. She looked a little frightened now. There were two pretty little puckers above her eyes. I leaned forward to kiss them away. She pushed me back.

'A bird is a girl, Mitchum, a chick, a lady. Those of us who are sensible take the Pill each day to stop getting pregnant.'

I suddenly felt ridiculously jealous. So I was just another easy lay. At eighteen? And then I came to my senses. If she had been a virgin I wouldn't be here. 'They think of everything these days,' I said.

'So what is it?' she said. 'You've never heard of a bird, or the Pill, or LSD. You don't know what grotty means, or groovy, or fab or gear. Everyone else does. Everyone in the world. Where've you been? Have you been asleep for twenty years? Or for twenty centuries?' she shivered. 'Christ, you could be Rip van Winkle, for all I know, millions of years old.'

'Even older than your father.'

'Stop bullshitting me, Mitchum.' She had a nice turn of phrase. I looked at her legs to remind myself that she was still a woman. They convinced me. 'I bet you've never even heard of the Beatles,' she said.

Beetles? What was this turn in the conversation? 'Of course I have,' I said.

'What are their names, then?' Her eyes were challenging.

'Names?'

'What are they called?'

'Beetles?'

'*The* Beatles. What are their Christian names?'

Perhaps she was right. This wasn't the 1940s. Nobody ever gave cockroaches Christian names in the 1940s. They didn't even call them Rover or Fido. They just stamped on them.

'You haven't a bloody clue, have you?' she said. 'You haven't the faintest idea what I'm talking about.'

She had me there. I couldn't stall any more. She'd begun to get me worried too. The way she looked, the way she dressed, the way she spoke, the way she danced, the way she . . . well, everything, it all started telling me to wake up, punk, you've somehow lost twenty years.

'Do you have a calendar?' I said. 'Or a diary?'

She looked puzzled.

25

'Don't say you've got pills to do that for you too,' I said. 'I need to check the date.'

She disappeared into the other room and came back with a newspaper. It had headlines bigger than I'd ever seen, and big pictures of girls with no clothes on. Perhaps the Commies had finally taken over. Perhaps the beetles were called Ivan or Mikhail. The date on the paper told me she was right. It *was* the 1960s. I had mislaid twenty years.

'Okay,' I said. 'You win. I've never heard of the beetles.'

She seemed to soften. Women always do when you surrender. They just need to see you with your hands up first. 'Why, Mitchum?' she said gently. 'Why haven't you heard of the Beatles? Everyone else has. They're the most famous band in the world. They've changed everything, the way we think, the way we live. Nothing will ever be the same again. It's a revolution of youth, and peace, and love. Because of them there'll never be wars again. Because of them the politicians will be forced to ban the Bomb.'

'Tell that to Stalin.'

She looked at me with pity. 'Stalin's dead,' she said softly. She took my hand and stroked the back of it. She looked at me again with eyes as old as Time. She was Eve. 'You can tell me the truth, Mitchum,' she said. 'I want to help. There's a lot of mysticism around these days, psychedelic drugs, Maharishis, gurus going on about ESP, but I don't believe any of that crap. I think I know where you've been all these years. You've been in prison, haven't you? You've been locked up for years and they wouldn't let you see any newspapers or TV and they've only just let you out in the old clothes you were wearing when they locked you up all those years ago. It's true, isn't it? That's why you're so out of date.'

I looked away. If that's what she wanted to believe, why not? Broads always believe what they want to believe, anyway, and sometimes a lie is best told without words.

'Look at me,' she said kindly, turning my face. Her fingers were hot, her eyes tender. 'It's true, isn't it? I won't mind, Mitchum, honest I won't. We understand these things these days. I just want to know the truth. All you need these days is love. It *is* true, isn't it?'

I blinked and looked away.

'I knew it,' she said. 'You poor man.' She slid close and hugged me tight. I began to reckon that perhaps there was something to

26

be said for being twenty years older than I was. She put her hand
on my chest and her head on my shoulder. Her hair was as fine as
a spider's web against my neck, and the touch of her long white
leg against mine started sending messages around my body.

'Poor, poor Mitchum,' she said. 'It must have been terrible.'

I grunted.

'What did you do to make them lock you up for so long?' She
raised her head and kissed me, and held me again with her eyes.
She seemed old and young and ageless. 'Did you kill someone?
You must have killed someone.'

I looked away.

'You killed someone, didn't you? Why do you always look away
when you're telling the truth? I don't mind, Mitchum, honest.
They must have deserved it. You wouldn't kill someone if they
didn't deserve it. Was it a man or a woman?'

'I need a drink,' I said.

She jumped up and took my glass. 'I'll get it,' she said. 'Don't
move. You relax.' I loved the way she sashayed across the room.
No wonder they'd had to invent this pill once they'd started
wearing skirts as short as that.

When she came back she handed me the glass and bent over
and her chests swung towards me and she kissed my brow. 'I'll bet
it was a woman,' she said. 'It was, wasn't it?'

I grunted, and took a belt from the glass.

'Was she really grotty to you, Mitch? Did she make you really
unhappy? Were you married?'

'I don't want to talk about it,' I said. In a way she was almost
right. Of course I'd never killed anyone, but a long time ago I'd
killed a woman's love and the effect is the same. When we broke
up it was as though I'd murdered her. The grief was just as bad as
death and perhaps the guilt was worse.

She took my glass and put it aside, and gripped my hand and
pulled me up off the couch, and led me through to the bedroom,
and gently took my clothes off and then her own, and she said
nothing all the while, and naked she was even more perfect than I
had imagined. Her beauty was not just because of her youth and
her shapes but because of her soft kindness. Promiscuous or not,
she was clean, honest and generous. She wanted to make a
stranger happy in the best way she knew how. She smelled of love
and hope.

'Who are you really?' she whispered.

'Search me,' I said, so she did. This time it was quiet and easy, slow and gentle, like friends, and when it was over she sighed and held me close and said 'Sleep now, Mitch, go to sleep, my love,' and I murmured 'Farewell, my lovely,' and slept, and in that sleep I dreamed I was a stranger on the run in an unknown city and looking for a name without a body.

(2)

I woke with a start to feel a nameless body in the bed beside me. I propped myself up and stared at her blearily. A slice of sunlight cut through a gap in the curtains and nagged at my hangover. She was still asleep. She was frighteningly young, seventeen or eighteen at the most, and very beautiful. Her fine blonde hair wisped across her cheek and lips and the soft damp corner of her mouth stirred my blood. Who the hell was she? And where the hell was I?

And then it all came back. I'd done it, really done it at last. I'd left my wife, sunk the boat, caught a plane to a city where nobody knew me, and I'd picked up the girl in the hotel bar and she'd taken me to a crazy pseudo-'60s nightclub and then back here to her place. We'd made love – twice! God, I hadn't done it twice for years. And now I wanted to do it again. I touched her under the bedclothes and after a while she hummed softly and turned towards me and stretched and slowly opened her eyes. They were deep and somehow innocent. She smiled sleepily. 'Hello again,' she said, and pulled me towards her. My heart lifted, and so did everything else.

I checked out of the hotel and we stayed together for more than a week, and those days and nights were among the happiest of my life. I knew I was far too old for her, but she didn't seem to mind, and she made me feel so much younger myself that it didn't matter and the world seemed fresh and new. The air itself smelled sweeter, cigar smoke richer, petrol fumes sharper. The daylight took on a new translucence that made every colour brighter, and you could almost feel the velvety warmth of the nights. I found myself giving money to tramps and relishing meals

28

as never before, revelling in the textures of meat, the flavours of fish and the juicy plenty of fruit, and enjoying strange dishes I would never have dreamed of even trying before. The city itself seemed to buzz with excitement and I fell a little in love with its parks and fountains and statues and cafes because it was her city and she showed it to me as generously as she gave herself, and I was already more than a little in love with her. I loved the colours of her eyes, the shapes of her lips, the whiteness of her grin and the gleam of her chuckle. I gloried in the softness of her hair and the endless promise of her marvellous long legs, and I was dumb with pride and felt taller when she walked beside me and took my hand, and because she was with me other women looked at me with new interest and seemed no longer to see just the tired, middle-aged bore I had been for too long. I loved her silly jokes, and I woke each morning with eagerness and rejoiced to find her beside me, and I slept each night with a smile. We drifted through each day without making plans, luxuriating in idle irresponsi-bility, and yet everything seemed to happen perfectly, unplanned. We did such stupid, childish, wonderful things, like going to a funfair and riding the rockets and having our fortunes told and clutching each other shrieking in the ghost-train dark, and licking candyfloss. We played together with soap and boats in the bath, and giggled like kids, and when we made love it was with that intense but carefree eagerness that only the young in heart ever know. My hormones, sluggish for years, seemed to have been given an electric jolt.

'I've fallen in love with you,' I said one night, and it was true. At least it was true at the time, and what else matters?

'I love you too,' she said, 'very much,' and I think that was true as well. At least it was possible. Anything at all seemed possible then.

It's beyond my power to describe deep joy, so I won't go on any more about it. Complete, overwhelming happiness is so subjec-tive, and perhaps so rare, that it's monstrously difficult to try to convey it in words. It can only be sensed from the twinkle in the eye and the spring in the step, and from laughter, and print is inadequate for that. So you'll just have to take my word for it that during those exuberant days and nights with her I was suffused with a glow of love and optimism. I felt a completely different person, and it can't just have been because I had taken a different name. Could it? No, surely not. A dead man's name could surely make no difference at all.

It couldn't last, of course. I didn't expect it to. I was far too old for her, and not naïve enough to think there was anything I could offer for ever to a girl as young as she. I looked on each day with her as a bonus, and just as I made no plans for tomorrow, so too I was overjoyed and grateful to find her still with me each separate morning. I knew it would have to end eventually, and the fact that she let me love her as long as she did was a gift to treasure. When she told me gently that it was over I didn't even ask her why, and certainly not whether she had found another man – or, even worse, some glamorous boy. She had taught me respect, not only for her but for myself. She had given me back too much dignity to tarnish my memories of our happiness together with questions or protests.

'I still love you,' she said, 'but in a different way. I'll always love you. We just won't be together, that's all.'

It was a very Sixties-ish thing to say.

I kissed her lightly. 'Thank you for everything,' I said. 'Farewell, my lovely.'

When I left to move back into the hotel I confess there were tears in my eyes, but I didn't let her see them. I would have been ashamed to leave her feeling guilty, or to make her last memory of me one of pity.

'God bless you,' I said, and for a moment I wished that He existed.

There is little point in hiding the fact that I was very unhappy for some time afterwards. I felt desperately bereft and lonely, and on a couple of nights I drank a bit too much and made the mistake of telephoning her, hating it when she wasn't in, and then the next day feeling immensely relieved that I hadn't spoken to her. That would have spoiled it. The best love affairs should rocket across our lives like comets and quickly burn themselves out. The bad ones crawl like snails and leave a trail of slime.

I tried to discover new parts of the city for myself, going to theatres, cinemas, art galleries, museums, but found myself returning compulsively too often to places we had shared. I sat alone on benches where she had sat, but the wood was cold. The park where we had ridden on a miniature railway and had shaken with laughter now seemed deserted and tired. I started noticing litter, and resented other people's happiness. I ate alone in a restaurant where we had had a stupendous meal together, but now the food was insipid and the waiters ignored me. Even the fairground seemed tawdry, the stallholders greedy, the ghost-train an unimaginative rip-off of tape-recorded wails and groans and cobwebs made of sacking.

Unable to stop myself, I went to the fortune teller again. The woman didn't recognise me. Of course not. She must have told hundreds of fortunes since last we had met. She seemed bored, peering irritably into her crystal ball. Last time she had told me that I had a glowing future, and she had described all manner of warmth and happiness to come. But now she looked gloomy.

'You will go on a journey,' she said.

That certainly wasn't worth the entrance fee. We are all of us on a journey of one sort or another.

'I see water,' she said. She looked at me and frowned, annoyed. 'I see water in the past, and water in the future.'

I confess I felt a superstitious tremor. But then it could mean anything to anyone. We all have some sort of water in our lives – ponds, lakes, lagoons, rivers, seas. Water is even some sort of Freudian symbol, if I remember rightly.

'I see a separation,' she said, 'and a joining together.'

What nonsense, I told myself. That too could apply to anyone anywhere.

Yes, said the voice in my head suddenly, the voice I hadn't heard since the night of my disappearance. My conscience? The still small voice? *We're together again*, it said. *It's been a long time.*

'Beware of a certain stranger,' she said. She shook her head and tapped the crystal ball with puzzlement. 'I'm sorry,' she said. 'It's gone all cloudy. There's nothing there.'

I paid her, even though she seemed oddly reluctant to take my money. 'I've told you nothing you don't know already,' she said. 'There seems to be something in the way, between us.'

'That's not your fault,' I said, and paid her, old charlatan that she was.

It's time to move on, said the voice. *It's getting colder. We need to get closer to the sun.*

Your subconscious often knows things before you do, and it seems to warn you in dreams of things you only become fully aware of later. I hadn't dreamed much for many years, or at least I hadn't remembered my dreams, but now they seemed to come almost every night in Technicolor, and sometimes they were close to being nightmares. I dreamed of the stranger's green gravel grave, of corpses washed up by the sea, of making love to a woman who was either my wife or my teenage blonde or both or possibly neither. In one recurring dream there was always a dark tropical lagoon that shimmered with heat and filtered sunlight. It seemed to beckon me and I began to yearn for the warmth it promised and knew that it was indeed time to move on. I came to terms with the loss of my teenage love, and was no longer distraught, and my loneliness turned to aloneness, which is not the same at all. There is a cool pleasure to be derived from being alone and separate and a welcome selfishness in having no one to answer to or care about. But I had taken all I needed from her city, and it was time to move on. I had come to terms with myself and I had learned a new pride and independence, but it was time now to put it to use and to live for something more than mere self-gratification.

I did pick up two other women, but it was not the same. Promiscuity is not the answer. We all learned that in the Sixties, and I learned it again with the second of the two, a stylish and attractive but oddly vulnerable woman with an air of sadness and a defensive wounded look in her eyes.

Afterwards she lit two cigarettes and passed me one. 'My God,' she said, 'anyone would think you'd been in a monastery or in prison for the last twenty years.'

'Close,' I said. 'I was married.'

'Me too,' she said, 'but my husband left me. One day he just told me he couldn't stand it any more, and walked out. Just like that. After twelve years.'

Her eyes were bruised with disappointment. I had to look away. Did my wife look like this now? Beaten and betrayed?

'Children?' I said.

'No, thank God. But it's still different for a woman. At first I made the most of it. I told myself I was liberated. But I wasn't. I was miserable. As a woman gets older she needs a man of her own.'

'That shouldn't be difficult,' I said gallantly. 'I wouldn't have thought you'd have any trouble at all.'

'Oh, I get my share of men all right,' she said, laughing nervously. 'But when it comes to the crunch they all shy away. I lost more than just a husband when he walked out on me. I lost my confidence and self-respect. I began to think he was right to go, and that I was worthless.'

Dear God, the things we do to each other. I felt mean and tarnished. I had used her, as all her other men had used her. A shadow passed over my grave, or was it over the stranger's grave? Had he betrayed someone too? Why not? We all do at some time, in one way or another. Betrayal seems an inevitable part of being human, and he too had been young in the shabby, promiscuous, selfish Sixties, and he had committed suicide. You don't commit suicide unless you feel dirty, mean and worthless.

'It's not just the infidelity,' my wife had said when she discovered I'd been having an affair with a friend's wife. 'Most husbands are unfaithful at least once or twice. Maybe it's natural. No, what disgusts me is who you chose. For Christ's sake, he was a friend of yours. You ate his food and drank his booze. And you didn't even bother to take her to a hotel. You did it in his bed. That has to be something else. Every man betrays his wife, but betraying his friend is unforgivable. It means you've betrayed yourself too. I can hardly respect you if you don't respect yourself.'

The deserted woman lay back beside me, not touching, staring at the ceiling and blowing smoke. She looked so small and easily hurt in that double bed that I felt a deep twinge of pity for her, and pity is no good for desire. I could see why her other men had run away from her. Failure and disappointment are contagious. I felt sorry for her, but I wanted her to go. Physically and emotionally I suddenly felt older than my years, with a wisdom and maturity I had never known.

She stubbed out her cigarette and turned towards me again and clutched me with a kind of desperation, just as I had clutched my wife in terror in the small hours of the night when the clock read 2.22 or 3.33 or 4.44.

'Make love to me again, please,' she said tremulously.

I hesitated.

'Please,' she said.

How could I deny her? I owed her something. Without lust, but with iron efficiency and self-control, I serviced her again just as

33

my wife so often had serviced me.

Now you know what it was like for her, said the voice in my head.

'Mmmm,' I said afterwards, 'that was good.'

We might have been sharing a bar of chocolate.

We didn't embarrass each other with long goodbyes. When we were dressed I asked her half-heartedly if I could see her again. It seemed only kind, and if I really hoped to change my life I had to learn to be kind again. Being born again means more than just changing your name and walking out on your old life and responsibilities. You have to build new ones.

'What about tonight?' I heard myself say. Me? The voice in my mind? My conscience?

She shook her head. She knew. 'Best not,' she said, and kissed me politely on the cheek. Already we were almost strangers again. Already I found it difficult to imagine her naked.

'I've settled for one-night stands,' she said. 'It's safer that way. You don't get hurt.'

'I'm sorry,' I said, and I was. In ten years' time she would have to settle for one-night stands with old men, or pay for young ones.

'So'm I,' she said, and was gone.

And I was damned if I could remember her name.

I hung around for a few more days, drifting wherever my whim took me, but the city had begun to pall. There were too many cars, too much pollution, noise and bustle, too many young couples holding hands, too many glimpses of distant girls who seemed to look like my teenage love. I was free, I had no demands, I had nothing to prove, but it still wasn't enough.

We need more warmth, said the voice in my head, *more air, more light, more elegance.*

I caught a train that would take me nearer the sun.

3

I took my leave of that city by way of the cheapest form of transport available to those desirous of reaching their destinations before too great a length of time, that is to say by way of the railway, or the iron horse as it was once so quaintly known!

The terminus whence my journey began was a fine, new, vaulted edifice ringing with the confident clamour of this great age of industry and energy into which we have all been so fortunate as to be born. It bustled with the optimistic passage of persons travelling to and from the great metropolis, and it seemed to mark a junction of all the ages, past, present and future, with its thrusting congress of extravagant humanity, business, trade, errand and quest that caused the great domed concourse to echo with vigorous intent.

The bright morning, neither still spring nor yet quite summer, was crisp and clear yet one of those that threaten later cold wet squalls, and so it was with eagerness that I purchased my passage towards the sun and made my way through the jostling throng with many an apology to claim a sleeping compartment upon one of the famed rapide expresses of those parts, a sumptuously appointed caravan of carriages drawn by a proud, majestic locomotive breathing steam. My spirits were raised by the mere sight of the locomotive's gleaming bronze and its rich scarlet, azure and golden livery and the acrid odour of smoke, as it wheezed and strained with ill-concealed impatience to embark upon its lengthy mission into the unknown hinterland. I also was eager to take my leave of the city, despite the diversions it had offered me. The reason for my own impatience, it seemed to me, was not so much a matter of place as of time. Had I discovered it when I were either younger or older it may have sufficed, but in these years of my prime it seemed meretricious and unworthy of

35

me. I sought a setting of greater depth and warmth.

Already my heart felt lighter as the great locomotive coughed out of the terminus, for there is a grand nobility of purpose attached to steam locomotion that has less to do with vulgar speed than with stern endeavour and firmness of purpose, virtues not always held perhaps in quite as high esteem in these modern days as heretofore. There is a hint of brutal poetry in the shudder of iron, the panting steam, the billowing smoke, the glowing furnace, the darting pistons, the flashing orbs and the twin fidelity of rails, rigid yet supple, snaking faithfully together like a mature marriage towards a common purpose and horizon, utterly certain of their cause and destination. Would that Man himself were always so determined and confident! What a paradise this world could be, were Man equally firm and driven not by fleshy weakness but by the strong machinery of an iron resolve. Yet all is possible, and who can tell? Our modern progress is such that perhaps our scientists one day will continue such omnipotent constructions, mechanical men maybe and contraptions able to know all in the twinkling of an instant, so that all men may be freed from toil to bask by the millions in joyful leisured unemployment. Tut, what melodrama!

I was truly fortunate in having acquired for myself a sleeping compartment which I was not required to share with another soul. I am not an unsociable man and am able to enjoy intercourse with others as blithely as any; indeed, on occasions I positively crave the company of fellow creatures and go to certain lengths to seek them out; but I was happy to find myself alone as we hurtled through space at an unconscionable speed; for I suffer occasionally from a dread of confined spaces; and companionship should be deliberately chosen, for there is always an awkward joviality in finding oneself sharing sleeping quarters and nakedness with strangers, unless, of course, the stranger be of the fair s**! No, I jest, of course.

For some time in the comfort of my quarters I enjoyed the sensations of travel, revelling in the rocking of the carriage, the clicking of the wheels, the flashing by of fields, pastures, meadows, hills, cattle, villages. How strange that objects close to the observer pass with such speed while those at a greater distance appear barely to move, just as I, observed from an equal distance, must appear to be scarcely moving myself. The world is indeed only what we make of it and exists only in so far as we observe it from a particular vantage point. The world appears utterly different to the cow and the tree and the insect, yet it be the same world. So too with Time: the insect's life is but a minute to that of the cow and but a second to that of the tree, yet to the insect life is equally a taste of eternity.

Enough philosophy! I do not doubt that it weakens the brain, like a novel by Dickens!

In the fullness of time I repaired to the dining carriage, as the darkness crept across the face of the earth and the velvet curtains were drawn across the windows and the gaslamps lit. I was heartened by the cosy warmth of that restaurant on wheels with silver gleaming against mahogany and crisp linen tucked into crystal and the sight of elegant ladies and gentlemen decked out in travelling finery. Here there was no vulgar hint of toil or commerce. All was elegant leisure and genteel unemployment.

'Will you partake of dinner, sir?' enquired the *maître*.

'Certainly,' I quipped, 'for surely I had not anticipated breakfast at such an hour!'

He smiled obsequiously and bowed me towards a table for four that was already three-quarters occupied by a lady and two gentlemen. I could barely credit my good fortune, for the lady was one of the most delicious creatures upon whom I have ever been privileged to set my eyes. Her own were large and generously spaced, her nose perfection, her lips and complexion such as painters dream of. I confess my heart missed a beat, though possibly my reaction was also occasioned by the sight of the two gentlemen with her. Beside her was an elderly person, with protruding eyes and a beard, of such gross corpulence that the couple barely succeeded in sitting side by side together in the eating booth, and opposite him was placed a much younger but villainous-looking character, well-dressed enough (as indeed they all were) and sufficiently well-spoken to be taken for a gentleman, but whose gaunt, sallow face and ridiculous little moustache and beady eyes betrayed a blackness of soul. I suspected he might be a Jew.

'I trust I do not inconvenience you?' I said to them all. 'I have no wish to intrude and would happily await a later hour should you prefer to dine alone.'

'Be seated, sir,' said The Beard, a trifle testily, but the heavenly apparition beside him smiled so sweetly that I was damned if I would take offence at his curmudgeonliness.

37

'I am obliged, madam,' said I, ignoring The Beard and seating myself beside the Israelite villain, where I could gaze directly into the lady's peerless eyes without any sense of impropriety. Indeed, to do otherwise would have been impolite, sitting as I was directly facing her. I confess that I fell in love with her upon the instant.

I introduced myself.

'Mrs Langtry,' she said. Her voice was as angelic as her appearance.

'Honoured, ma'am,' said I.

The Beard mumbled something, Edward something, followed by an unpronounceable Germanic surname of gutturals and hyphens that I had no intention of remembering since I did not intend to do him the honour of addressing him by his name. I merely inclined my head briefly in his direction. 'Sir,' I said. No man treats me with testy condescension with impunity.

'Druitt,' remarked the Jewish villain in a cultured but chillingly treacly voice. 'Montague Druitt, Barrister-at-law.'

'Sir,' I said brusquely. I had no intention either of addressing him other than formally. His hair, parted centrally, did not increase his attraction, and I have never been greatly enamoured of the legal profession. They resemble butchers in their eagerness for pounds of flesh.

'May I enquire whether you are all travelling together, Mrs Langtry?' I asked.

'Confound it, sir!' said The Beard, glaring with those protruding eyes. 'May I ask what business it is of yours?'

'Teddy, *please*,' said she.

'Damned impertinence!' said The Beard.

At any other time I surmise I should have invited the tetchy, bloated oaf to step outside to settle the matter, but this seemed inadvisable since the railway carriage was progressing at speed, and I had no intention of brawling in a corridor. In addition I surmised that Mrs Langtry would be less impressed by a show of brute strength and wounded pride than she would be by a display of nonchalant wit, and from that moment I made it my business to impress her. Further than that I only dared to dream, but I fully intended to diminish the oaf in her eyes and to advance my own cause and charms.

I fixed The Beard with a cold smile. 'I have no wish to intrude upon your affairs whatever, sir,' I said icily, '*whatever* they may be.' Her lips flickered with interest. 'I assure you that your secrets are of no consequence to me whatever, sir.'

He bristled and his beard twitched and his eyes appeared about to dislodge themselves from their sockets, but Mrs Langtry swiftly intervened.

'We are travelling to the coast for the Season,' she said. 'But we have only this evening had the pleasure of making the acquaintance of Mr Druitt, who has joined us, as indeed you yourself have done, merely to dine.'

'Oh, I hope not, Mrs Langtry,' said I lightly. 'I very much hope that this shall not be merely a fleeting acquaintance and that I shall see more of you. Congenial intercourse is so important when one is travelling, do you not agree?'

'Oh, indeed, sir,' said she, staring at me so boldly that the Israelite villain Druitt beside me stirred with a hint of malevolence that made me suspect that he too had entertained romantic hopes for himself and was now discommoded by the sudden appearance of a possible rival. It seemed obvious that Mrs Langtry must be The Beard's mistress, for otherwise how could they travel together alone? But a mistress may be seduced as simply as a wife, and if The Beard had succeeded with her, why should I be daunted by the challenge? He must have been exceedingly rich, for he possessed neither a pleasant countenance nor any obvious attractions of charm or temperament. I prayed that they were not accommodated in the same sleeping compartment. He was so corpulent it certainly seemed unlikely.

'Mr Druitt was speaking of cricket,' said Mrs Langtry, in a tone that suggested that she might be partial to my concocting some mischief at the semitic villain's expense. 'He has played for Winchester.'

'Indeed,' I ventured. 'For the cathedral?'

Mrs Langtry laughed prettily and I gleamed with triumph, but the villain's expression was so suffused with anger that I counted myself fortunate I was not meeting him alone on a foggy night in a slum alleyway.

'Winchester College,' he hissed. 'I played for the First XI at Lord's in '76.'

'My apologies, sir,' I continued. The man was a natural butt, like so many Hebrews. He took himself with exquisite seriousness. 'Undoubtedly you were also a prefect?'

Druitt seemed suddenly to spring to life at memories of his childhood triumphs. I sensed that he was a man already conscious

39

of failure, despite his callow years. Winchester College had represented the pinnacle of his life's achievement, and already he suspected that his future would be a series of anti-climaxes and disappointments. Already he was a man in decline.

'Prefect of Chapel,' he said with that mock modesty that is so easily identifiable as self-important vanity. Prefect of Chapel? Surely not. A Jew? 'I was fortunate enough to win a scholarship. Indeed, I won a further scholarship to New College, Oxford. Fate has been good to me.'

'Capital, sir, capital!' I cried. 'You are obviously not only brilliant but also a man of true humility and commendable gratitude.' I glanced at Mrs Langtry. She was too well-bred to laugh but her eyes were twinkling. 'Is young Mr Druitt not a shining example to the rising generation, Mrs Langtry?'

'To be sure, sir,' she said. 'We should thank the Almighty that he has seen fit to place the future in the hands of such paragons as he.'

I beamed at Druitt. I regret to confess that bore-baiting can be most satisfying, but I pardoned myself with the thought that it could only be beneficial to this son of Abraham to be shown that his public opinion of himself was offensively high. His face had taken on so pale a hue that I feared he might faint, but upon his cheeks there were two spots of colour so vivid that I acknowledged a deep sense of hatred in him. One of his hands was gripping the edge of the table and the fingers of the other clenched his linen napkin with such ferocious concern that it seemed as though he wished to choke the life out of it. The sinews stood out on either hand with equal and surprising ambidextrous power. He stared at me with a chilling intensity that I confess alarmed me in a far greater degree than had The Beard. Two new enemies made in as many minutes!

'You insult me!' hissed Druitt. 'Me, sir! I would have you know that I hold an honours degree in Greats. I have been called to the Bar. I am a member of the Inner Temple, with chambers in King's Bench Walk. I am not some snivelling stripling of no accomplishments. I come of exceedingly good family. My father is a medical man of much renown, not to mention a Justice of the Peace and a governor of Wimborne Grammar School.'

The time was upon me when I should make amends. Mrs Langtry was wearing the over-solemn expression of a lady about to burst with merriment, but the game had proceeded far enough.

Druitt was clearly on the brink of insanity. It may be sport to taunt a pompous bore but not a fellow in danger of losing his hold upon reason.

'Mr Druitt, sir, please,' I soothed. 'I meant no insult.'

'Yes, you did.'

'Not I, sir.'

'You did.'

'I didn't.'

'You did.'

'I didn't.'

'You did.'

Since the conversation appeared to have reached the conclusion of its natural life I appealed to Mrs Langtry, who gave the impression of being about to come adrift beneath her stays.

'Madam,' said I, 'I throw myself upon your gentle feminine nature and soft intuition. If I gave the impression of attempting to insult Mr Druitt, I beg you to chastise me and I shall make full restitution. It may be that some nuance of tone or reference unknown to me led me to give unwittingly the impression that has undoubtedly been taken so ill. I beg you to be my judge. Only speak, and pronounce my sentence.'

'Balderdash,' said The Beard, though to whom or what he was referring I could not be certain. 'Waiter! We expire from hunger!'

'You shall apologise,' hissed Druitt.

'Certainly, sir,' said I, 'if Mrs Langtry finds me guilty.'

What a lady she was, that lady, what a delicious admixture of translucent beauty, charm, humour, vivacity and immaculate tact. She smiled so winningly at Druitt that I wager a monk would have broken his vows on her behalf.

'Dear Mr Druitt,' she said, with eyes like stars, 'you are quite entitled to feel offended, and I shall beg the gentleman to proffer you a full and proper apology. But may I also urge you to consider that no offence was truly intended and that it was occasioned only through thoughtlessness? Most men would not have been offended by what was said, but I venture to suggest that you are of so greater a masculine bent than the majority of men that you saw, quite understandably, offence where none was intended, just as the strongest, most powerful beast will roar with rage even when stepping upon a thorn. It is precisely because you are a proud lion among men, Mr Druitt, that you roar.'

And then that delightful nymph proceeded to kick me beneath

the table.

Druitt seemed to grow visibly in stature. His spine straightened, his breast expanded, his Shylock nose lifted. He gazed at me. 'Well?'

'I apologise with all my heart,' said I with an exultation I endeavoured not to show. The goddess had struck me upon the shin! There could be no mistaking the import of that gesture. She would be mine before the celestial orb lifted again above the horizon. I had, as the Americans say so vulgarly, cracked it.

'Mrs Langtry has found me guilty,' I added, 'and I must bow to her verdict and crave your indulgence and forgiveness.'

Druitt wore the expression of a man about to soil himself with self-justification. A vision immediately visited me that here was a solitary man who probably consorted in the night with women of the streets.

'Well, sir? Do you forgive me? I am abject in my apology.'

He smiled crookedly, an insubstantial man whose moments of small achievement were obviously so rare that he must wallow in the few that passed his way.

'I forgive you,' he said. 'Pray do not allow it to happen again.'

I looked suitably contrite, and felt Mrs Langtry's silken leg slide beside my own.

Druitt, being Druitt, could not leave the matter there. 'What is more, sir,' he added with a ghastly condescension, 'I shall shake your hand as a token of my magnanimity to allow bygones to be bygones.'

I took his hand with as little distaste as I could feign. It was, of course, unpleasantly damp, but his grip was uncomfortably firm, like that of many inadequate men. There arose before my eyes a vivid vision of Druitt, crazed, committing murder with those powerful hands, by strangulation.

'May we dine now?' asked The Beard irritably. 'Is all this foolery finally settled? Confound it, Lillie, I shall waste away.'

'Not you, Tum-Tum,' she chuckled, and patted his vast stomach.

Tum-Tum? Damme, but I felt more than a tweak of the green-eyed vice to hear the affection of that ridiculous pet-name and to see her fingers upon that ponderous paunch. I consoled myself with the reflection that no man whose mistress calls him Tum-Tum could possibly be of any account between the sheets. Tum-Tum, indeed! One would not find it difficult to envisage

42

alternative portions of the anatomy by which one would infinitely prefer to be known affectionately to one's paramour.

Tum-Tum's temper improved with his intake of provender. He assaulted the first three courses with such dedication that his conversation was limited to animal sounds of grunting and slurping. His stomach rumbled and echoed as though it were a concert hall, and his breathing, forced by necessity to rely solely upon his nasal orifices, wheezed like the bellows of an aged church organ. But by the sixth course his gustatory energy was slackening and he was finding time to smile, nod, and once even to laugh, when Mrs Langtry remarked that she hoped he was not feeling indisposed since he appeared to have such a poor appetite this evening.

'There is nothing whatever amiss with my appetites, Lillie m'dear,' he leered, 'as well you know.'

I despised him. He was not only a boor but a vulgar, boastful boor.

Druitt too was more cheerful, in a ghoulish fashion. Established now in his own mind as Mrs Langtry's hero and as my conqueror, he delivered a series of arrogantly gauche remarks and kept gazing hungrily at her neck and bosom. I do believe that he entertained hopes himself of advancement in that quarter: Lord, how we mislead ourselves! He prattled on about his own importance even to the extent of informing us that at Winchester he had not only won the school's Fives singles championship but had also played an acclaimed Sir Toby Belch. He fawned upon Mrs Langtry in the most awkward fashion, making eyes and addressing her as 'dear lady', but Tum-Tum appeared unconcerned by this unlikely courtship, as though he too considered Druitt of no importance and certainly of no danger as a rival. Mrs Langtry's leg did not approach mine again but I was constantly conscious of the promise of the impishness in her magnificent eyes whenever she glanced at me. Druitt of course saw nothing: she was but a beautifully ornate mirror for his own poor vanity. After each of his remarks there was that fractional silence that unites listeners in a common embarrassment at the presence of a champion bore. Druitt unknowingly made allies of Mrs Langtry and myself even as he attemped to press his own suit. I would not have put it past the Shylock to have thought to offer Mrs Langtry money for her favours.

Eventually Tum-Tum sat back and ventured a sigh as gargantuan as if he carried upon his shoulders all the cares of the Empire. He belched and patted his navel, the size of which by now must have matched the rim of Vesuvius. He called for brandy and cigars and had mellowed to such an extent that he suggested we should all adjourn to the smoking carriage for a hand or two of cards before retiring.

'Ripping,' said Druitt in a sepulchral tone. I waited for him to announce that he had also been the Winchester College cribbage champion, but unhappily this time he failed me.

'Very well, Tum-Tum,' said Mrs Langtry, 'but I shall first repair to my boudoir to refresh myself.' She required as little refreshment as a daisy at dawn, but I suspected I knew the meaning of her ploy of absence. My blood quickened. Did she expect me to make an excuse and follow? 'I shall return in twenty minutes,' she said, looking at me.

Druitt and I stood as she departed, and her ambulation transpired to be quite as exquisite as I had anticipated. I decided, for decency's sake, to wait for five minutes before joining her. My blood thundered. Tum-Tum merely waved his cigar, firmly anchored as he was by his banquet.

Druitt and I seated ourselves again and listened to a lengthy discourse by Tum-Tum regarding his prowess with a gun and his ability to slaughter regiments of tame birds in outlandish areas like Scotland and Norfolk, but now it was a very different Druitt who fidgeted beside me. He was pale again, afflicted with a wondrous nervousness, and apparently suffering a nightmare of indecision as he drummed his fingers on the mahogany and sniffed and twitched, and in a moment of insight I apprehended his problem: Druitt, being Druitt, assumed that Mrs Langtry had absented herself for the express purpose of a clandestine meeting with *him* in her boudoir! Yet Druitt, also being Druitt, could not be absolutely certain that he was not mistaken and that if he followed her he would not find himself in some difficult situation of exceeding embarrassment. His mind was in a turmoil in which lustful vanity did battle with cowardly prudence. I made a silent wager with myself that cowardice would win. I lost: after a few moments of silent agony, and just as I was about to rise and follow Mrs Langtry myself, Druitt stood with a rigid expression upon his

44

white, sweating brow. Even Tum-Tum noticed his discomfiture.

'Here, Druitt, you indisposed?' he rumbled. 'Not sickenin', I hope, what?'

'Not at all,' stammered Druitt. 'Must just . . . get something . . . be back.'

He squeezed past me and even his knees were trembling. I wished with all my heart that I were able to observe his imminent encounter with Mrs Langtry. What sport would there be! I imagined him fumbling through an awkward declaration of passion and she laughing in his sweaty, pasty, Israelite face. As for myself, I was content to wait. Anticipation is to be savoured, and what could be achieved in ten minutes? I should bide my time and win the entire night.

'Rum sort of feller, that,' said Tum-Tum, scratching himself. 'Never could abide confounded lawyers.'

'I suspect he may be one of the Chosen People,' said I.

'Ha!' said Tum-Tum. 'That could explain it. Worse than niggers.'

We repaired to the smoking carriage.

Druitt joined us there ten minutes later. He was flushed and flustered and a damp patch on his collar betrayed the fact that he had been cooling the vivid embarrassment of his face with water. How I wished I could have observed his encounter with Mrs Langtry! If Fortune smiled upon me it was possible I might be able to persuade her later to describe the scene in all its excruciating detail. Druitt resembled a youth apprehended with his fingers trapped in his employer's safe-box. He could not bring himself to look directly at Tum-Tum, no doubt mortified as he was with guilty failure.

Mrs Langtry was not much further delayed, and when she joined us at the gaming table she was calm as a nun. She offered me a little smile that betrayed nothing. Already in her brief absence I had forgotten precisely how matchless was her beauty and the renewed sight of her smote at something within me. In beauty and breeding and bearing she was incomparable. She smiled even at Druitt as a matter of common courtesy despite the probability that barely minutes hence his grasping fingers had been importunate upon her bodice, but he could not bring

45

himself to acknowledge her and turned away with burning face. I wagered that before any great space of time had passed he would make his excuse and repair to some fiendish solitary solace in the privacy of his own sleeping chamber.

Tum-Tum had decreed that we should play baccarat and had already called for a shoe and fresh packets of playing cards stylishly printed in the scarlet, azure and golden livery of the railway company. Baccarat is not my favourite game of chance, relying as it does less on skill than on fortune, but there is always a warm glow in the pool of light above the gaming table and the crisp clicking and slithering of fresh cards upon the baize, and I experienced then a deep emotion of contentment as the carriages rattled and rocked through the balmy night and the locomotive hooted distantly on occasion and cigar smoke twirled at sensual leisure around the gas lamps gleaming on starched cuffs and golden signet rings. For a fleeting moment I enjoyed one of those rare apprehensions of infinity, when the universe seems suddenly utterly understandable and in harmony, as it can at night by the sea when the stars are so sharp that they appear to lie beside the hand of God. Time itself seemed to hold its breath and grant us all an extra second of eternity. In that moment I had a deep knowledge of myself: I was for a second a god myself, a man at the peak of his prime, to whom nothing could be denied and for whom there was no threat or danger. Mrs Langtry's long, smooth neck shone like an exquisite treasure.

She sat at the gaming table opposite Tum-Tum, who had elected himself to play banker, and Druitt and I took our places on either side of him, Druitt flinching almost physically from such proximity to the man he would have cuckolded. I wondered whether Druitt had ever lain with a willing woman, of her own choice, and doubted it.

Tum-Tum had summoned several other travellers to join the game as punters and they stood around the table in varying degrees of joviality. I remember particularly a large, heavy individual with curly hair and pouting lips who obviously accounted himself a wit but many of whose quips and epigrams were far beyond the understanding of a man such as Tum-Tum. He was accompanied by a slim, epicene youth, much given to dramatic gestures, of whom the other seemed inordinately fond, and both wore green carnations in their buttonholes, which I took, tolerant though I pride myself to be, to be somewhat flamboyant. They were not the quality of company I should normally have selected for myself, but Tum-Tum seemed oblivious to the unsavoury nature of their relationship, and I told myself charitably that perhaps they were merely uncle and nephew, or possibly cousins, though the shrill cries of the younger suggested otherwise.

'Oh, no,' he whined. 'Do we *have* to? Baccarat is so *tedious*.'

'Bacca*ra*, my boy, not bacca*rat*. The "t" is silent, as in Whistler.'

For the first time since encountering Tum-Tum and Mrs Langtry my resolve faltered, for at last I could see for certain the source and cause of his fascination for her as he placed before him upon the gaming table a vast pile of banknotes that would have engaged the interest even of a Rothschild, and he matched them with several towers of gleaming sovereigns, the sight of which caused Druitt's eager Shylock nose to twitch. No one would be calling 'banco' tonight. If this were the sum Tum-Tum was prepared to wager merely on a polite after-dinner hand or two of baccarat it seemed no longer a mystery that such a man should seem alluring to Mrs Langtry. I stole a glance at her, and my spirit soared again, for she too was gazing at me and in her eyes I detected a depth of promise that weakened my knees. I could not match Tum-Tum's fortune, but in my own way that night I, not he, might be king.

Druitt appeared to be mesmerised by Tum-Tum's wealth lying so close before him and I wondered whether he might not on an instant seize it all and jump from the carriage to take his chances in the night. His open greed, so characteristic of his venal race, betrayed the fact that he must be a failure as a barrister, too. Such men of small accomplishment and bitter disappointment are as much to be feared as despised, for when they are driven finally to the deepest depths of regret and shame they are liable to seek out almost any means of making themselves known to the world, however villainous or monstrous those means may be. I hoped that Druitt might be fortunate enough to win some small share of Tum-Tum's wealth that night, for if not, following his rebuff by Mrs Langtry, who could tell how his resentment would fester in an already unstable breast, one day to spew forth in a black fury of revenge against Fate and his fellow men? I could imagine Druitt on the gallows, with a rope about his neck. I resolved to be kind to him.

'Good luck, Mr Druitt,' I ventured. 'The riches of the Orient lie before us!'

Druitt nodded briefly and licked his lips.

Tum-Tum shuffled the cards together, placed them in the shoe, and began to deal, one to Druitt, one to me, one to himself, one to Druitt, one to me, one to himself.

'A sovereign on the left hand,' offered one of the punters.

His overblown confidence in my cards was not reassuring. I wagered little myself, intending to eke out the sum I was prepared to lose until it was time to claim a richer prize. Other punters laid their various bets, only Mrs Langtry abstaining. It was not until then that I realised that she was the only lady present: even so, had there been others, I vow I should not have noticed them.

Druitt looked at his cards, his powerful fingers shaking. He placed them face down again. 'Stand,' he said.

'*Non!*' growled Tum-Tum. 'We say *non*, Mr Druitt, and *carte* when we require an additional card.'

'*Non*,' said Druitt viciously.

'Oh, *dear*', said the catamite.

I glanced at my cards. A Queen and a 4. I had to call for another.

'*Carte*,' I said.

'This suspense is terrible,' chuckled Mrs Langtry. 'I hope it will last.'

Tum-Tum dealt me a third card, face up. A benighted 10. The catamite groaned dramatically. Tum-Tum showed his own cards, an immediate natural of 9: a 7 and a 2. He had beaten us all.

Tum-Tum accepted his winnings with grace, almost with a sort of nonchalant majesty, as though they were of no great matter, which indeed, of course, set beside the total of his bank, they were not, even though in one play he had accumulated the equivalent of a housemaid's annual remuneration.

'Come, Lillie,' he beamed jovially, smoothing his moustaches, 'you must join the play.'

'I shall support Mr Druitt, then,' she said, causing that individual to turn scarlet with her acknowledgement of him despite his own base intentions of only minutes earlier. 'I suspect Mr Druitt may be lucky tonight.'

What a saucy, treacherous minx!

Druitt knew not where to place his gaze, causing Tum-Tum to turn playful.

'You should not flirt with Mr Druitt, my dear,' he guffawed. 'You are the most wicked tease, that is the pure and simple truth.'

'The truth is never pure and rarely simple,' said Mrs Langtry mischievously.

I would not have believed the good fortune that Mrs Langtry brought to Druitt thenceforth had I not witnessed it myself. For an hour it seemed that he could not lose, and she followed his every wager as though taunting him. Play after play went his way until both he and Mrs Langtry were in possession of a tidy mound of Tum-Tum's fortune. Even when Tum-Tum cheated (and on several occasions I observed him dealing from the bottom of the pack, though I said nothing, since it seemed to be of no avail to him) he nevertheless continued to lose. It was almost as though she had put the evil eye on her paramour, and even I myself accumulated from him a profit sufficient to cover my journey several times over. In earlier ages they would have burned her as a witch.

The catamite and his companion were less fortunate, generally wagering on Druitt's hand only on the rare occasions that he lost, and they and several others soon drifted away to their repose, with the pouting fellow declaring: 'I must repair to bed: I must look after my youth,' at which Mrs Langtry and I shared a glance that threatened to explode in laughter.

Eventually there were only the four of us remaining at the gaming table, and apart from the creaking of the carriage and the clockety-clock, clockety-clock of the wheels and the faint sound of the panting locomotive far before us, there descended a portentous silence that seemed to enter Druitt's very being to render him insane. Already he was feverish with his successes: his winnings would have bought him a substantial house in a less fashionable area of almost any city. His eyes gleamed, his fingers twitched, his breathing was fast and he seemed inebriated with triumph though his consumption of brandy had been but moderate. But what Druitt did then can only be ascribed to lunacy. He stared hotly at Tum-Tum.

'I wager my entire winnings against the next turn of the cards,' he croaked.

Tum-Tum stared at him for a full half-minute. 'A bold venture, Mr Druitt,' he growled. 'Should you win you would then be in a position to call *banco*.'

'Should I win,' said Druitt haltingly, like a man walking in his

49

sleep, 'I should not require your money, sir.'

'The devil you wouldn't!' said Tum-Tum. 'What are you driving at, sir?'

Druitt swallowed hard. 'I wish to game with you for Mrs Langtry,' he said.

The silence was shocking. Even she coloured. It was the first time I had ever seen her confounded, and hardly surprisingly. She rose from her seat in confusion and fled from the carriage.

'How dare you, sir?' I heard myself say. 'How dare you!'

'Scoundrel!' bellowed Tum-Tum. 'Blackguard! Gad, sir, what a scoundrel!' He attempted to rise and to strike Druitt at the same instant, but lost his balance, falling back into his seat.

'How dare you, you Jewish swine,' I said. Words come slowly in such a situation, so instead I struck Druitt in the teeth.

'Guard!' called Tum-Tum. 'Guard! Help! Murder!'

Druitt advanced upon me with loathing in his Israelite eyes. I had been right about his possible talent for strangulation: his fingers flexed towards my neck and their sinews appeared monstrously powerful. Fortunately, the railway company's employees were soon upon him, restraining him, pinning his arms and leading him away towards the rear, where I believe they store manacles for just such an emergency, but I knew now I had been prescient about Druitt's future. His madness would undoubtedly lead him one day to the gallows.

'She is a whore!' he shrieked as they dragged him away. 'Whore! Prostitute! I hate her! I curse all whores! Jezebels! I shall rid the earth of them! Painted harlots! I shall rip their hearts from their breasts and tear their wombs from their bowels! I shall . . . .'

His voice trailed away as the guards fought with him and dragged him down distant corridors.

'My God,' said Tum-Tum, scooping up all the money, including Druitt's substantial winnings. 'It is a good thing you restrained me. I should have killed the blackguard. Where is that infernal brandy bottle?'

I abandoned all hope of Mrs Langtry for that night, deeming it would be outrageous licence to continue to press my suit upon her after all that she had endured, and scheming how I might best tomorrow obtain her address when we reached the coast. But an hour or so after I had finally retired, having to half-carry the drunken weight of Tum-Tum to their carriage, as he muttered constantly '*Evil be to him who evil thinks*,' she came to me.

Due to my occasional dread of confined spaces I had not locked my door and I woke from my slumber to find her slipping into my bunk and whispering endearments. I surmised at first that this must be some heavenly dream, but her voice and texture and kisses soon obliterated that fantasy, and I lit the lamp the better to adore her and blessed whichever god or devil it might be that had delivered this angel to my arms.

'Your eyes change colour, sir,' she whispered. 'In passion they become an ardent golden brown.'

I have promised myself that in my new life I shall cling to honesty if I cling to no other virtue at all, so honesty it shall be.

For hours that night, lulled by the rocking train, inspired by my earlier hopes and the confident prime of my manhood, and spurred by her caresses, of which she employed an infinite paradise of variety, I held within my arms the most beautiful woman I had ever seen, a woman so exquisite that even a decrepit Pope would not have failed her. Yet I must force myself to record that I failed her, and failed myself. Had she been a virgin, she would have remained a virgin still. Despite every encouragement I remained infirm. I felt a deep sense of shame that in its fashion was as black as that of Druitt.

Such a calamity had previously befallen me only once, when I was a callow youth and had taken too much wine. I felt both as young as I had been then and also immeasurably old, for impotence is the curse of age, and within myself I sensed a hollow sound of mocking laughter at my own arrogance.

When she left just before dawn I fell on the bunk in despair. The most beautiful woman I had ever met would always remember me as an eunuch. She would smile at the mention of my name and mock me to her friends. Could it be that she was too beautiful? Had she shamed my base desires with her perfection? I tossed and turned in search of excuses for my feebleness as the sun rose bright on a clear and glorious summer dawn. But none of my reasonings brought me any satisfaction. None of the rivals I had so easily despised would have failed her. Not Druitt, certainly, and even now perhaps she lay beneath the gargantuan wheezing engine of Tum-Tum.

I hid in my compartment long after the train had reached its destination on the coast, and felt in my mind like dust the crumblings of my pride.

(2)

I felt inexplicably uneasy during my stay at the coast. When I checked into the hotel I signed the register unthinkingly with my old name and was forced to stick with it to prevent drawing attention to myself. So for several days I was myself at the hotel but the stranger whenever I cashed a cheque. It was unnerving trying to be two people at once. Somehow the overnight train journey had unsettled me, and at first I couldn't understand why, especially as I had managed to win some money at cards off some people I had bumped into in the dining car, and the woman with them had made it plain that she found me attractive, though I didn't pursue the obvious offer and it came to nothing. So why should I feel so restless? Perhaps it had something to do with the journey itself. It was probably ten years since I had last travelled by overnight sleeper and the confined but speeding atmosphere of the train, both alien and intimate, like a capsule hurtling through space and time, kept reminding me of that last overnight train journey. It had been during the most uneasy period of my life and the woman with me was nagging me to leave my wife and live with her.

We'd been having a spasmodic affair for several months. For me it was simply a brief stimulus to relieve the boredom of my life, my job and my marriage, but for her it was becoming serious. She kept insisting that this was love, the Real Thing. Women do. It makes them feel less furtive. And she knew too that I dreamed even then of changing my life. I had reached that crossroads where I was no longer young but not yet middle-aged, where I had established myself firmly in my career and was successful and prosperous enough but was beginning to wonder what next? I had recognition, money, wife, family, and enough leisure to satisfy all but the idlest Victorian gentleman. I had achieved most of what I had ever expected to achieve, but somehow it wasn't enough. I felt uneasy and no longer master of my fate. I suspected I needed to be extended more, challenged more, to be less safe. But I didn't have the courage then (or perhaps the foolhardiness) to change anything.

'Leave her and live with me,' said my mistress.

We had stolen a weekend away together – the usual excuse, a conference somewhere – but now the interval was over and we were returning like children going back to school after half-term.

'We've been through all that,' I sighed. 'It wouldn't be fair.'

'On who?' she demanded. She had drunk too much and was alternating between maudlin sentimentality and foul-mouthed belligerence. Her drinking and swearing were becoming embarrassing. They also made me feel guilty. She had never drunk much at the beginning of our affair, but the tensions, deceptions and disappointments of our adultery were driving her increasingly to the bottle and four-letter words. Feminism had not been kind to women and I envied the Victorians their complaisant wives and patient mistresses. Nowadays a mistress demands not just your body but also your soul.

'It wouldn't be fair on the children,' I said. 'They're still too young to understand. I'm not going to screw up their lives.'

'And what about my life? You don't seem to mind screwing me or screwing me up. How long do you expect me to go on like this?'

'Until they're old enough not to be too hurt.'

'Shit, that could be ten years or more. The classic married man's excuse. Do you really expect me to hang around for ten years or more on the off-chance that you might still fancy me?'

'I don't expect you to do anything.'

'You really are a bastard, aren't you?' she snapped. 'You don't give a damn about me. In fact you don't give a damn about anybody, least of all your precious children. When did you last spend any time with them? When did you last even take them to the zoo?'

'I don't approve of zoos.'

'Don't give me that crap. You know what I mean. If you walked out on them tomorrow they wouldn't even notice.'

'Oh, thank you.'

'And don't start getting all hurt and sulky, either. Jesus, I know you so well. You're a taker. When did you ever *give* anything? And I don't mean presents. When did you last give some of your time or some of yourself to anyone without expecting something back in return?'

'You're drunk again.'

'Too fucking right I am. You're such a pain in the arse I'm surprised your wife isn't as pissed as a parrot from dawn to dusk

53

as well.'

'She's too strong-willed for that.'

'So now I'm weak-willed as well, am I?'

'I didn't say that at all.'

'Yes you bloody well did. If your wife's so wonderful what the fuck are you doing fucking me?'

'You're disgustingly pathetic when you're drunk.'

'You're disgustingly pathetic even when you're sober. So I'm weak-willed, am I? I'll tell you who's weak-willed, you wanker. You. You're too fucking weak to be faithful to your wife and you're too fucking weak to leave her. You're too weak to have any real friends or even any real enemies. You want to change your life but you haven't got the balls to do anything about it. Christ, you're wet. You're so bloody indecisive about everything except the high opinion you hold of yourself. And what about your job? You're not exactly setting the world alight.'

'I do all right.'

'All *right*? What sort of great peak of achievement is *all right*?'

'I do bloody well, then.'

'Oh, sure, great, yes, you make a bit of money. You've got a nice house. You can afford to buy me decent dinners and pay for hotel rooms, though I wouldn't be surprised if you claim me as expenses against tax. But who really respects you, or what you do? Do strangers whisper admiringly when you walk into a room? Do they fuck.'

'They certainly whisper when you stagger into a room,' I said.

She hit me. 'You bastard,' she shouted.

I raised my hand to strike her back, and lowered it. The occupant in the next sleeper compartment was banging angrily on the wall. I had not hit a woman in years, and I wasn't going to start again now. The last time I had felt horribly ashamed afterwards.

'You're even too feeble to hit me back,' she jeered. 'Christ, a real man would give me a good hiding.'

'I'm going to find another compartment,' I said.

'That's right,' she sneered, 'run away. You've been running away all your life, haven't you? What happened to the bright young high-flier who was going to take the world by storm? What happened to the young eagle who was going to soar gloriously into the heights? You've turned into just one more flabby, material-istic, self-indulgent fascist. Do you know what's the most pathetic thing about you? It's not that you've been unfaithful to your wife,

54

your children, even me. It's that you've been unfaithful to yourself. You've betrayed your own promise. What was it Oscar Wilde said? "Each man kills the thing he loves." You love yourself all right, and you're killing yourself, your talent and your soul. You've had things far too easy and you're too bloody comfortable. You're not some leisured landed Victorian gentleman who can afford to waste his life playing baccarat and screwing the peasants and sneering at Jews and negroes and homosexuals and patronising women. This is the twentieth century, sunshine, and if you're going to do anything worthwhile you've got to get out there and fight before it's too late. Will you ever have the guts to do it? Will you hell. You still think you're a promising lad and God's gift. Jesus! You're almost past it already. And when you're old you'll sit around boasting about your non-existent triumphs when you were younger and secretly blaming everyone but yourself that you didn't do better. Go on, then. Fuck off. Find another compartment. Run away, as usual. Fucking wanker.'

I had slammed the door behind me and walked the length of the train, trembling with anger, not because she was cruelly unfair but because she was right. I found the guard and asked for another compartment, but the train was full and I sat in the dining car and swigged a couple of large brandies to calm myself and waste the time until she would have fallen into a drunken stupor and I could slide into my bunk quietly.

The affair was finished. I didn't need her to tell me what I knew already: that I was drifting, bored, destroying what promise and talent I had ever had. I had become self-indulgent and materialistic and it wasn't making me or anyone else happy. I was wasting my life, and fooling myself that an occasional adulterous excitement could give it meaning. When your wife understands you, that may just be the beginning of harmony and contentment. When your mistress understands you too that means trouble. I had to end it.

Nearly an hour later I crept back into the compartment. It stank of whisky. She was snoring loudly. Dear God, how had I ever desired her? I undressed quickly and slipped into the top bunk, and vowed once again to change my life completely, not knowing it would take another ten years before I summoned the courage to do it.

In the morning she had been as contrite as she always was the next day. 'God, darling, please forgive me,' she said. 'I can't remember even half of what I said, and I didn't mean any of it. Please forgive me.'

In the taxi, when I had dropped her off at her office, she had hugged and kissed me like a woman drowning. 'I love you,' she had said. 'I love you so much.'

I never saw her again. I was neither brave nor confident enough to end it any way but brutally. My secretary acted as an impenetrable barrier to her pleadings, and eventually the telephone stopped ringing, though my wife once answered it at home late at night and came back into the room with a little smile.

'Who was it?' I had said.

'Some drunken woman. She wouldn't give her name. She said I should know you were a selfish, useless bastard.'

'Oh?' I had said uncomfortably.

'I told her I knew already.'

Our marriage was never quite the same again.

Why should another overnight train journey, ten years later, revive that old guilt and feeling of impotence? Perhaps because it reminded me that I had wasted another ten years before fulfilling my vow to change myself and be born again? Or because I had already been dreaming then of reaching for some sort of perfection in my life but had kept failing to grasp it until it was nearly too late? Or was it because already I was beginning to wonder whether that perfection even existed? I was looking for something, but I didn't know what.

You're looking for me, said the voice in my head.

Perhaps that was true. Perhaps I really was on a quest to rediscover my conscience.

There were several odd things about my stay on the coast that made me feel uneasy. The sun glittered each day, the sea was blue, the beaches inviting, the girls young and pretty, and I had all the time I wanted to do anything I chose. But I felt curiously displaced and distanced from everything that was going on around me. I strolled up and down the promenade as carelessly as a leisured Edwardian, I gambled a bit in the casino, I bought a panama hat and sat at pavement cafés sipping foreign drinks, watching. But I felt remote, as though I were living in someone else's dream. Everything seemed to belong to another age. I felt

56

out of time. And there was certainly something almost Victorian about my strict self-control. I watched the girls cavorting on the beaches and laughing in the waves, but I lived like a monk for all the weeks I lingered there, declining even the approaches of the prostitutes who loitered all night on the streets and in the bars. My experience in the city had left me with a determination to be chaste. Perhaps it was guilt at the way I had used the woman who had been abandoned by her husband, or maybe I was afraid of taking the chance of falling in love again, or perhaps I had simply grown up at last and realised that there is something undignified and pathetic about a middle-aged man who is determinedly promiscuous. I was able to enjoy watching the girls with their beautiful young bodies and smiles and eyes, but I might have been impotent for all the physical desire I felt for them. I saw them not as objects of lust but as other men's daughters, to be admired but protected and cherished. Perhaps my conscience was indeed beginning to work again. Or perhaps I was just growing prematurely old.

Celibacy is supposed to heighten your awareness, and if it goes on long enough to bring you the sort of visions and hallucinations that are apparently experienced by monks and Hindu holy men. I never saw God, nor even a saint, but the dreamlike quality of those days at the coast was heightened when I kept experiencing a weird sense of *déjà vu* as I rounded a street corner or came upon a quiet tree-shaded square which I knew I had never been to before. Why did I keep thinking that I had? Why did several people nod at me as though they knew me? Twice complete strangers waved across the street and called me greetings, and one night I dined in a small restaurant where the *maître d'hôtel* treated me like an old and valued customer.

'Welcome, sir,' he said. 'It it very good to see you again. You have been away?'

I nearly told him I had never seen him or his restaurant before in my life, but suddenly I wanted to know why he thought he knew me and who he thought I was.

'Yes, away,' I said.

'It must be a year, maybe more.'

'Really? That long?'

'At least a year.'

'I suppose you're right. Time passes so fast.'

'Ah, yes, alas. The older we become, the quicker the days

vanish. When we are young a month can seem like a century. Perhaps when we are old a century may seem like a month. Your usual table at the window?'

He guided me to a small table set for two. I sat with my back to the wall, like an animal seeking security, with only a potted plant for company, and deeply conscious of the empty place before me and the separateness of eating alone.

'A dry sherry as usual?' he asked.

I had not drunk sherry for years. 'Of course,' I said.

He handed me a menu and smiled. 'It is good to see you again,' he said, and eased away.

I looked around the restaurant. It did seem familiar, but then restaurants often seem familiar. There are only so many possible combinations of tables, chairs, cutlery, napkins and decor in restaurants, and so many resemble each other. I knew even before I saw it that the little cocktail bar would be on the right, but then in a restaurant this size the cocktail bar would have to be on the right: there was nowhere else for it. And the door to the lavatories, I knew, were beyond the bar, but then that was the only possible place for them, too. I was certain I had never been here before, but I had eaten in dozens of other restaurants just like it.

I glanced at the menu.

The duck is very good, said the voice in my head. *With a sauce of lime and white wine. Let's have the duck.*

I suffered an irrational moment of panic. Why was I beginning to hear voices again? Was this the onset of senility? Would it only be a matter of time before I started moving my lips, and then actually mumbling to myself, like a mad old man?

The spinach mousse with prawns is pretty good as well.

I became aware that beneath the table my fist was clenched tight with anxiety. All this solitariness was beginning to make me neurotic. I vowed to start meeting people again, to strike up acquaintanceships, talk to others and not just to myself. What a terrible irony it would be to escape the jail of my old life only to lock myself into a new prison of lonely paranoia. I forced myself to study every item on the menu, looking for alternatives, determined to choose anything other than the spinach mousse and the breast of duck. When the wine waiter brought my sherry my hand shook as I sipped it. His expression depressed me. He looked at me as though he thought I must be an alcoholic.

The *maître* approached again, smiling, a pad at the ready. 'Will

58

you order now, sir?'

'Please. I'll have . . . . '

'I can recommend the veal. It is the new chef's speciality.' He kissed his fingertips. 'Delicious.'

Not the veal. They cut their throats and let them bleed to death.

'No, I think I'll settle for the duck,' I heard myself say, 'with the spinach mousse and prawns to start.'

'An excellent choice,' he said, scribbling. 'And a selection of vegetables?'

'Please.'

'And the house red as usual? Or do you wish the wine list?'

'No, the house red,' I said, 'as usual.'

'Very good, sir. And later I will suggest the chocolate gateau with chopped nuts and cream. It is so light it will make you float.' He smiled professionally. '*Bon appétit*,' he said, and was gone.

I sipped the sherry again and spilled a little down my chin. Damn the trembling of my hand. I felt completely disorientated. He was so certain he knew me that I was beginning to doubt my own memory. Was it really possible I had indeed been here before and simply couldn't remember? Was I suffering some sort of amnesia? They say that guilt can so overload the circuits of the mind that they simply erase unacceptable memories. And yet I was certain I had never been here before.

The food and wine when they came were excellent, and after the meal I felt more confident. I chose a cigar and the lingering blue smoke and the hot black coffee quelled my nerves. I summoned the *maître*, determined to find out more.

'I have a confession to make,' I said.

He looked pious.

'Since I was last here I've been ill,' I said.

He looked suitably concerned. 'I am so sorry. Is there anything . . . ?'

'No, it's nothing really serious. But I've suffered from amnesia. I've lost whole areas of my past. I can't even remember my name.'

He shook his head with sympathy. 'That must be terrible.'

I nibbled at the cigar, like an infant worrying a nipple.

'You see,' I said, 'I'm terribly sorry, it's awful, I know, but I don't even remember you at all. I don't remember ever eating here before.'

'But, sir . . . .'

'My memory is a complete blank. And yet you seem to know me.'

He looked wary. 'This is most extraordinary,' he said. 'For a month or more, a year ago, at least, perhaps longer, you would dine here almost every night. You always sat at this table. We could set our watches by your arrival. *Antonio*, I would say to the chef, *he has arrived. It is time for the cheeses to breathe*.'

'A year ago?'

'Not much more.'

'And my name?'

'You never gave a name. You would never book a table, but would merely arrive. You arrived so regularly that we would always keep this one free for you.'

'Did you find out anything about me?'

He looked suspicious. 'This is a joke?'

'It's no joke, I can assure you,' I said. 'I've lost my memory. When I walked in here today you were a complete stranger to me. It was most disconcerting to find that you seemed to know me well.'

'The doctors?'

'They know nothing about the mind. It's as though an entire tape of memory has been wiped clean. Did you learn anything about me?'

'You were very brown. You had come from the sun. By sea, you said. I understood you had been sailing in the tropics. You were very fit.'

'I had money?'

He spread his hands. 'You ate here almost every night, sir,' he said. 'And you . . . you were very generous with . . . ah, the gratuities.'

'I was rich?'

'You were not uncomfortable.'

'I don't remember it at all.'

Now he was uneasy. His eyes flickered politely with disbelief or maybe with fear. He was trying to decide whether I was making fun of him or perhaps if amnesia might be contagious.

'Was I always alone?'

He wanted to end the conversation, and I didn't blame him. For most people any sort of mental aberration is a form of

60

madness, and while we can find it in ourselves to be kind and understanding about cripples, the blind, the deaf, we have a superstitious dread of any mental disorder. It reminds us too sharply of the frighteningly frail barrier between sanity and the nightmare of the asylum.

'At first, yes, you were always alone,' he said. 'Later . . . there was a lady.'

'Ah,' I smiled. I had to lighten the atmosphere. 'So at least I was normal in those days.'

He grinned with relief. I might be mad but at least I was humorously mad. 'Very normal,' he said. 'She was beautiful. You really do not remember her at all?' I shook my head. 'This is impossible. She was quite unforgettable. She was perfect, with a laugh like the sound of jewels and with mischief in her eyes.'

'You were obviously in love with her.'

'We all were, sir. The waiters would stand with their mouths open.'

'And I was in love with her too?'

'It would seem so, sir. She was certainly very taken with you. We were all most jealous.'

'Was she a local woman?'

'We had never seen her before, and never saw her again. I seem to remember she was only here on holiday for the Season.'

'Do you remember her name?'

'Ah, yes. Her name was Lily. It was perfect for her. Lily.'

'I have never in my life met any woman called Lily,' I said, and was puzzled to hear it sound like a lie.

I told myself later that he had obviously simply mistaken me for someone else. They say that everyone has at least one double somewhere, perhaps more than one. That's not surprising. There are only so many faces to go round, just as there are only so many types of restaurant. But I began to speculate about my double. Would two people who look alike have similar characters and lead similar lives? Why not? Your looks surely affect the way other people see you and treat you, just as sharing the same name must inevitably give you something in common. I wondered about the stranger's past, and during the next few days I found myself strolling increasingly often towards the docks where he must have

61

arrived from the tropics, drawn there by their busy promise of strangeness and adventure and by memories, perhaps from childhood, of the cry of seagulls and the rich smells of rope and hot tar and foreign cargoes, animal hides, spices. I stood for hours looking out to sea, inhaling the ozone and wondering what lay beyond. The waves seemed to beckon me to a different sort of freedom, their crests curling like fingers. I was free already and had nowhere to go and nothing to do, but freedom alone, like self-indulgence, was not enough. I had to use it to some purpose. People, like ships, are not meant merely to drift. They need destinations.

I was attracted back time and again to one particular vessel, the *Marie Antoinette*, a passenger liner that was due to sail in a couple of days for the tropics. Her elegant livery of cream and green seemed cool and welcoming, and there was something jaunty about the way she rode the water and something rakish in the way the sun winked at me from her portholes.

That's the one.

What?

That's the ship. The 'Marie Antoinette.'

Why not? Wasn't this what I had been seeking when I took a new name and changed my life? The chance to act on impulse, for no reason at all? Why shouldn't I jump on a ship, as casually as you jump on a plane or train, and sail with her towards the warm seas and hot white beaches and palm trees and girls with soft black breasts? I was restless with the land, and tired of humdrum civilisation and long aimless days and nights alone watching the rest of the world. I hankered for sunshine and warmth and a more primitive freedom, and at least on a ship I would be heading somewhere.

I climbed the gangway to look for the purser, and as I stepped onto the deck I was overwhelmed yet again by the feeling that I knew the ship already. To the left was the small swimming pool, covered over in port but promising the cold tingle of water on blazing tropical days, and to the right was the play area for deck quoits and shuffleboard, just as I expected. Two decks above my head, I knew, two rows of lifeboats stood guard beside the funnel; on hot starry nights they would shelter the shipboard romances of junior officers, smart in their white tropical uniforms, and the prettiest girls among the passengers. Yes, all liners, like restaurants, are similar, yet for some inexplicable reason I felt a glow of recognition, as though I were going home.

The purser was in his office where I knew it would be, beside the little shop on the main deck. There was still a vacant cabin for most of the voyage. I booked it. I gave him my name. He looked up at me quickly.

'How strange,' he said. 'Four or five trips ago – no, maybe six – we had a passenger with exactly the same name as yours.' He stared at me, and then shook his head. 'Nothing like you at all, of course. Not the slightest resemblance. Just a coincidence. Or a distant relative, perhaps?'

'Where did he come from?'

'We picked him up at one of the ports near the Equator. I can't remember which one. He sailed with us here. A year ago, maybe, perhaps more.'

I felt curiously calm. This was right. I belonged.

'No,' I said, 'I can't think who he might have been.'

But I knew by then who he was, all right. You win, I thought. I submit. You win. But what is it that you want?

To explain. I need to make someone understand.

Suddenly I didn't feel lonely any more. It was as though there were two of me, and we had each other for company. In a way it was like the early years of my marriage, when my wife and I had been separate and yet one, when each act of love had been less a physical invasion than a fusing together of two halves that fitted and belonged. Perhaps Man is made incomplete, and needs The Other to become whole. Perhaps that is why unhappy or mismatched husbands and wives always seem to be something a little less than human when they are together, mere fractions of themselves, and only become real again when they are apart.

The smell of the sea alone made me feel years younger, and seemed to promise to give me back something I had lost. When we sailed two days later I turned my back on the land and faced the breeze and the rolling open ocean and laughed for sheer joy.

4

(1)

We set sail upon the good ship *Marie Antoinette* with a fair wind on a good day of glorious High Summer, notwithstanding to be sure that there were those among the Crew that muttered superstitiously as to the advisability of setting forth upon the Thirteenth day of any Month. Seafaring folk are much given to such Godless fancies. The Master, an ancient mariner much skilled in the handling of men, had them soundly whipped before the mast ere twenty-four hours were passed. I vow I never saw nor heard of such sparkling seas and azure skies and golden suns as witnessed our passage in that Glorious Year of Our Lord, who surely smiled upon our Venture as we trimmed and tacked and ran before the kindly wind towards the Tropics, nor do I recall in all my days such a Vigour of Youth as that which filled my every Waking Hour, suffusing my every Organ with unconscionable strength and sensation. Sun was never warmer, nor limbs surer, nor eyes brighter, nor odours more pungent, nor Love sweeter, than upon that Voyage unto the Lands of the Equator in search of nothing more than a way to fill my youthful days.

There were others among our Party who travelled with more serious Intent: a godly Missionary and his devout but desiccated Wife, a Woman of such dryness of countenance and temperament her flesh must surely repel even the Cannibals amongst whom they had elected to take the Word; and their daughter, a blossom of no more than fourteen years, who could count on being consumed almost immediately; a Trader in beads and skins and ivory, whose promises would undoubtedly transpire to be as shallow as his mind; four Maids setting forth upon that horrendous voyage, Marriage, taking ship in faith to join intended Husbands, one fair, one dark, one red of hair, one nondescript as the mouse that scurries from the vestry to the

64

graveyard, hiding her little pink nose; five Soldiers bound to join their regiment, Mercenaries by the villainous look of them; a Mineral Prospector, lured by rumours of gold as wispy as his whiskers; a family of emigrants, Man, Wife and two Boys, in search of some dream of their own; a Grandmother, homely as a pudding and quite as circular, venturing forth unto some godforsaken colony for reasons only grandmothers might ascertain; a Remittance Man, a younger son of noble birth sent forth since neither Land, nor Church, nor Army, nor City could discover a position for him; a brace of Hussies about whose occupation none could be in any doubt; and finally half a dozen convicts, mild-looking men all six, but chained below in damp and darkness for pilfering pennyworths.

I rogered both strumpets that very eve, both separately and then together, erupting thrice like an angry volcano within the hour with the lights of Civilisation still twinkling along the fading shore as I pounded joyously first in the fo'c'stle and then against the mainmast and finally in the stern with the chilly breeze caressing six cheeks.

'Ah, *sir*!' cried the one, and 'oh, *aye*!' gasped the other, and only for fourpence the pair.

Thus I cleared the decks, so to speak, on the very first night, and looked to cheaper but more profitable communions henceforth and ate a hearty meal of fowl and beef, and in the morning importuned the Chirurgeon for a tincture against the Pox.

So commenced the Voyage of my Life, with a spilling of stale seed and an infusion of fresh meats, and the knowledge that the World was mine and the Devil Himself needs must wait a while for my Soul, for my bones were young and my sinews strong and my heart was light and gay.

Daily, as we crept towards the warmer climes, with both seas and skies seemingly turning lighter by the hour, my fellow travellers promenaded the deck of the good ship *Marie Antoinette* in the manner of Latins at dusk around the village piazza, except for the gold prospector, who lay below for most of the day embracing a bottle, and the mousy girl, who lay below retching with sickness and wailing for her Mother.

As I lounged in the bows there first came the emigrants,

pioneers even here, the Husband a clear-eyed confident sort, the Wife a cheerful soul, and Boys aglow with the excitement of adventure.

'Will you not join us, sir, in our perambulation?' called the Husband. 'The idleness of a sea Voyage demands constant exercise.'

'Thank you kindly, sir,' replied I, 'and you are right, but already this morning before breakfast I have ran an hundred circuits of the deck.'

'Most commendable, sir,' said he. 'Perchance one day we may arrange a Grand Contest for the fleetest of foot.'

'An excellent notion,' said I. 'May I rely on you to make the necessary arrangements?'

'Indeed,' said he eagerly. 'I shall speak to the Master this very day, and perchance we may also prepare for other contests of skill.'

'Wrestling,' said one of the Boys.

'Boxing,' cried the Other.

'Quoits!'

'Catchball!'

'Pig in the middle!'

'Stay, stay!' laughed the Mother. 'You would have us turn this vessel into a bear garden.'

'An entire day of sport!' cried the Father. 'I shall make the preparations.'

I liked them all. They were forward and vigorous and filled with hope despite the hardships that must surely have caused them to abandon family and home to seek a fairer fortune in a harsher land.

They were followed by three of the four Maids together with the young Nobleman, who had already moved swiftly to make his tryst with them and was conducting himself with the utmost gallantry. Before too long, to be sure, he would attempt to exercise the *droit de seigneur*, I had no doubt.

'Sheer greed, sir,' I called, 'to appropriate to oneself no fewer than three beauties.'

'You are welcome to join us,' said he graciously.

'You are kind,' said I, 'but anon, anon. For the present I am perfectly content to feast my eyes.'

Two of the girls twittered prettily but the flame-haired beauty ignored my little pleasantry and passed by with an iciness that excited me. The sweetest waters are always cool, and I promised myself that of the four I should ravish her first.

After came the Missionary, dressed in a poor frockcoat, with his visage constantly buried in the Good Book, trusting to the Lord to direct him around the bollards and stanchions and coils of rope and stacks of sheets that lay in his way. His Wife paraded at his side looking neither right nor left but gazing with a solitary purpose toward the horizon as though expecting the imminent arrival of the Son of God Himself. Behind them followed the budding girl-child with hands clasped before her, across her quim, and eyes demurely fixed upon the planks beneath her feet: mayhap her Faith and Trust were not yet as firm as those of her Father, or more likely her Mother had instructed her never to catch the eye of a Man. I caught her peering crookedly at me from the side of her downcast eye and I gave her my smile and she swiftly averted her gaze in blushing confusion and hastened after her Parents.

'Ha, pretty thing!' I called. 'You will not scuttle so in a year or two!'

'Shame, sir,' said one of the strumpets, coming upon me. 'She is but a child.'

'Ah, yet also the daughter of a preacher.'

'Is it true what they say about preachers' daughters?'

'Indeed it is. So much so that I would hazard that you yourself must be the offspring of a vicar.'

She sniggered.

'Or even a Bishop?'

'I cannot believe a word that you say, sir. Your words have all the substance of those of a jester.'

'Yet I have no balls upon my cap.'

'Oh, *you*!'

Behind the Hussies strolled the Hussars, tall, rangy youths still given to nudging at the sight of a female limb. The sun and heat and Fuzzy-Wuzzies would doubtless soon cause hair to sprout upon their chins. They exhibited the air of brazen bumptiousness of a gaggle of country lads come into town for market day, whose shared courage would swiftly evaporate were they to be taken singly.

'Oi,' called their leader, a spotty bumpkin with breeches as tight as a miser's purse.

'Do you speak to me?' asked I.

67

'Who else?' asked Spotty. 'There is no other oik that I can see.'

His companions gave vent to strange cries that I took for mirth at his flashing wit.

'Oik?' said I. 'What word is that? I do not know its meaning.'

'It denotes an ignorant peasant,' said Spotty.

I smiled. 'Ah,' said I, 'no wonder you know its meaning and I do not.'

Spotty and his comrades gathered about me. 'I have a mind to give you a thrashing,' said he.

'You are welcome to attempt it,' said I. 'The last man who did so is lame in his right arm.' I stood to face him. I am of only an average stature but my body is strong and my muscles firm, and I never turned away from a challenge.

'Leave him be,' said one of his companions, 'he is not worth it.'

'Not worth a lame arm?' I enquired.

Spotty sneered. 'Beware, oik,' said he. 'Beware of a dark night.'

'On a dashing white charger?' said I.

'Do not say I have not warned you.'

'I shall be prepared,' said I. 'I am always prepared.'

They shambled away, as military as an orphans' outing. I vowed not to venture forth in future without my snickersnee: one I could thrash, two I might overcome, but three or more would be beyond my pugilistic power; an important rule of combat is never to underestimate your enemy.

Finally, in the rear, there waddled the Grandmother, as yet alone but smiling still with so translucent a goodness and contentment it could never be feigned. Why had the Missionary and his Wife not asked her in a Christian fashion to join them on their perambulation? Such people care more for fire and brimstone than for common charity.

'A fine day, Madam,' I ventured.

She offered me a smile of true radiance. I hoped she had a tribe of grandchildren who would love her dearly and properly as feebleness claimed her.

'May I be so bold as to join you upon your circuit?' I enquired.

'Pray do,' she granted. 'I should be honoured by your escort.'

And so it was that, despite such abundance of fragrant young flesh, I took the wrinkled arm of an old lady in mine and promenaded her about the vessel for a turn or two.

The Soldiers sniggered and gave catcalls at such a sight, and the flame-haired girl raised her nose a trifle, but I should deal with them all in time in the appropriate fashion.

Did I say that I travelled upon the *Marie Antoinette* merely through Youthful Exuberance? That is not the entire truth, not the pure and simple truth, for I had experienced strange yearnings that seemed to draw me towards the Equator. In sleep I dreamed of a humid night beside a distant lake or sea, and of some Destiny beckoning me.

'A strange coincidence,' quoth the Master when I booked my passage upon his vessel. 'Upon a recent voyage hither, from the Tropics, there was upon this ship a seaman whose name were identical with yours.'

'He worked his passage?'

The Master laughed unpleasantly. 'Worked? Aye, that were the notion, but the fellow were a rogue, idle and disputatious. Twice the bo'sun were moved to give him a taste of the Cat. He were a proud, arrogant, angry villain.'

'Did he travel alone?'

'He did, praise the Lord. More than one such would have resulted in mutiny.'

'I wish to take passage to the port where he embarked,' said I, knowing not why I did so but reasoning it as good a destination as any.

'It is far down the coast,' said the Master, 'as warm as the kitchens of Hell and half as welcoming, a place of savages and sickness.'

'Nevertheless.'

'So be it,' said he, 'but you will thank me not.'

To purchase my Passage I gave him half the gold I had won at a gaming table.

The Master's blessing was soon given to the Running Contest as a means of restraining passions that are otherwise oft uncontrolled in the idleness of Shipboard life, even to the extent of his providing small prizes of wine and cloth for the victors, and allowing the more respectable of the Crew to contest with us, and the Emigrant set to preparing for the event with a gusto that would serve his Family well in the days to come when they would face a patch of bare and barren alien Earth and learn to call it Home.

'We shall have a Handicap,' he announced, 'devised by means of Age, so that those on either side of Vigorous Manhood shall be staggered equally to allow fair chances for all. We shall have a Starting Line occupied by yourself and the Soldiers, and before you those in their thirtieth years together with those in their adolescence, and before them further still the old men of forty or more and the Boys.'

'And the Gold Prospector a yard before the Finishing Line?' I suggested.

He laughed. 'The Gold Prospector will doubtless still be seeking his fortune at the bottom of a bottle.'

'Would it not be less difficult and equally just to start all from the same line?' I asked, 'but merely require some to complete a fewer total of circuits? Perchance we in our sturdy Primes might be required to complete an hundred circuits, those less so merely ninety, and the ancient and childish only eighty or less?'

'Excellent!' he cried. 'For it would add the pure intensity of Mathematics to the physical excitement of the chase!'

'And a chase for the ladies also?'

'God bless you, sir!' he said. 'What sport! And also a chase for the ladies.'

Such a man was worth a dozen mercenaries, a score of matelots and fifty fops. His Wife was dearly proud of him, and rightly so.

Thus we took our places upon the appointed Morning, yet another of those golden tropical days of which I spoke before, which appeared in long succession as we skimmed the parabola of the Globe towards the Equator and mysteries and adventures as yet unimagined let alone apprehended.

Barefoot, I stripped to my breeches alone and was not ashamed of the darkening hue of my upper body or the glances it attracted from the ladies, not least from the older ladies. Even the Crew were a motley mob of skin and bone, apart from one seaman built like a brick privy, and I surmised the Master had eliminated the rougher element as too unseemly for the ladies to witness. Lined up beside me the Mercenaries, required otherwise to wear uniform all day, were a pale breed, and the Nobleman so white he seemed ghostly, though he had the advantage upon us, being younger, of being required to complete fewer circuits, together with the Emigrant himself, the Trader, and the Emigrant's Boys, and the younger sailors. The Missionary, though not yet forty, declined to join us, declaiming in a lofty, reedy voice of the Race of Life in which seemingly he already deemed himself a winner, though I wondered whether he knew the meaning of the word.

'Perchance it would be more appropriate to procure a private chase between yourself and the Gold Prospector,' I ventured cruelly.

'I contest only the Lord with drunkards,' said the Missionary. He possessed that variety of visage that constantly demands to be assaulted, though even I would hesitate to strike a Man of God, despite occasionally doubting the wisdom of Heaven's choices.

There was some jostling for position at the Starting Line, notably from the Mercenaries, one of whom behind my back contrived to bring his boot down painfully upon my ankle and heel. Each Lady had been allotted to keep a tally of the circuits completed by two contestants, so to placate the Goddess of Fortune I blew a kiss to mine, the mousy Maid, only recently risen from her sickbed and looking less winsome, if that were possible, than even the Missionary's Wife. The girl appeared so confused by this gesture of gallantry that she dropped her tally paper and required to be consoled by her flame-headed companion, who instructed her coldly that it was about time she ceased to be a Goose.

The Bosun fired the flintlock and we were off, another boot on my leg, raked viciously downward, but no time to turn and apprehend the villain for the wind was in my hair and the glorious smell of the sea upon my nostrils and the pounding of hard warm timbers beneath my feet and the sight of the ladies crying and jumping up and down and within my mind no thought possible but that I would win the day, for it seemed that nothing could ever defeat me, no not Death itself.

Before me the beefy matelot ran, three yards or so in front, setting the pace for circuit after circuit, and beside me, matching step for step, the spotty Mercenary, more of a Man that I had allowed. On circuit after circuit we passed again and again not only the Boys and the Trader and the Nobleman but also the younger Sailors. Never once, though, did I see the Emigrant, and I came to realise that it must be he wheezing and gasping not ten yards behind me, game as ever despite his years.

I counted the circuits myself, not trusting the mousy girl to count beyond ten, and soon the chase settled into a stirring rhythm that seemed of greater volume within my mind than all the cheers and shouts of the bystanders. Their features blurred as we

71

pounded by, in a fuzz of shape and colour, but on occasion one visage might be glimpsed whole for a second in all its naked revelation before flashing by: the Grandmother smiling and willing me on; the Gold Prospector waving his bottle; the Missionary's wife with her hard dry lips so slightly open with flicking tongue like a lizard and short quick breaths almost as laboured as my own. And the flame-haired girl, just one glance between us on the fifty-ninth circuit and held therein the instant knowledge in that small fraction of a moment that we would lie together one night when the moment was good.

By the sixty-fifth circuit half the field was gone: Boys, Sailors, the Trader, and two of the Mercenaries, who would need a sight more stamina to flee the murderous Fuzzy-Wuzzies. By now the beefy matelot and Spotty and I, matching each other pace for pace, now gaining, now falling back, but always with barely a few yards between us, were passing again and again the others, amongst them at last the Emigrant, whose gait now resembled that of a drunken camel but who struggled resolutely on, determined to complete his course and contesting now only a grim race against himself.

My own lungs now seemed fit to burst, for the matelot set a fearful pace, but I knew of old this to be the moment decisive for victory, where pain must be set aside and weariness banished and the body pushed harder yet onto that plateau where courage conquers weakness and the limbs move swift and sure beyond the threshold of agony as though it were for ever. No man who does not constantly defy that barrier can ever call himself a Man.

For five or six circuits I ran through a fog of pain, each step a leaden misery, each breath stabbing at my guts and resolution, the faces flashing by no more now than a blur of blindness, and the thundering within my ears drowning with blood the cries of the crowd, but I knew that such must also be the suffering of my opponents, and so it proved, for on the seventy-ninth circuit the giant matelot at last lost wind and we drew towards him like frigates overtaking a galleon, the spotty mercenary and I, closer with every step until we passed him and he uttered a groan that seemed to be dredged from Neptune's kingdom on the ocean bed, and the fog cleared for me as I passed the barrier of suffering and my legs seemed filled with a new strength, the second wind in my breast, the agony receding from my belly, and the eyes of the girl with the flaming hair caught mine and smiled as I sprinted past.

So just the two of us, then, Spotty and I, and he running a devilish cunning chase still only yards behind my shoulder but forcing me now to set the pace and holding on, waiting, always waiting, and I dared not turn my head to ascertain his position for it was obvious from his breathing, heavy as a carthorse, and the echo of his footsteps after mine.

'Oik,' he gasped.

'Onanist,' I panted.

And we ran and ran with the knowledge that only this mattered and that the world could go to the Devil.

It was on the ninety-seventh circuit that the matter turned sour. By then I was willing to shake his hand and embrace him close when the chase was done, for he had proved a worthy rival, but there was one position on the circuit, behind the wheel, where for five seconds we were invisible from the spectators as we rounded the stern, and there he lashed his boot at my ankle, causing my feet to clash and my knees to buckle and I toppled like felled timber as he passed me and my ear to the deck resounded with the sound of his feet thudding away towards victory.

A shout went up.

'The soldier!'

'The military will win!'

'Where is the other?'

'Stricken!'

Foul play, then. So, swiftly, still out of sight, I grasped a rope and knotted it across the route, a mere foot above the deck and just at the spot where the vile mercenary would least be able to see it in time as he approached the turn, and then I set off in strong pursuit, a good half circuit behind him and by any judgement now a clear loser.

'See, the other still comes!'

'A fall, perchance.'

'It will not suffice.'

'He is lost.'

'But how he ventures!'

The pain in my twisted ankle was excruciating but the anger in my heart was greater and as he approached the distant turn by the wheel I bellowed 'Rogue – I shall kill you,' and he turned his head to sneer and tripped himself over the rope and fell sprawled with shock and shrieking. As I bounded toward him he attempted to stand but his knee appeared to be out of joint and he fell forward again, moaning.

I skipped lightly over the rope myself and ventured a kick at his posterior, which sent him sprawling again, and ran on to the incredulous bellows of the crowd as he crawled and then hobbled after me, defeated.

For the final two circuits I ran alone, my arms aloft, twice passing the hobbling mercenary, and they clapped fit to rival the theatre, bellowing my name in unison and in time to their hands. The red-haired girl pushed my mousy tally-girl forward and she held up a single finger and shouted in a tiny voice 'One further circuit alone, sir,' so I completed an extra one though I knew she were wrong, swiftly releasing the rope as I passed, and then a second, a lap of victory, for now I felt I could run for ever to the end of the Earth, and the flame-haired girl was laughing deliciously. When I stopped, to the slapping of my back and laughter and cheers (and a large and liquid kiss from one of the strumpets, damn her) the Bosun approached with a stern expression but also a glint in his eye by which I hazarded that he knew precisely what had taken place.

'A complaint has been lodged, sir,' he said.

'A complaint?' gasped I.

'The soldier objects that you placed an obstacle in his way upon the circuit that was last but three, to whit a rope fixed across his path, thus causing him to fall.'

'The man is crazed with disappointment,' I panted. 'There is indeed a coil of rope where he fell, but he tripped upon it of his own accord and fell to damage his knee, just as I had done on the previous circuit with no help from him. I suggest you investigate the matter yourself.'

A sailor ran up from the direction of the wheel. 'The winner tells the truth,' he said. 'The rope lies loose but is not fixed.'

'He tied it across the path!' snarled Spotty, grimacing with pain.

'Come, sir,' said the bo'sun, 'would you add dishonour to honourable defeat? Will you not shake hands?'

Spotty surveyed the crowd and saw it to be against him. Grudgingly he offered his hand, and we shook. 'Oik,' he muttered as the crowd cheered again. 'Beware. This is not the end of the matter.'

'I fear only those I respect,' said I, and received from the

74

Master my prize of a bottle of port-wine, and my red-head beauty smiled again.

The Ladies' Chase was a delicious affair, a dainty business of only five circuits entered with much exuberance and many a pretty feminine shriek and lifted skirts and ankles and delicate pink flushes.

The Missionary's Wife refused to play and forbade her girlchild to enter the fray with many a scowl.

'But Mama!' cried the child.

'No, child.'

'But Mama . . . .'

'Silence, girl!' This from her Father. In the child's frown I detected a pleasing hint of rebellion. One day soon, among the Cannibals, she would startle them both, I had no doubt.

But the Emigrant's Wife joined in with much laughter and gave a good account of herself for three circuits before acknowledging with mock dismay the physical superiority of Youth. The Chase was dominated by the flame-haired girl and one of the strumpets, both of whom ran with such admirable lack of modesty, tucking their skirts into their knickers, that the Missionary averted his eye and muttered. The strumpets' limbs I had already observed, indeed felt their strength upon my back, but they were no match for those of the red-haired girl, whose shapely calves and thighs were not built merely for comfort but also for speed. She ran with the grace and dignity of a deer, springing from step to step with a subtleness sufficient to stiffen my Member immediately. How I yearned to enter that particular paradise!

'Come on!' I cried. 'One more! Just one!'

The strumpet faded on the final circuit, no match for purity of soul and body, and my beloved stretched those lovely limbs to take the prize by several yards, a bolt of finest Lancashire cloth most prettily designed.

'We are the champions!' I cried, clasping her in my arms and kissing her full upon the mouth with a taste of nectar. 'Well sped, girl!'

'Come, child,' said the Missionary's Wife, with lips as pursed as a parrot's arse, 'You shall not witness Babylon,' and they hurried away, the girl with simmering resentment.

'Have you done, sir?' said my love, for I clasped her still.

'Oh, no,' I murmured, 'not yet, not by far.'

'Desist, sir, now!' Her eyes were a deep green. How I wished to see them flutter and roll and to hear her groan! I freed her.

'This calls for celebration,' called the Master. 'Tonight we shall feast in style, and the carpenter shall play the fiddle.'

'Tonight I would play a different tune with you,' I murmured, and she laughed with such gaiety I burst into laughter myself.

'My instrument plays not for any bow,' she whispered.

'But mine is the finest in the World,' I said, and believed at that instant my words to be entirely true.

I sat beside her that night at the banquet and made her laugh and glow so greatly that I swore my moment with her was almost come. Her skin was as smooth and fragrant as a peach. We ate right royally of the last of the vessel's fresh victuals, hoarding the taste and texture of venison and beef and luscious fruits against the long approaching days of salted pork and biscuits, always biscuits. We drank copiously of wine and her cheeks flushed with heat and imagination and her fingers touched mine and her leg lay warm upon the bench against my own. We danced to the fiddle, none of your vulgar modern capers but the graceful jigs of olden days, and my Love for her swelled until I would burst. The green ice of her eyes was melted soft and the dampness of her exertions gave off a fragrant exhalation that rendered me giddy with its wistful odour. For politeness' sake I danced also with her companions, except the Mouse, who started back with fear when I requested a turn, and I skipped with the Emigrant's Wife and cut a sedate caper with the Grandmother, who chuckled and winked, but my eyes were only for my green-eyed Goddess and the green-eyed monster of jealousy pierced me to see her in the arms of another, for she teased me by twinkling with the Emigrant and chuckling with the Trader and flirting with the Nobleman.

Finally, well after midnight, I could contain my Passion no more, and whispered in her delicate ear, so pink and tasty.

'Why, sir, but we are strangers,' she said with feigned surprise.

'We may swiftly remedy that,' I prayed.

'But I have known you barely a few hours,' she said. Her damnable, heavenly eyes were playing games with me. 'And I am promised to another, whom I journey to join.'

'But not yet wed. I have loved you since the moment I saw you,' said I.

76

'Loved?' she said mockingly. 'You mean True Love, sir?'

'Yes, yes,' said I, besotted with surging blood. 'I would do anything for you,' said I. One does, when one is young and urgent.

'If that were true you would tarry,' she said softly. 'You would court me with leisure and proper patience and prove your consideration for me.'

'Dammit,' I said heatedly. 'You tease me. You toy with my Passion.'

'Not I,' said she, and the ice glinted again in her eye. 'But I shall not be treated as one of those Whores.'

'You equate my Love for you with the fleeting coupling of Strumpets?'

'I do,' said she, 'unless you care to prove it otherwise.' She touched my fingers gently beneath the board. 'Do not be in such *haste*,' she whispered. 'I like you truly, but I am no bawd. And now I shall retire to my rest, and torment you no further. We shall start again anew tomorrow.'

'Perchance,' said I, petulantly, 'and then mayhap not.'

'It seems your Love is brief, sir,' said she, and was gone, with a swirling of skirts that tortured me further.

I reached for the bottle and proceeded to drink with the urgency of the Gold Prospector, who was by now comatose upon the deck.

'My friend requires her rest,' said the dark-haired Maid to my left. She smiled. 'Her beauty is such that she needs much repose to preserve it, while I, though no beauty, crave rest much the less and may go the distance with many.'

She was indeed no beauty but if my Love were a peach then this were a dark rose and she was young and wholesome and we finished the bottle between us and then on a pile of canvas beneath the stars I delivered swiftly into her keeping the boiling brew stirred by my Beloved as I closed my eyes and thought of tresses that were copper-gold, not dark, and eyes of green.

After the dark-haired Maid were gone, carrying with her my precious load, I lay sprawled back upon the canvas with its odour of fish and gazed drunkenly at the stars, lighter with relief but heavier in my heart, cursing myself that the dark-haired Maid might boast to her companions and thus lose me forever the affections of my Love. Do Maids speak together of such things? Even when already betrothed? I knew not, and as I pondered how best to assure her silence five figures emerged from the night

77

shadows, one hobbling upon a stick, and stood about me.

'Now is the reckoning, oik,' said Spotty.

One does not parley in such a situation, not with four advancing upon one (for I judged that Spotty with his injured limb would be of little account) and I leapt with sudden ambush to my feet, startling them, and drew my knife and plunged it deep into the arm of the nearest Mercenary, whose howl was wondrous to perceive, like a stuck hog.

I know not how it is, but sudden brisk activity is a potent relief for drunkenness, and I was aware of a swift evaporation in the blood of the vinous fumes as I went for the second Mercenary, snickersnee flashing across his face, taking with it part of his nose, and he bled like an ox and staggered away, shrieking.

'Come, come,' I bellowed, sturdy with the certain sharpness of my knife and the Vigour coursing through me, 'who next, and what part of the anatomy? A severed finger for you, sir? A blinded eye? A second navel for that belly? Come, sirs, choose!'

'Kill him,' said Spotty.

The largest Mercenary advanced upon me with a pungent odour of sweat and as I lunged at his breast the fourth gripped my arm and Spotty hobbled forward and struck my wrist with his cane. I clung to the knife, my only hope of salvation, but the largest clamped his yellowed teeth deep into the bone and I yelped myself and dropped the knife and the two held me back and down while Spotty proceeded to beat me with fists and stick and the others provided a chorus of thudding boots.

'The reckoning, oik,' said Spotty with a marvellous malice.

Fortunately the clamour had aroused some attention and it was the Emigrant who appeared from the gloom crying: 'Halt! What is this?'

'Murder!' I shouted. 'They mean to kill me!'

The Emigrant, stout fellow, may his Memory be enshrined for Eternity within these Pages, hesitated not at all but first knocked down Spotty and wrenched his stick away and proceeded to club and belabour the others, allowing me to turn upon the largest and kick him in the privates. I winced even for him as I did so, for the groan of agony that proceeded from his lips would soften the heart of a monster, and I understood myself only too well the pulsing grief of such a blow from past experience, and he crawled away, bent double, moaning piteously, while the last, seeing which way the matter proceeded, took to his heels.

'Are you injured?' panted the Emigrant.

'Injured?' I growled. 'See this,' and I walked across to Spotty as he lay prone and booted him thrice, viciously, in the ribs, as they had done to me, and then the pain of their blows and utmost weariness flowed over me, and the wine flooded back into my brain and I fell to the deck, insensible.

I awoke in my cabin to the sensation of an army of termites tramping through my body, gnawing my bones. I endeavoured to rise but pain lanced at my ribs, my breast, my wrist, my cheeks and my eyes, and the thunder in my head would not have disgraced a battlefield. I groaned and lay back, determined not to move a jot, while my buttocks burned with fire against the hardness of the bunk.

'Lie still!'

It was the Mousy Maid, her head hovering above mine, her hands applying a cool, wet cloth to my brow with a gentle certainty of purpose that amazed me.

'You are not to move!' she instructed firmly. Was this the same timid Girl who had flinched from a mere jig not half a day previously? She seemed uncannily imbued with a strange authority.

'My father is a Physician,' she said, 'and the Chirurgeon has deputed me to care for you until you are well.'

I turned my head as she moved away, and groaned again. The sensation was excrutiating.

'I warned you,' she said piously. 'You do not know how badly you are hurt. Here, see.'

She held above my eyes a mirror, and I would hardly have known myself. I stared at the face of a Stranger: eyes black and bloated, cheekbones swollen blue, lips puffed and livid, blood caked purple across the brow and chin. A tooth was missing.

'The rest of you is quite as bad,' she chided. 'Your breast and ribs resemble a geographical chart, so colourful are they. Heaven knows, why must you fight?'

'A man must do what a man must do,' said I stiffly. My lips felt as though a sweatshop of tailors were sewing them together.

She chuckled in a surprisingly deep and mischievous fashion. 'Your enemies are no more whole,' she announced. 'Two are

79

confined to their bunks, one carries a sling, and one walks like a bowlegged Elephant.'

I laughed and immediately regretted it. The tailors at work on my lips were employing needles as blunt as pitchforks.

'Now I must cleanse you,' she said. 'Do not flinch, or the pain will be worse,' and she stripped back the sheet from my poor bruised body so that I lay exposed to her in all my Nakedness and discovered, for the first time in my life and to my discomfiture, an unexpected embarrassment to be naked before the eyes of a Woman. Even my Member seemed to shrink so that I felt ashamed for its paucity of size.

'Ow,' I cried, 'Ow,' and 'Ow!' again as she applied both hot and cold compresses to my wounds and washed me beneath the arms and around the neck and in other places I hesitate to mention, though she did so without any unseemly contact of flesh and the experience was that of an infant bathed by its mother so that even my unruly Member did not have the Impertinence to rise but cowered, like a tremulous worm.

'You need not blush,' said she. Lord, how she had changed with just this chance to exhibit her skill and knowledge and power over one who was helpless! 'My father opines that a time will come when Women shall perform such services for wounded and sickened Men as a matter of course, unworthy of comment.'

'No married woman would be allowed to perform such services for strangers,' I grimaced. 'Their Husbands would not allow them.'

'The time will come when Husbands will have no choice,' she avowed grimly, poking me in an especially tender spot so that I shouted out. 'And why should it be considered unseemly? Your nakedness is nothing to me. You are merely a lump of battered flesh requiring refurbishment.'

'I am flattered to hear it,' I winced.

And then, with utmost gentleness, she caressed my wounds and bruises with creams and ointments, cool unguents that soothed my skin with a delicious mix of pleasure and pain, so that I closed my eyes, and thanked the Lord for such sensations and for being alive, and sighed.

'That pleases you?' she asked, her fingers moving upon my body.

'Mmmm,' said I languorously.

She slapped my hand. 'Then I shall cease,' she said. 'I sense you to be a man already greatly surfeited with too much pleasure. It is bad for the Soul.'

When she had gone, I slept, and dreamed again of a misty jungle, and a dark lagoon, and the hazy visage of a man I did not know, a Stranger.

For several days I lay imprisoned within my cabin, as my hurts throbbed, and stabbed, and tingled, and then began to itch. Each day the Chirurgeon inspected me, and it was an education to see how the Mouse reverted to her previous timid manner in the company of others, for she flitted nervously behind the Chirurgeon and answered his questions in so apprehensive a voice that I could not credit her Independence when we were alone and she in sole command. I suspected her to be one of those poor feminine Souls deprived of gruff fatherly affection and rough brotherly example, for whom three persons were a mob and only in her own solitary company was she truly content. Even when her dark-haired companion called upon me to bring condolences she faded into greyness and held back both in presence and conversation.

'My poor love,' whispered the dark-haired Maid with troubling familiarity. 'Did they do this on account of me? Perchance from jealousy, my sweet?'

Love? Sweet? This dark rose hath hidden thorns. I prayed she would not become possessive and importunate for no reason other than a quick roll in the canvas. I never could abide a clinging Woman.

'Why else?' asked I, with the cowardly attempt that thus I should deflect her affections. 'The large Mercenary, the one with the bowed legs, has conceived a deep Passion for you.'

Her eyes gleamed. 'I should not dream of lying with any Man but you, my precious,' she whispered. 'Except my Betrothed, naturally.'

Lord save me. 'It must be a secret, then, between us,' I mumbled. 'Not a word to any of our Passion.'

'I would first rather die,' said she. She looked behind her swiftly, saw that the Mouse was turned away and otherwise occupied, and bent to give me a kiss, of the deep and liquid Frenchified variety, that tasted of pepper and was not wholly unpleasant but that rasped my lips like sandpaper so that I needs must swallow a cry.

'I shall wait, my Treasure,' said she, and winked, 'until my treasure is full upstanding once more.'

I should have trouble from that one, anon.

The Emigrant also came, bearing a bottle of wine, which I sipped with him more for his pleasure than my own, since it stung my lips most cruelly.

'You saved my life,' said I. 'I am much obliged.'

'Fiddle-faddle.'

'It is true. They would kill me. I am in your debt.'

'It were merely a scheme of boyish villainy,' said he, over eager to make allowances. He was a good man. I should have no qualms to enter any jungle with the Emigrant by my side.

'The Master is eager to punish them,' he said. 'He speaks of a flogging when they are whole again.'

'Excellent,' said I, with venom. 'A touch of the cat would work a miracle. Personally I should not settle for less than a keel-hauling for the leader.'

He laughed. 'Such youthful anger! It will stand you in good stead in later years, when it matures and mellows to a virtue more profitable.'

'And what might that be?'

'Steadfastness. Determination. A refusal to surrender, whatever the circumstances.'

I envied his Boys to have such a Father.

Less pleasurable was an unexpected visit from the Missionary and his Wife. They came upon the Third Day, perchance expecting me to rise again.

'We would not bring the Child,' said he. 'It were not seemly.'

I should have been happier without their gazing. He considered me haughtily and his Wife appeared mesmerised by my wounds and bruises as a rabbit is besotted by a fox. She licked her dry lips quickly and her breath was laboured. Gadzooks, but she were ugly! Blotches of scarlet mottled her parchment skin, though she cannot long have said farewell to Thirty, and a musty odour rose from her as though from a damp closet. I gained the impression that she could barely restrain herself from reaching out and pinching my hurts, to make me squeal.

'The Lord be praised,' intoned the Missionary. 'He bringeth evil to the wicked and smiteth the wrongdoer.'

'I were ambushed by ruffians,' said I hotly.

'Yet carried a knife? The Lord sees all, and punishes the impure of heart. O Lord, take pity upon this worthless creature and show him the Light and bring him unto Thy Way.'

'Amen,' breathed his Wife.

'Go boil your heads,' said I, 'you *and* your God, whatever he may be.'

The Missionary gasped and his Wife whimpered.

'No God of thine could ever be mine,' said I. 'My God is a joyful God, a God of grace and spirit and laughter. My God would never invent your Hell.'

'O Jesus!' said she.

'Satan!' cried the Missionary. 'Beelzebub! Baal! Nebuchadnezzar!'

'Pish!' said I.

They backed from the cabin, the Missionary holding before him the Good Book as though it were a talisman to protect him from demons, and crying loudly on the Lord to strike me down in my iniquity. I confess I experienced a certain qualm at this, believing it perhaps incumbent upon the Lord to come to the assistance of His assistants whenever they called upon His Name, and it was in a certain state of agitation that I felt myself when the Mouse returned to salve my wounds.

'Hush, hush,' she said, 'such rage.'

'He called upon the Lord to strike me down!'

'There, there,' said she, 'lie still, the ointments will soothe you,' and she began those firm but tender caresses with oils and such that caused me so exquisite a mix of pleasure and pain, her fingers smoothing my bloated eyes and gently rubbing the cuts on cheeks and chin, massaging the reddened welts on breast and ribs until I fain would fall asleep beneath her magic touch until I ascertained that her fingers were straying further South than ever before, tracing patterns around my navel and tangling with gentle tugs the edges of my Bush. I could scarce believe it. The timid Mouse? My unruly Member strived to meet her hesitant touch.

'Now, what is this?' she whispered. 'A creature nests in the jungle, its little pink nose rising to test the air.'

She told the truth, too. The treacherous beast were uncoiling

83

itself with uncouth rapidity. O mercy, not the little Mouse! Fie, sir! I closed my eyes and cursed my Vigorous Youth.

'And look!' said she. 'Its little eye grows larger, glaring at me. O such a big dark eye. Is it angry with me? It pops up and looks angrily around. Naughty! Naughty!' and she smacked it lightly with the obvious result that I stood as firmly to attention as a Guardsman at Windsor.

'Now it won't lie down,' she said crossly. 'But we know a way to make it lie down, do we not? Indeed we do,' and she took my globes in her small soft hand and taunted my extremity with light flicks of her tongue.

'Come to me, my little Mouse,' I muttered thickly. 'Not like that, girl, come lie with me.'

'Little Mouse?' said she, ignoring me, 'you are not a little Mouse, now, are you? More a great Giraffe with sinewed neck and great smooth head nodding at the trees. Ahhh!'

'Stay!' begged I. 'Come, lie.'

'I hear a distant voice,' she said, 'urging me to sin. But I am a Virgin, and promised to be married, and a Virgin I shall go to my Wedding Bed. Yet neither Book nor Preacher ever yet forbade a little sporting in the jungle with a Giraffe,' and she took me in her teeth with orchid lips and her fingers played and the throbbing of my wounds were concentrated in one mighty burst of pleasure, greater than ever, always, it seemed, greater than ever before.

She lay still, her hair across my loins, and then she started weeping.

'Ah, girl, girl,' said I, and pulled her to me, but she started back, terrified again, the Mouse that first I knew, shaking and trembling, a child again tormented by hellish fears. Her eyes were stricken.

'No, no!' she wept, 'oh God, oh God,' and she fled the cabin in a flurry of indecision and torment.

Dear Lord: these women! Now I had an hysteric on my hands, as well, not to mention the dark-haired Maid who claimed me as her own.

And my green-eyed, red-haired Goddess never came once in all those days to visit me.

Within the week I walked again, despite sundry twinges and a deep aching in the bitten wrist, and my pains seemed all the lighter when I observed my enemies: Spotty, as I , had recovered sufficiently to display a new malevolence towards me, but the others were mightily subdued, especially the fellow with the bandaged nose, whom I jested appeared to have the noseless Pox, and the large Mercenary whose privates had suffered less than his pride and who now avoided me, so proving yet again that big men are often the soonest cowed. Spotty's anger was not relieved when the Master conducted an inquiry into the matter, the Emigrant and I giving evidence of their assault.

'I shall not tolerate brawling upon my vessel,' announced the Master, and he sentenced Spotty to twenty lashes and his companions to ten each. 'And you, sir,' he said to me, with brows of disturbing ferocity, 'you may consider yourself fortunate to escape the Cat yourself.'

'I, sir? It was I were ambushed and placed in fear of my Life.'

'I credit you this time,' he warned, 'but would not again.'

I shall not dissemble: only one of the Mercenaries took his punishment like anything less than a Man, the Coward who had remained uninjured and who had fled the battle, who shrieked and wept for mercy even before the first lash; but the others bore their torment with courage, especially Spotty, who stared at me with a chilly intent as they strapped him to the frame and who bit his lip bloody without releasing so much as a whimper. I had to admit a small admiration for him. The Fuzzy-wuzzies would be well advised to beware of such a man.

The entire Ship's company gathered to witness their penance, including the Passengers, by order of the Master, who thus intended to serve an example, and the sight of the Bosun's burly arm and the stinging welts that sprang upon the instant beneath his lash appeared for a moment to sober even the Gold Prospector, who constantly enquired as to the victims' crimes and constantly forgot again. We watched in silence as the Cat mewed through the sunlit air, and there was a murmur of fearful approval at the completion of each sentence. Most remarkable of all was the manner of the Missionary's Wife, whose Husband stood by the punishment frame together with the Chirurgeon, muttering prayers: she stood immediately before me in the press, breathing heavily, as though she herself were receiving the blows, and several times, I could have sworn, as the lash bit into bloody flesh, she pressed backwards to brush her buttocks against my thighs, giving a little grunt. My flesh, I fear, knew no shame, for even she, dry and ugly though she were, succeeded in stirring the proud expectations of my voracious Giraffe, and I prayed that soon the day would come when the animal would prove to be more discriminating in the type of foliage for which it raised its head. I suspected that the Missionary's Wife would visit the injured Mercenaries to gaze with rapture upon their new wounds as soon as she were able to persuade her Husband that it were his Christian duty so to do.

'Thank the Lord that is over,' said the Emigrant. 'Let us pray there are no grudges borne, but all forgiven if not forgotten.'

I doubted his hopeful expectations. Spotty would neither forgive nor forget.

Anon I sought out my red-headed Love. 'You have avoided me,' I said.

She turned those eyes upon me, verdant as tropical lagoons. 'I did not wish to see you suffering,' said she.

'I should have suffered the less had you cared sufficiently to console me.'

'Did not the Physician's daughter care for all your needs?' she asked, without a smile. Lord, did she know? Had the Mouse been sufficiently overwrought to speak to her companions of the matter? I could not believe that Maids would speak together of such things, for subsequently the Mouse had reverted to her timid manner once more, refusing to speak of it and ministering only to my most distant needs. She smelled of fear and shame, like a fallen apple. After that single encounter she had never again applied the ointments or touched me, insisting I were sufficiently healed to perform such duties for myself.

'She cared for me tenderly,' said I, 'but not for my heart.'

'And that too is bruised?'

'Do not taunt me. You know of my Love.'

'Ah, Love,' said she, 'how easily the word falls from your lips.'

'I have never used it before,' said I, not entirely truthfully, for on occasion it is most efficacious in procuring a Maiden's favours.

'Is that so?' she mocked. 'In that case, sir, I must doubt your knowledge of the meaning of the word.'

'Damn you,' said I. 'Will you walk with me?'

She laughed, and my heart trembled. 'Why, sir, surely I will, if that is the only exercise you have a mind for.'

I had met these teasers before, but never one for whom I was so easily to become a willing fool. We walked, and spoke, and I ascertained my affection to become an obsession, for still she parried my importunities so that I began to wonder whether all my previous conquests had been mere imagination and that perchance in fact I were dull and slow and ugly and suffering from some unsavoury physical odour. She consented to sit by me at supper and while I ventured to sparkle and pressed my thigh upon hers the dark-haired Maid sat equally importunate upon my other side pressing *her* thigh against mine and fingering my knee and making outrageous promises with her eyes. I cursed the weakness that had allowed me to entertain her previously, for it seemed she considered that to be a mark of her possession of me. Damnation, when my Beloved retired again early, to her cabin, the thought of her and the wine and the willingness of the dark-haired Maid led me once again to tumble with her into the canvas, thus compounding my earlier folly. Perchance the Church is wiser than we credit in warning against Fornication.

'Mine, mine, mine!' muttered the dark-haired Maid hoarsely with a certainty that rendered me undoubtedly uneasy even as I emptied into her pouch. I vowed to discover some means to reject her affection.

It were several nights later that the Tragedy occurred, that villainous treachery that even now brings me to the verge of tears. I had spent the intervening days pursuing my Beloved on a different tack, withholding passionate declarations of Love but making myself useful and congenial to her, perambulating with her, conversing, reading passages aloud as she sat at her embroidery, wooing her in a fashion I judged she wished to be wooed, and it was thus that I was so foolishly employed on womanly things that tragedy claimed that wondrous good man, the Emigrant.

In the darkness of one night the watch perceived him to fall overboard with a cry, and two shadowy figures were observed running from the scene. There shone above a bright tropical moon and the sea was so calm that in normal circumstances it would have been a matter of but half an hour to halt the vessel and return to rescue him from the ocean, but by now we were in waters infested by man-eating tropical Monsters, and before the very eyes of the Watch the Emigrant was dragged, howling, by finned creatures beneath the waves, never to be seen again.

Oh god, the agony of his Wife, and Boys. In one moment of murderous villainy their Light had been extinguished, for how now could they brave alone the unknown trials of an alien Land? All three wept piteously upon my shoulder, I being judged the Emigrant's closest acquaintance after our joint encounter with the Mercenaries, and I swore to bring the guilty to justice. In my own moment of danger the Emigrant had rushed valiantly to my rescue; in his I had been occupied below in a childish game of chance with my Beloved.

'It were you!' I raged at Spotty, 'you and your cowardly villains!'

'Prove it,' said he.

I struck him, and when he refused to strike me in return I knew for sure that he and his murderous companions were guilty, for he seemed unwilling to draw attention to himself.

I made my accusation before the Master and his Officers. Though the Watch had failed to identify the Assassins I urged them to consider that all but the Mercenaries could offer witnesses to testify as to their whereabouts at the time of the murder.

'For murder it was,' I insisted. 'This man did not merely fall overboard. He was punished by these villains on account of his support of me in a previous contest, and his evidence on my behalf, that led to their lashing. Two figures were seen fleeing the place, and two of these scum deserve to hang.'

The Master's pronouncement rivalled that of Solomon in its wisdom.

'Two of you five are found guilty of murder,' he told the Mercenaries. 'Are you willing to admit to the names of the two?'

They stood silent, trusting in numbers and a belief that even the Master would not hang two innocent men.

'Will none of you bear witness against your guilty companions?'

They said nothing.

'Very well,' said the Master. 'You are Soldiers who must surely understand the need for discipline aboard a vessel on a long journey such as ours. I cannot allow murder to remain unpunished. You have robbed a man of his Life, and a Family of their Guide and Protector and Future. Two of you were guilty, and two shall hang. You shall draw lots.'

The Coward broke immediately. 'It was not I!' he howled. 'I

shall not draw! I am innocent! It was not I!'

'In that event, name the guilty,' said the Master.

'I do not know,' wept the Coward. 'I swear upon my Mother's grave. I was not with them. I was below, asleep.'

'Do you have a witness?'

'No, no. But I swear it. Upon my Mother's grave.'

'Your Mother still lives,' said Spotty contemptuously. He stared at the Master. 'I am not afraid to draw. Let it happen, and damn the consequence.'

'No, no,' cried the Coward. 'In God's name. Mercy! It was not I.'

Two matelots restrained him while five playing cards were placed in a bag, two Jacks for Death, three assorted others for Reprieve. The Coward sobbed quietly within the grip of the matelots and refused to draw. His four companions, with faces pale, reached one by one into the bag to learn their Fate. Spotty drew first – a 4 – which he threw contemptuously upon the deck. The noseless Mercenary drew next – a 7 – and gave a most unsoldierly whimper of relief. The Coward, realising that only three cards now remained, two of them deadly Jacks, struggled with his captors and wept bitterly. The large Soldier approached the bag with the delicacy of a cat, hesitating, plunging his hand, rummaging around as though by mere touch could he choose salvation. Finally, with sudden decision, he grasped a card and pulled it forth. A Jack! He turned, stricken, lumbering like a hunted beast towards the door, seeking God knows what pitiful sanctuary on a vessel far from sight of any shore. Six matelots struggled to subdue him, finally forcing him to the deck and keeping him there.

'That man will hang,' said the Master, 'and one further. Draw!'

The Coward now was silent, as though in a trance, calculating that now his chances of escape were equal. His final companion, now by circumstance his deadliest enemy, trembled as he reached into the bag to discover his Fortune, and removed the second Jack. He swayed briefly, and fell in a dead faint.

'Did I not tell you?' cried the Coward with rediscovered spirit. He shook off the restraints of the matelots, and advanced aggressively upon the Master. 'I swore my innocence, yet you credited it not, and now God has seen fit to bear witness to it.'

'Let us hope He protects you equally in battle,' sneered Spotty.

The two Mercenaries were hanged that very evening, as the sun hovered above the pink and purple horizon in that brief and beautiful twilight of the Tropics that lights up the skies with a blaze of brilliance and promises another day of shimmering gold and blue. What a melancholy sight for young men about to die. How terrible to see beyond the final rope such a Kaleidoscope of colour and to know their eyes would never see again, and they still so young. I thought of the Emigrant, shredded by Monsters of the Deep, and hardened my heart.

The large Mercenary met his Fate with quiet dignity, and I had little doubt of his guilt, for surely he would have protested had he been innocent, as did his companion, who struggled and fought and had to be dragged to the Yard-arm, protesting loudly his innocence and cursing his fellows that did not speak up on his behalf. I felt certain he were indeed innocent, and that he were being hanged by mere chance of Fortune in place of Spotty, who stared at the victim who had taken his place and refused to answer his taunts and accusations.

'There is your murderer!' cried the Condemned Man, as the Bosun placed the Rope about his neck, 'there is the one who should hang!' and he pointed at Spotty, who gazed back at him with such clear steadfastness I knew for sure he must be guilty, yet beyond punishment himself now unless it be by his own admission.

'Was he not your companion?' cried the victim to his fellow condemned. 'In the name of God, admit it now. Save me.'

'It is not for me to betray another man,' said his fellow.

'Is it true?' asked the Master.

The big Soldier spat contemptuously.

'Is it true what this fellow says?' the Master asked of the other two Mercenaries.

The Coward shrugged. 'I was not there. I told you so.'

The Other shook his head. 'Nor I,' said he. 'I know not the truth.'

The Master stood before Spotty. 'Would you allow another to swing in your place? On the salvation of your Immortal Soul, will you admit your crime?'

Spotty stared at him with arrogance. 'I admit nothing,' said he. 'It is not I that hangs him. Look to your own justice, which condemned him. And may the Lord have mercy upon you if you hang an innocent man.'

Had I been Spotty, would I then have admitted my guilt? To save the innocent Other? Knowing that I myself should instantly forfeit my Life? Honesty, honesty: no, of course I should not have, much though I would wish it; few men, certainly not I, have courage of that order.

I stepped forward. The Missionary was already at the foot of the Gallows, intoning a passage from the Good Book, the second Condemned feverishly repeating the words in terror, and matelots stood behind prepared to remove the supports and launch them into Eternity.

'That man is innocent,' said I to the Master. 'It is the Leader who should hang.'

The Master regarded me with eyes as hard as diamonds. He knew I were right. 'What proof is there?' he asked.

'None,' said I, 'but Common Justice.'

'I can do no other.'

'You would hang an innocent man?'

He stared at me. His expression chilled me. 'Aye,' said he, 'if necessary.'

Few men have courage of that order, either, and in desperate times the weak require a despot to govern them, perchance benevolent but capable also of ruthlessness.

We gathered around in silence, all the Passengers and the entire Crew, to witness a second murder that could not be prevented. We heard only the voice of the Missionary, praying now, and the voice of the second Condemned, hoarse with horror, and the slight crack of the breeze in the sheets and the creak of timbers and the lapping of water upon the hull. The sun was already half dipped beneath the horizon and the large Mercenary gazed upon it with a terrible hunger. Many of the women were weeping, led by the Emigrant's miserable Widow, all but my Beloved, whose lips moved with the words of the prayer, and the Missionary's Wife, whose eager eyes and gloating manner betrayed the fact that she were revelling in the sacrifice. I knew then why I hated her and her Husband and their God: for theirs was a Worship of Death.

'Amen,' we muttered, and the Master nodded his head, and the two condemned men swung instantly in space, the one swiftly despatched, the other struggling and choking and groaning for a full ten minutes. Their corpses were left to sway aloft all night.

I regarded Spotty and Spotty regarded me. We both knew.

Few of us could eat that night, and certainly not I. Nor could I face the further wailing of the Emigrant's widow, much as I wished to give her Comfort, and my Beloved sat with her instead, together with the other Maids. I lay in my cabin and could not sleep, and rose after midnight to take the night air upon the deck. I lay in the stern and watched the stars, so bright and so different in these latitudes, and the shapes of the two dead men creaking from the Yard-arm. I found myself musing upon the natures of Good and Evil, philosophical thoughts occasioned by this desperate day, and could see no answers. The World seemed a deadly place of careless Chance and malignant Accident.

Presently there came from below a dark figure, a woman, to stand near the corpses, and I saw her move into the shadows and raise her skirts with a white flash of petticoats. Was there a man with her? I strained my eyes in the darkness, but could see no other. She was alone. I thought I could hear her breathing, and then a low moan, and then she lurched towards the stern like a drunkard.

I stood, and as she approached I saw it was the Missionary's Wife. Her hair was loose, her eyes wild, her gait ungainly, and her voice was slurred. When she saw me in the darkness she did not start away but approached all the closer, peering into my eyes.

'Ah, you!' she exclaimed. 'Yes, you will suffice,' and she raised her petticoats again full in my face.

I have rarely hated a Woman, but I hated her with a deep loathing then, yet even so the sight of her slim white naked legs in the starlight stirred something within me even more Primitive than Lust: a pure violence, a desire to stab and wound, for the sake of all that is Good against all that is Evil, and I stared at her ugly face and the twisted expression thereon and knew that I faced a Power of Darkness that I could only quell by equal wickedness.

'Do it,' she said.

'Bitch,' said I.

'Yea, but do it,' said she, so I threw her to the deck and forced her over upon her knees and serviced her from the rear like the Bitch she was. She smelled of decay and corruption, like an ageing cheese, but in that unholy coupling my own pleasure was greater than ever before as I thought of her Husband the Missionary muttering his prayers perchance immediately beneath.

Afterwards she said not a word, and offered not even a glance, but raised herself, smoothed her skirts, and lurched away. We might indeed have been two Hellish creatures meeting once in the darkness of a graveyard and never again.

The dangling corpses seemed to be watching me, and I imagined their Spirits, and hurried below.

The hangings seemed to lance some boil of poison upon that good ship *Marie Antoinette*, for the remaining weeks of the voyage were passed in wondrous tranquillity, except for an attack by Pirates and a puny attempt at Mutiny by the sorry convicts below, and they were all flogged. It seems that Despotism and even Cruel injustice is essential for the common good in some Times and Places.

Spotty, for all his arrogance, was mightily subdued, as well he might be, knowing Another had suffered Death in his place, and despite a certain tension between us we never again exchanged harsh words or blows, and indeed, it were almost as though we shared some common bond in the deaths of the Emigrant and the two Condemned, for I could not find it in me to despise his actions, knowing I also might have done likewise. When the Pirates attacked us upon a steaming morning of high Tropical summer Spotty and I fought side by side against them and I blessed the fact that his companion, not he, had been hanged, for his courage and strength twice saved me from Death that day as he parried and slaughtered dark assailants who would have despatched me. I, in turn, succeeded in rescuing the fair-haired Maid from the clutches of a Blackamoor villain whose interest in her was certainly not fatherly, and her gratitude was such that later that night she lay with me, the third of the betrothed Maids to serve my pleasure, and sweetly so, too, with an hesitant, blushing grace that offered me an almost sisterly tenderness and affection and added an incestuous excitement to the union, which I gladly repeated thrice more before the voyage was done, and she always gently pure, in her way, with a taste of young grapes.

The battle with the Blackamoor Pirates was not won, but a

93

truce agreed after fighting had reached a standstill, with Crew and Passengers at one extreme of the vessel and Pirates and Convicts gathered at the other.

'Gold we wish,' bellowed the Pirate Chief, in accents barbarous, 'and virgins.'

'We have no gold,' lied the Master. 'But beads in plenty.'

In the course of Time, after much dispute, the Pirates accepted the beads, bright but tawdry baubles of no value whatever, and when they refused to quit the vessel without the said Virgins, the two strumpets, God bless them, offered themselves for the afternoon and crossed the gap towards that vile band and pleasured them all on my own pile of canvas within a circle of cheering, whooping scoundrels. Their bold sacrifices, and Spotty's courage, made me wonder again on the nature of Good and Evil, and vow never more to judge any other too swiftly. By nightfall the Pirates had gone, and the strumpets, though grimacing with pains, were feasted as best we were able on salted meat and weevil-infested biscuits made palatable only by copious draughts of sour wine.

During those remaining weeks of the voyage, with the Sun now like molten metal beating down upon us, and whales blowing spouts of mist upon the horizon, and dolphins dancing about the craft, and fish with wings, most wondrous to behold, skimming the warm ocean, my body turned as brown as an Arab. The temperature of those climes affected even the ladies, who shed much of their apparel and also most of their morals, so that I suspected even the Gold Prospector of knowing the Missionary's Wife. Almost every night I took my pleasure with one or other of them, though never again with the Missionary's Wife or the Mouse, who hid her face in shame from me, and one heavy afternoon, in a sweaty moment of grief and despair, the Emigrant's Widow wept on my breast as I comforted her in the only way I knew. In that very cabin, a few days later, I happened in to find dishevelled together one of the Emigrant's Boys with the Missionary's girl child, though now she seemed no longer a child but a blossoming woman, and when I beheld his callow clumsiness I barred the door and dropped my breeches and said, 'Here, I shall show you how best it is done,' and despite small protests eventually the Missionary's child took me willingly into her precious little purse, as tight and smooth and fragrant as a tulip at dawn, with tiny cries of painful pleasure as I offered all my

94

skill most lovingly, as a gift to her on her Coming of Age, and the Boy marvelled at his Lesson, attending with greater concentration than ever schoolroom inspired. 'Go to it,' said I when it was done, 'and remember, Boy, never hasten unless it be with a stranger or unless the Lady begs you thrice, for Love is destroyed by speed,' and I left them there, glad in their knowledge and delighted myself to have rogered both the Missionary's Wife and the Missionary's Daughter. So much for sin.

Yet of all those young delights upon that Voyage I never did enjoy my Beloved with the hair like an equatorial sunset and the eyes like green lagoons and the fragrance and texture of peaches. For weeks I wooed her with the utmost consideration, and for five successive nights I withheld myself from the other Maids to prove my fidelity to her, and she did allow small familiarities, a kiss now, a touch then, but never that which besotted me, even in that stifling heat that surged through every other.

'I am sorry,' she said, 'but I must remain true to myself.'

'I would marry you,' said I, and possibly even meant it.

'What, only so as to lie with me?'

'So as to live with you.'

'We should both regret it within a short while.'

'Not I.'

She placed her hand tenderly upon mine. 'Aye, both of us,' said she, gently, 'For I love another, and go to wed, and you would never wish for a Wife whose heart was elsewhere. You see, I know about them all, all the others, even the Physician's daughter. Maids speak to each other of these things. I have always known.'

One night, in drink, and fuddled with frustration, I essayed to take her by force, but she lay there so still, with those wondrous green eyes so calm and cold that even I could not proceed, despite the urgency in my loins, and I took myself away in shame and silence, never to speak with her again, but always to dream of what had never been, and to curse the clerk or cobbler or shopkeeper to whom she went to spend her days and spend at last her Passion.

The rest is swiftly told. I enquired of various members of the Crew who had known the Stranger who had served with them upon a previous voyage, to whose port of embarkation I was bound, but their reports of him were muddled and contradictory: one reported him to have been a vicious man, another a sulky fellow, another the finest comrade he had known, but to none had he spoken of his past, as though he wished to hide and forget it.

Hide what? Forget what foul secret? Had he murdered, like the Master? Betrayed, like Spotty? Sold himself, like the whores? Lost his Soul, like the Missionary's Wife? Or merely, like I, soiled that which he loved the most? I felt it might be any of these, or all, or none.

In penitence, I made my peace with the only God I knew by one act of selfless charity before the Voyage was done. Sickness had ravaged several of our number, and particularly stricken with scurvy was the gentle Grandmother, who had lain often below alone in her weakness, attended by the Chirurgeon and the Mouse. On the night before I was due to disembark at that tropical harbour from whence the Stranger had sailed, the Grandmother sent for me to attend her in her cabin. She was lying weak upon her bunk, with bleeding gums from the scurvy, but with great effort she had essayed to colour her cheeks and lips with dyes and her hair was brushed fine.

'You are a good man,' she said.

'I?' said I, startled.

'I have observed you during this voyage,' she smiled. 'You laugh, and jest, and sing. You have also given great pleasure.' She chuckled, and winked.

I was dumb.

'I shall not survive this voyage,' she said.

'Fiddle-faddle,' said I, a trifle uneasy, suspecting it to be true.

'I shall die before I reach my destination,' she said firmly, 'and I shall never see again those I love. So take this. My parting gift to you, so that One at least will remember me.'

She handed me a clinking bag of coins.

'I could not . . . .'

'Take it,' she admonished. 'If you do not, it would only be stolen when I die.'

'I . . . .'

'To refuse would distress me greatly, for there is none other I would pass it to.'

The look that passed between us denied refusal.

'I know not what to say,' said I.

'There is nothing necessary.'

'Thank you. Er . . . my deepest thanks, ma'am. Is there any service I may perform for you in return?'

She smiled so softly that I vowed to grant her any request at all.

'I hesitate to mention it,' said she.

'I will do whatever you wish. Only speak.'

'It is not shame that restrains me. I am past shame. It is simply that I would not distress you, for you are so Young and Vigorous, and I so old and ugly and feeble.'

I was truly shocked. I, shocked! I! I may even have blushed, like a girl.

'I shall never know another Man,' said she. 'Unless he be you.'

I swallowed, yet my throat was dry. To lie with a dying woman, and a Grandmother!

'Go,' she said quietly. 'God be with you. I had not the right.'

Coward! cried my conscience. Weakling! Ingrate!

'I should be honoured,' said I.

It was her turn to blush. 'Truly?'

'Truly. For I have lain with many, but never yet with a Lady.'

It was not so difficult, nor horrendous. I extinguished the lamp and although she smelled of dust and camphor it is true that in the dark they are not so different, whatever age they may be, and her tremulous delight in the youthful strength of my body and the vigour of my sinews was a pleasure in itself, for my mere young naked presence alone seemed to give her great joy and she bare refrained from touching my every part.

'I had forgotten,' she whispered. 'It has been so long. So much forgotten, yet always remembered.'

And here is an oddity: my lack of honest, surging desire rendered me like iron for what seemed an eternity, so that our excursion together was long and leisurely, and finally it was she who begged and begged for the flood, and when it came the interminable delay rendered it so great that I myself cried out, in true ecstacy, as the tide seemed to ebb from my very toes. It were a fitting climax to that Voyage, teaching me that every Woman, no matter how old or ugly, is worthy of Love and should be cherished. Every woman, that is, excepting the Missionary's monstrous Wife.

I lay with the Grandmother all that final night, so greatly did she revel in my warmth and strength, and served her again as the dawn crept up across the approaching land and touched with pink the shadows of the distant palms.

She was ancient and haggard in the dawn, but I knew that her heart glowed with Love.

'I would that I should die this instant,' said she fondly. 'Perchance in an Age to come it will be common custom to give the old release when they choose their time, and to allow them a final night such as this. Your memory will warm me alway.'

'And yours me,' said I, and truly meant it.

'There is a Goodness in you,' she said. 'I always knew. You are as much a Child of God as the Missionary's Wife.'

'Whom?'

'The Missionary's Wife. She has been so kind to me in my sickness. She is truly devout, a Saint.'

I was dumbfounded. The Missionary's Wife? That ghoulish bitch? A Saint?

'When my final moment comes,' said she, 'I shall leave her the other half of my gold. You and she shall be my Heirs, partners in compassion.'

Back in my cabin I discovered the dark-haired Maid. Her eyes were vicious, her visage harsh.

'Where have you been?' she demanded, in a voice that would scrape splinters from a slab of marble. 'I have waited all night. Where have you been?'

'You would never believe me.'

'With one of those Harlots no doubt,' she spat. 'Lord, have you no shame? Then this will shame you, and it will cost you more than ever harlot did. I am with child.'

'Ah.'

'Yours.'

'Indeed.'

'You shall wed me.'

'Let us not be hasty.'

'*Hasty?* Why, how can I tarry? And how may I wed another now? I have spoken already with the Missionary. He will perform the ceremony at noon.'

I parried for time. Wed to her? Never. And how should we name a child conceived only in disappointment?

'Very well,' said I. 'At noon.'

'You agree?'

'I have no choice. I cannot abandon you alone with child.'

She threw her arms around me, then, covering me with kisses and exclamations of joy and prophecies of our future happiness and declarations that she had never truly cared for her Betrothed, whom she journeyed to wed, but only for me, ever since that first night upon the canvas. Her embrace was distasteful, with the sickly odour of lilies. I could never wed one such as she.

'Until noon, then,' said I, but as we docked in the sorry little Tropical harbour I was first off the vessel ('to purchase a wedding gift,' I told her) and by Noon I was well hidden in a poor shack in a mean quarter of the town, where none would think to seek me.

I did not credit her story, believing it only a ploy to ensnare me, but even were it true I could not conceive of a lifetime with such a Trollop. Did I do wrong? Yes, and also no: for our union would only have caused misery to all three, and a misery tripled is surely not a mischief halved. What was done, if it were indeed done, could not be undone, and I wrapped the Grandmother's bag of gold in a box and addressed it to the Maid, as a forfeit against any future poverty for her and the child, and handed it to the Bosun to pass to her at noon.

'She will find another to take your place,' he grinned. 'It is said the Mercenary has fired a shot or two in that direction, and the trader also has exchanged with her somewhat more than the hour o'clock.'

I stepped ashore, amazed at the infinite devious variety of human perfidy, mine own, of course, included, and enjoyed much mirth at the prospect that Spotty might be forced to marry the dark-haired Maid and find himself the father of my Child. The land, so strange for so many weeks, rolled beneath my feet, so I staggered, but the dusty streets of that distant barbaric town teemed with lusty young beauties of every hue, black as coal, brown as toffee, gold as Autumn leaves, many of them naked above the waist, and I laughed aloud at the heat and the sun and at being alive and young and free with all my life before me, and I vow the Stranger would surely have approved.

(2)

If you're ever depressed take a sea voyage to the Tropics, as I did aboard the liner *Marie Antoinette*. The grey Victorian gloom that had enveloped me at the coast was soon evaporated. Each day as we sailed towards the Equator the sea became a paler grey until it shaded gently into deepening blues and eventually a thin translucent green. Each day the sky lightened along with my spirits, the sun rose higher and brighter until at last it stood right overhead and blazed with the full glory of life itself. As each day passed I seemed to lose another care and another year, so that after a week I was forgetting I was middle-aged, and after a fortnight I was behaving quite outrageously, as though I were in my twenties again and eager for everything. I was filled with energy and nerve and every sense was heightened. Even the mildest flavours were suffused again with taste and the faintest smell was rich with promise. I relished the dangerous warmth of the sun on my skin, the smooth cool whisper of the water in the swimming pool, the burning firmness of the deck with the tar almost bubbling in the heat, the frosted mist on a cold glass of beer, the unbelievable softness of women's skin.

Yes, there were women, of course there were women, no fewer than five of them in a fortnight, and the sign of my new confidence is that I don't feel at all ashamed or guilty about any of them, even though one was disgracefully young and one turned out to be embarrassingly old. They all enjoyed me quite as much as I enjoyed them, with sheer physical relish and plenty of laughter and no regrets, and none of us was harmed. It was sex as God must surely have meant it to be.

Something happens to women during a long Tropical sea voyage. The sun seems to make their juices flow, the salty air to soften them, and the long procession of idle day after idle pampered day eases their languid limbs and spreads them wide. As they shed their clothes they shed their morals, too. The heat has a lot to do with it, but there is also something other-worldly and dreamlike about life aboard ship. It becomes a small closed Universe with separate rules bounded only by the endless circle of the smudged horizon. The everyday restraints of ordinary life are cast off like the ropes that once kept the vessel in touch with the shore and reality, and maybe because ships are still ruled at sea by Captains whose powers are as wide as those of eighteenth-century tyrants should they choose to use them, the passengers, no longer responsible for making even the smallest decision, respond by behaving like rumbustious eighteenth-century roisterers. Women who wouldn't have looked at me twice ashore were suddenly smiling and winking, and I found myself buying drinks for girls I wouldn't even have considered before: fat girls, plain girls, ugly girls. Each of them suddenly seemed especially desirable in her own way, perhaps for the softness of her hair or the colour of her eyes or the sound of her laughter. I discovered again how beautiful every woman is, each in her own unique fashion, and learned anew that every one of them deserved the sort of man I once had been and was becoming again.

It wasn't only the surge of lust that made the voyage so rejuvenating. It was the entire atmosphere aboard, the shameless exuberance of almost every moment of every day. I would wake each morning early, so as not to miss a minute of it, and breathe deep and stretch with languorous pleasure at the open porthole of my cabin, sniffing the ocean and luxuriating in the sound of the rush of the waves beside the hull and the blood-red grin of the Tropical sun peering over the horizon at dawn.

Each morning I went for an early run around the deck, revelling in the exercise and the silence and the power of the ship as it surged on through the sea with a constant tremor and a hum from its engines and a wisp of smoke from the funnel. There were usually two or three other early risers and we waved and greeted each other with the common smug camaraderie of those who are up while the rest of the world wastes its life in sleep. One of those dawn joggers was a jolly girl with freckles and gleaming eyes and a dirty chuckle and she ran wearing only a bikini and it wasn't long before we met by chance on the Boat Deck one morning when the breeze was still and the sea calm and flat and there was no one in sight and we looked at each other and laughed and did it there on sudden impulse, on the deck behind a lifeboat, for the sheer hell of it and because it seemed marvellously right with the sun coming up on a fresh and clean new world.

'Ya-hooooo!' she yelled afterwards, and raced to plunge in the swimming pool, and we swam against each other, up and down, for length after length, until I could breathe no more and surrendered.

'Weakling!' she yelled. 'I bet you couldn't do it again.'

'Tomorrow,' I gasped.

'And tomorrow and tomorrow. Ya-hooooo!' And for three tomorrows we did, every morning behind the lifeboat, until she decided I had had my share of her and started to work seriously through as many of the passengers and crew as she could manage, and the joy of it was that I didn't mind at all. Why shouldn't she? Why shouldn't I? My malignant pride had evaporated along with my guilt, and anyway by then I was about to embark myself on my second romance.

This may all sound a bit sordid, five casual women in a fortnight, but it wasn't, I swear it wasn't. It was simply *fun*, high juvenile spirits and firm affectionate flesh, and it certainly wasn't the most important part of the voyage. It was an expression of the physical well-being that glowed through my body during those weeks and had me whistling out of tune again. Some mornings I spent half an hour in the ship's little gymnasium, until I could almost feel the blood pounding through my veins, and I fell on breakfasts with huge appetite, savouring the glorious sunny textures of paw-paws and melons and devouring enough eggs and sausages and buttered toast to give a heart specialist a coronary.

I spent most mornings in or around the swimming pool, wary of the sun at first but increasingly confident as my body coloured and turned eventually a deep hard brown that had several of the girls aboard glancing at my groin. One of them was a shy, blushing blonde whose skin was so fair she had to stay out of the sun, in the shade of umbrellas. She was sailing to meet her fiancé but her eyes kept flickering towards my darkening body as though she were mesmerised by the possibilities of my blackness against her pale white skin. Who was I to refuse a lady? I parked myself on a deck-chair beside her, still dripping from the pool, and bought her one of the rich, steaming beef teas they served on deck at about eleven o'clock each morning.

'Haven't we met somewhere before?' I said, and then laughed at the corny approach. But what the hell – you have to start somehow.

'It must have been in a previous life,' she murmured.

'Reincarnation? Do you believe in it?'

'Sometimes.' She was blushing. She was irresistible. Her eyelashes fluttered like nervous butterflies.

'So what were you before? A slave girl? Cleopatra?'

She giggled. 'Nothing glamorous like that, worst luck. No, I think I was a doctor. Or a nurse. I don't know why. Sometimes . . . . '

'I'm sure you were a marvellous nurse. In fact, I've got a bit of an ache you might look at for me. Perhaps you could cure it.'

She went a glorious deep pink and I knew then it was only a matter of time, and two days later, after lots of jokes and cold drinks and games of deck quoits and shuffleboard I found myself on a sultry afternoon in her cabin and her shyness gave her a delicate grace and modesty that made me rampant, and every afternoon for a week we shared enormous lunches and then delicious sweaty siestas in her cabin where she marvelled at the blackened frontiers of my skin where my swimming trunks had been, and whimpered as the sea breeze and the ocean whispered through the porthole and the flying fish and dolphins skipped and splashed beside the ship as though rejoicing at being alive, and now and then the distant humps of whales blew mist at the sky.

'Who do you think I might have been in a previous life?' I asked one afternoon, afterwards.

She giggled and poked me in the ribs. 'You!' she said. 'I bet you were a Negro gigolo.'

'Then I'd better earn my keep again,' I said.

I loved the ghostly whiteness of her skin in the gloom of her cabin and the pinkness of her parts and the faint gold hairs on her cheeks, and her gentleness, but she was going out to the Tropics to get married and she had to disembark before I did.

'Let's meet again in our next lives,' I joked.

'That's a definite date,' she whispered, and clung to me.

It wasn't just the sex. Those lusty afternoons were unforgettable, but so too were the evenings chastely sipping cocktails as the setting sun glittered across the turquoise sea, and the warm purple nights when we all dressed for dinner and sat down to five courses and the cutlery shone as much as the ladies' eyes and the wine gleamed against the virgin tablecloths. Afterwards we would dance to a six-piece band that played tunes from the past and the world seemed younger, with a gallant courtesy it seems to have lost. Or some of us would play cards, or watch a film in the ship's small cinema, or join in the quiz or bingo games that the purser ran in the main lounge. And one night there was a Fancy Dress Ball that started my third romance.

I went as Jack the Ripper, with just a dinner jacket and a borrowed cloak, top hat, cane and butcher's knife, but she had taken much more trouble. She was wearing a high-necked dress like an eighteenth-century lady of the court, complete with long gloves and a black velvet mask glittering with sequins, and I fell for her liquid voice and the flashing sparkle of her hidden eyes. She was a widow alone on a world cruise, and although I danced with other women – a nun who fondled my buttocks and a girl dressed as a tart who started to take her part seriously despite my Jack the Ripper knife – I was constantly drawn back to my eighteenth-century lady, powerless to resist the fascination of her voice. Where had I heard it before? And when? *Had* I heard it before? And her eyes reminded me of someone I had once known, someone I had loved. We seemed instantly at ease together, like old friends meeting after decades. Or was it just the mystery of her mask that made her so appealing, and the lure of those elegant layers of petticoats that begged to be stripped away?

So we danced together again and again, and even her embrace seemed wondrously familiar, her scent an old acquaintance, and the movement of her thighs with mine was so knowing we could already have been lovers of many years ago. The band was playing a soft, haunting version of *Greensleeves*, that magical melody that wafts across the centuries promising a timeless unity of the ages and hinting at the common poignancy of human loves and hopes and death. The music, the rhythm, her scent, the movement, the closeness of her, made me dizzy with a brief illusion of immortality, and it seemed that the night could never end and must have existed for ever.

'I feel I've known you all my life,' I said.

'I'm glad.' Her voice was as smooth as a stream on pebbles, her lips as soft as moss.

'Will you take your mask off? I want to see you.'

Her eyes twinkled. 'Later,' she smiled. 'Later you can take it off for me.'

'I'd like to make love to you.'

'Thank you.'

'Now.'

'Later.'

'Soon. Please.'

'Later. A lady should never be hurried.'

A memory flashed through my brain, some remembrance from time out of mind, and was gone before I could grasp it.

'Love is destroyed by speed,' she said.

I was not alone in admiring her elegance. There was a young man dressed as a soldier who danced with her too often for my liking and who glared at me now and then, but I refused to believe that she cared for him. *She's mine. She's mine tonight, and she always has been, from long ago.* My subconscious knew. It was only a matter of time.

Well after midnight, in her cabin, she turned out the light.

'Now you can take it off,' she whispered.

'But I still won't be able to see you.'

'Later, my love.'

I removed the mask, and everything else she wore, and felt her face in the darkness, fingering her eyelids and cheekbones and nose like a blind man and building a portrait of her that was very beautiful. I sipped at her lips and imagined she might be anyone, any fantasy I cared to conjure. She could have been Marilyn Monroe or Brigitte Bardot or the Princess of Wales, for all I knew. In my mind she was anyone I wanted her to be. She was the eternal woman.

Afterwards the moonlight wandered across the cabin, a shaft of silver dancing with the waves.

'I want to look at you,' I said.

She sighed. 'All right. But I'm sorry. You won't like it.'

'What do you mean?'

'You'll see.'

She switched the light on.

I admit I was shocked. She was probably sixty, perhaps older. The skin on her neck, which had been hidden by the high collar of her fancy dress, was loose. Her hands, which had been camouflaged by long gloves, were discoloured with age. The eyelids I had caressed and kissed were grey and wrinkled, and I knew now where I had seen her eyes before. They were just like the eyes of my wife.

'So now you know why I wore a mask,' she said. 'Cinderella has turned into a pumpkin.'

'Nonsense,' I stammered. 'You're l-lovely.'

'And you're very gallant, my dear, and a very bad liar.' She laughed sadly. 'But at least I've still got my own teeth,' she said, and once again a sudden memory stung my mind, a sort of recognition, before evaporating like morning mist.

'You'll want to leave now,' she said.

I summoned all my moral strength. I had sworn to be born again, to become a better person. 'Leave? I was hoping to stay the night.'

She smiled gently, and the smile at least was that of a young girl. 'You're very kind,' she said.

She switched the light off again and I wrapped her in my arms, trying to forget the wrinkled skin and the liver spots, seeking only to make her feel wanted. In the dark she was just as soft as any girl, and her voice was as liquid as ever. It was only the light that was cruel.

'Age is a terrible thing,' she whispered. 'I still feel as though I'm in my prime, and yet I'm trapped in this hag-like body. I feel as though I'm still in my twenties but someone has suddenly dragged me off the street and made me up to look like a witch and then thrown me out again to fend for myself, and suddenly nobody looks at me any more. That's one of the horrors of being old. People just don't *look* at you properly any more, especially the young. Especially the young. For them you simply cease to exist. They look straight through you, as though you were a ghost, and maybe that's just what I am, a ghost from an earlier age that refuses to accept it ought to be dead.' She shivered, and I held her tighter. 'I still lust after the same sort of men I did as a girl but now they're usually thirty years younger than me and they don't even notice me. They don't realise that I'm really in my twenties and just made up to look old. I want to scream at them that everyone used to look at me once, that I was far more beautiful than the silly little girls they gaze at now and that men used to stare at me as though there was no one else in the room. Like you tonight. That's how they were. Like you tonight. I wish I could wear a mask all the time. I wish life was all one long fancy dress party.'

'It can be,' I said, 'if you want it to be. And now I'd like to make love you you again.'

In the middle of it she cried, and claimed she was happy, and I kissed her tears, which made her cry even more. For the first time in many years I liked myself. I was proud of my decency. If only I had been able to like myself before it would have changed my life, and I would have kept my old name and my wife and my soul.

I'm glad you didn't. I'm very glad you didn't, or we wouldn't be here together, and I really would be dead, and a ghost.

'What did you say?' I said.

'I didn't,' she said. 'I didn't say anything. I was thinking.'

'Thinking what?'

'I was thinking I really wouldn't mind dying right now.'

We never repeated that night. She had too much dignity for that. But whenever we met about the ship we always stopped for a chat and her hand would linger on my arm not with passion but with friendship and gratitude. The night before I disembarked she gave me a small package and forbade me to open it until I was ashore. Inside was a pair of embarrassingly expensive gold cufflinks, with a card that read: 'These were my dear dead husband's, so I'm sorry about the engraved initials, but I believe you can have them removed. He would have wanted you to have them. He loved me very much, and he would have liked me to thank you.'

Would my wife ever give my cufflinks away to a lover?

The engraved initials were the same as mine had been in my previous life, before I stole the stranger's name.

My skin crawled, and then I started laughing. *This* was precisely what I had been seeking when I had changed my life: not just idleness but the gloriously unpredictable.

Even the men on board seemed much more amusing than they might have been ashore: the pompous, trendy clergyman who appeared not to believe in God; the arms dealer who was obviously going to sell guns to some god-forsaken banana republic dictatorship but pretended rather touchingly to be a famine relief worker; the alcoholic saloon-bar philosopher who was a desperate bore when he was drunk but who told hilarious stories when he was half-sober, and who once remarked that reality is 'just an illusion created by a shortage of alcohol'.

In fact I can remember only one small sourness during the entire voyage. The young man who had been dressed as a soldier at the Fancy Dress Ball took exception to my success with the masked widow and attempted to take his revenge the next day during a morning of water sports in the swimming pool. In one of the events I was perched precariously on a greasy pole suspended above the pool and he challenged me with a light of ferocity in his eyes and there was more than just the simple urge to win in the blows he gave me with his soggy pillow. And in the Water-Polo match afterwards he deliberately ensured that he was in the opposing team and stationed himself in the right position to mark me and half-drown me every time we fought for the ball. I didn't have the heart to tell him who she was until I spotted him that evening frowning at all the women aboard, as though trying to imagine each in a sequinned mask. The only one he ignored was the widow. She had been right: he looked right through her, as though she didn't exist. So I took him aside and bought him a drink, and told him. At first he was angry, thinking I was taunting him. Then, when I persisted, he was doubtful, then incredulous. Eventually I persuaded him I was telling the truth and he burst into laughter, and later I saw him watching her thoughtfully with a sort of wonder.

He and I almost became friends after that, and when we crossed the Equator, and some of the crew dressed as King Neptune and his Court came up over the side of the ship for the Crossing the Line ceremony, like pirates, roaring for coins and virgins, we fought side by side in mock battle with them before we were both overpowered and ceremoniously pinioned, lathered, daubed with dye, and ducked in the pool by Neptune's demons.

I lost all capacity for smallness of mind or bitterness during that sea voyage. There was one stunning girl on board whom I pursued for days in vain, but even then I was able to shrug off my failure and disappointment and cut my losses. In some strange way, despite feeling younger, I also felt older and more mature. Win some, lose some, what's it really matter? For far too long I'd forgotten that nothing is really of much importance, that we all take ourselves and our petty ambitions and desires far too seriously, and that life is magnificent and to be enjoyed to the full, without remorse or melancholy. I learned again to look for the good in people and to accept their faults. I lost my guilts and intolerance on that voyage and started to live again. I could even think of my wife and children quite rationally and without pity. Why should I pity them? They were better off without the man I had been. It was not my wife's fault that our marriage had gone sour. I had gone sour. I had been so bound up in my job, my ambitions, myself, that I had selfishly denied her the dancing and laughter and irresponsibility and playful love I should have given her and had given instead to strangers. She too had deserved a man who was more like me.

And I stopped hearing any more voices in my head. It was as though my conscience and I were together again, in harmony.

I disembarked at the tropical port where the dead stranger, my namesake, my double, had boarded the *Marie Antoinette* on its earlier voyage going the other way. It seemed the right place to end the voyage, and the right time. To go any further would have been to start sailing away from the Equator again, and I was looking for heat, and by now I was curious about the dead man whose name had given me this new surge of life. Where had he come from, and why? What sort of man had he been? Now that I was getting so much closer to his roots there must surely be some records about him, some clues left behind. I felt a need to find some explanation for the source of this spring that had revitalised me, and I had a superstitious feeling that it was right to make a pilgrimage into his past to appease his spirit for stealing his name.

'You really want to disembark *here?*' said the Purser with a shudder. 'Rather you than me. It's a hellish dump, sweaty and filthy. You can actually taste the germs in the water.'

He was right.

It was one of those seedy, lethargic little tropical shanty-towns where mangy dogs prowl the dusty slums, scavenging, and the sun roasts the tin-roofed shacks and shabby bungalows, the sort of modern Frontier Town that marks the border between Land and Sea, between Old and New, between Civilisation and Savagery, where the dark-skinned Police Chief appears to be God and the few white women whine constantly about the humidity and drink gin and play Bridge all morning and sleep all afternoon and go quietly insane during the rainy season with the Monsoon thundering down.

But none of this depressed me, not even the rundown little boarding house in a drab back street where I chose to stay to conserve my dwindling funds. For the beaches were as white as sugar, the sea a pale green, the fish rich with the sharpness of the warm ocean.

Perhaps each of us has an ancient memory of a place like this, of the primeval seas and tropical shores from which we came so long ago, buried deep in our reptile subconscious. Far from feeling alien and repelled, I felt at home here. I knew this place, or somewhere very like it, or maybe my ancestors did. It was like coming back to the beginning.

5

1. Up, and it being a most fine day, to the harbour to trace the provenance of the stranger. All hustle in the streets and throngs of the dark-skinned peoples of these parts and such a commotion of traffic as would excite and alarm a country lad, though I held my wits about me and successfully avoided carts, wagons and barrows. Discreet enquiries in sundry taverns came to nought, though two or three declared they had heard the name. Thence to the Custom House, whence a surly blackamoor clerk attempted to send me about my business, claiming more important matters to engage his time. I stood my ground and demanded satisfaction, whereupon he reached for a baton near to hand and threatened to belabour me withal, wherewith I took my leave with dignity, informing him it were of little consequence yet I should report him to his superior. The uncouth wretch bellowed that he *were* his superior, thus vexing me greatly. So home and to bed, chafing, not least at the re-emergence upon my face of the angry pustules I had hoped to have shed with my coming to manhood.

2. Up betimes and to the shipping company, whence the stranger had sailed these shores upon the vessel *Marie A.* Thither encountered a chain of shackled blackamoors driven forth through the poor streets by a stout fellow, an uncouth slave-master; one of their number a fine dark wench with merry bubbies. I was desirous of relieving her plight and asked her price, an innocent enquiry that occasioned much mirth, the slave-master responding that the wench were destined for the King and not for some spotty changeling; which mockery I accepted with good humour, having no stomach for a beating and understanding that as a stranger, and on account of my youth, I had much to learn in this challenging new world, and so put a brave

countenance upon it, though partly on account of the slave-master's stout whip. Yet another cunning clerk at the shipping company did molest me tediously with delay of many an hour before deigning to search the record for intelligence of the stranger. Methinks he were of an age with me and of little more experience, but thus to display his position did play the snooty coxcomb, yet I considered it best advised to humour the wretch lest he deny entirely the requested intelligence. After much ado, this skellum, with many a sigh, was prevailed upon to deliver the intelligence that the stranger had indeed sailed upon the said vessel. This of course I already knew, so pressed for further knowledge, viz. his previous address, or any other intelligence of him, whereupon the clerk sneered that he were no secret agent and that if it were Intelligence I sought I should take myself to the King's Minister in charge of that department. Many a witty reply entered my mind too late but at that moment my tongue were as if paralysed, so I departed thence with as great a silent dignity as I could muster, vowing to learn myself better to answer such popinjays as I grew in years and experience. The day being far advanced, and I overheated with weary frustration, I took myself to a tavern and tarried overlong, remembering anon little but some merry songs with a brave band of travelling men and a fine meal of chicken and melon and a doxy that accepted my coin but never was seen again. And so to bed, a little wiser.

3. Lay long, sick in head and bowels. The meat in these parts is not alway in a noble condition. Sent the lodging-house slut for some physic, which rendered me into an even worse condition. Journeyed no further than the privy, though covered thither and thence many furlongs.

4. Up gingerly, much sickness. I vow never to countenance meat nor drink no more.

5. Up betimes, and abroad, judging it safe to venture further than a chain or two from the privy, to the King's Court to seek further intelligence of the stranger. I marvelled mightily at the bustle of the palace, deeming it a most noble place to embark on the road of life, though its odours held little in them of majesty. Petitioners thronged the corridors with much commotion and waving of arms. A friendly clerk, for some there be, much moved

by my bewilderment, did guide me into an ante-room where sat in some able splendour the King's Intelligencer, a furtive fellow with secret eyes, speaking only in whispers, and bent with the weariness of old age, being at least forty years. It is said he controls an army of spies and an empire of prisons where enemies of the King languish forgotten for many a year, yet he were civil enough to me when finally I achieved his throne and kissed his toe, as I understood to be the custom in these parts. The sudden merriment of the bystanders having dwindled, beneath his cunning gaze I felt a trifle apprehensive, as though trapped in interrogation by twin beams of light, but when I had persuaded him not to arrest me on account of impersonating the stranger whom I sought, he was greatly helpful and told me all he knew. 'I have never heard of the man,' quoth he, 'Next!' Such forthright honesty is not common among persons of great power, I believe. A goodly dinner of chicken with spices, and paw paw, and an afternoon of idleness, admiring the bustle of the town and the quaintness of its buildings.

6. To the King's Court again to seek some further advantage, to discover too late, after tarrying there until two o'clock, that it were the sabbath and no business done, so to another tavern where I drank deep, and foolishly ate not, and were robbed again.

7. *Lord's Day*. Lay abed all day, vowing to mend my ways. The slut rattled at me for idleness as she refurbished my lodging, but this I took for affection. She has a trim countenance but is over ancient for my needs, being surely thirty years at least. Later she softened sufficiently to serve a supper of chicken and guavas, with a draught of native ale.

8. Up betimes and to the King's Court, with which I am now most familiar. The pustules upon my chin have burst and I feel a hearty new confidence, certain in my errand and sure of excitement and advancement in the life that lies before me. I even display contempt for the guards at the palace gates who have no conscience for their duty but lounge on their spears and gossip. Within the palace beggars squat on earthen floors, some limbless, some eyeless, some stricken of the pox, all garnished with buzzing flies. It is said that the King has a one-legged mistress who once sat as they do until he caught sight of her and also a courtesan

whom he spied selling oranges in the market place, but for these gossips I cannot vouch, being careful not to toy with the King's dignity in idle speculation with strangers, who might well be informants for the King's Intelligencer. A stranger in these parts is held under constant suspicion, and already, in the streets, I believe I am followed by a knave with an eyeglass. All day in the palace seeking clerks and officers, and passed on from one to another. How may such a people ever become great? Yet the vigour and variety of life awes me, and I am warmed by the conceit that the entire hemisphere in my shellfish, requiring only to be prized open.

9. A commotion below even before rising, the slut in altercation with the knave with the eyeglass. Later she vowed he has been spying through her window and seemed anxious of her virtue, whereupon I did not enlighten her that it is I, not she, he seeks, for fear of presenting a false impression. Thence once more to the palace, nodding to the knave and remarking upon the fine day, whereupon he hid his face, as though assuming that if he cannot see he cannot be seen. I doubt this agent will progress far in his chosen calling.

Thence, to hinder his pursuit, in a carriage, first to the harbour; thence in another to the market; thence in a third to the King's Court; where I found the knave awaiting me. Such uncanny knowledge of my route is troubling, for witchcraft is said to be general in these parts. Discourse with sundry officials, none more useful than the last. A sorry day, relieved only by the smile of a dark-eyed wench whom I would fain have approached but for the presence of her husband. Men of greater experience think nothing of soliciting a rendezvous with other men's wives, but as yet I know not how, and fall to dreaming I were of greater experience, though not wishing my life away. Her smile reminds me that it is many weeks since I last faisais un coup avec a woman, so to the harbour again searching mightily but in vain before learning from a fisherman that all the bawds retire to their lodgings in the sultry afternoons. At night to the theatre, a poor comedy yet the savages accounted it very merry, and I fell in with a rare fine group of fellows with whom I supped on chicken and mangoes, thence with them to a maison d'assignation where I did tout que I wished avec une pretty little dark poulet, with whom I was greatly merry and pleased, despite the expense. And so to bed, mightily content.

10. Up, with an ingenious conceit, that I repair to the Exchequer, whence surely no man's name may escape, thanks to iniquitous taxes. Thence in a carriage and upon arrival the knave with the eyeglass were not to be seen, surely a goodly omen. Unlike the palace, the Exchequer were empty, allowing instant access unto the presence of the Chancellor himself, a fat but merry rascal whose cunning discourse ascertained first the fact that I am as yet not registered for taxes, and then the whereabouts of my lodging and then that I should pay a large impost for registration as a stranger to the town. I parted with this sum with good humour, for he is a brave rogue who must surely be of assistance, and he undertook to seek further Intelligence and to deliver it upon my return on the morrow. Thence, well pleased with my errand, to a tavern, where merry strangers coax me to join them at a cockfight, where I lose a goodly sum in wagers. Thence, out of temper, to my lodging, where the slut served a foul collation of chicken broth and demanded a week's payment. I fear that soon I needs must seek employment.

11. Abroad to the Exchequer, yet another fine day and my heart filled with hope, where the Chancellor hinted at discoveries but first required a fee for searching, which sum I paid, feeling my quest to be surely drawing to its close. The Chancellor chewed upon the coin, bending the metal fearfully, and angrily demanded another, together with a forfeit for attempting to pass a false piece which doubtless were passed to me at the cockfight. O that I were of greater experience, yet it will come with years. With heavy heart I parted with two more pieces, both of which satisfied, and he required me to return the following noon, being most busy today. On going thence the knave with the eyeglass approached me and boldly chid me for altering my movements, to which I riposted wittily that my movements were privy unto me alone, a sprankle with which I was greatly pleased, whereupon he threatened me with a knife so that I made apology, though did not mean it in my heart. I begin to tire of this town.

12. Up, and to the Exchequer, filled with pleasure and hope once more in the dawning of a new day and the sights and business of the town, among them a jade with a dancing ape. Each

day brings new delights and I thank God Almighty for life and youthful vigour and resilience. The Chancellor is unaccountably absent for the entire day upon some urgent business, but the Vice-Chancellor engaged to keep the matter open a further day upon payment of a fee. This I made, and with deep foreboding set out to find employment, for my funds run low and the slut will wait little longer. I enquired of taverns, coachmen, sailors, fishermen, but employment is rare, and betimes I returned to my lodging supperless. Thither a bawd offered herself and I was much desirous of her and would dearly baiser elle dans l'air plein if necessary, but I have no longer her price and she scorned me for a beggar. And so to bed, much vexed and troubled in my mind.

13. Up, and much distressed to discover now both Chancellor and Vice-Chancellor to be absent from the Exchequer, both 'upon urgent busyness'. An uncouth clerk solicited a further fee to keep the matter open, urging me to return on the morrow, and I had no choice but to part with yet a further piece. The Dutch themselves could learn these grasping savages little of the arts of thieving. In the dusty street an encounter with my shadow, the knave with the eyeglass, to whom I described my plight, whereupon he reasoned impertinently and with mirth my only solution to be to hew off a limb and become a beggar. Thither to my lodging, passing numerous trollops smiling and winking yet now I may barely purchase one finger of any, let alone ella cul de sac. One cried that since I refused their charms I must surely be one of those that prefer unnatural vices, occasioning much merriment among the others, which calumny I know not to be true. I considered a witty reply too late. O to be older and more experienced. At my lodgings the slut demanded payment, which I promised for the morrow. And so to bed again supperless, and my guts in a chafing condition, and now the cursed pustules reappear upon my chin, advertising my callow youth, of which all delight in taking advantage.

14. *Sunday*, which I had forgot. The Exchequer is closed. Much wracked with hunger, I purloined a chicken from the market and cooked it by the sea, finally consuming a sorry mix of raw flesh, charred skin, and sand. Thence to my lodging, where the slut threatened to lodge a complaint with the King. I vowed earnestly to make full payment on the morrow. 'And tomorrow

and tomorrow,' said she wittily, but without humour. It may be necessary to resort to a midnight flight. The pustules itch abominably.

15. All day abed, stricken with the grippe. This is a poxy town.

16. Up and abroad, and the Lord be praised, another mighty fine day and the streets entrancing with bands and dancers, some most merry, and pleasingest of all, the Chancellor is returned to the Exchequer, and before him a document upon which is inscribed a full sheet of the intelligence I seek. Mightily content at this, believing that my condition might be relieved upon the stranger's acquaintances or even family discovering I share his name, but first the Chancellor was desirous of a final fee, 'for inscription of the document', and a sum for the clerk, and an impost for the seal, and a tax upon the entire transaction. Upon emptying my pockets in proof of my inability to pay, he answered, 'It is an offence to refuse to pay lawful sums due to the King's Exchequer,' and summoned guards. Thence in chains, by wagon, to the common gaol, where I am mightily vexed to find myself lodged with felons and murderers, yet captivity has its compensations, for we were fed, albeit a noisome brew. And so to bed on a mat of straw.

17. Up, and an interrogation by the King's Intelligencer, attended by the knave with the looking glass. On being required to explain my every smallest movement, this time I accounted it unwise to jest. I threw myself upon their mercy, admitting also to the theft of the chicken, of which they were not informed, it having been the Lords Day and the knave not following, in the hope that it would go better for me to confess all, but the King's Intelligencer shook his head with sorrow. 'Theft too,' said he mournfully, 'and fraud, and debt, and personation, and idleness and licentiousness, and drunkenness.' The knave also shook his head. I took it that matters were not going well in this particular. Eight-legged beasts scuttle across the floor of this foul place, and distant cries of agony betoken ill for the future.

18. Up very betimes, and the King's Intelligencer and the knave returned and belaboured me with questions and occasional blows. I reminded them of my own King's mighty power, crying

116

'Civis Romanus sum', but they appeared unlettered and not to know the tag, and even after my translation they responded that powerful though my own King might be both he and his protection were a mighty distance hence, to which rejoinder I could find no reply, so they beat me again. They accused me of sundry vicious crimes, including the gathering of Intelligence, and enquired repeatedly as to what I may have done with the stranger whose name I share. My replies were ignored or disbelieved, beyond all reason, but then neither are reasonable men. When they were gone, a fellow prisoner also struck me for looking at him. Supper of stinking fish. On the whole I would rather be anywhere but here.

19. Today I am accused of treason. I denied it. They beat me, and still I denied it. They beat me further, and I denied it yet. After a further beating I admitted it. They appeared satisfied by this, and took their leave with many mutual congratulations. Supper of fried lizard and coconut milk, a dish I could not come to relish even after a month or two. A rat has taken up residence in a corner of my pestilent cell, and I attempt to befriend it, to no avail. Perhaps tomorrow. And so to bed.

20. Up, with a warning to prepare myself to appear before the King himself. A gaoler much given to smirking informed me that upon the previous day the King sentenced four to death for insolence. This troubled me more than I cared so I took the utmost pains with my toilet, combing my breeches and hair with my fingers, to appear at my best. Thence, with many others, to whom I am shackled with chains, by cart to the palace to learn my fate, only to discover that even the gaolers had forgotten this to be the Sabbath and the King absent hunting crocodile. Thither to our imprisonment, whereupon we were all soundly beaten for forgetting the Sabbath.

21. *Lord's Day*. Five times today forced to my knees and pointed in the alleged direction of Mecca, and required to touch the earth with my forehead. I considered offering to become a Moslem in exchange for my freedom, which development would at least allow me several wives, though their maintenance would prove vexatious in my present condition. Dogmeat for supper, with a flavour of camel dung, which I consumed with the utmost

despatch and a prayer that it might remain down. I mused as to the possibility of the lodging-house slut regretting my absence, and confessed it were unlikely. And so to bed, but soon up again, the dogmeat also. And so to bed again, with sleep difficult, a foul stench.

22. To the King's Court where the throng jostling in the palace gestured and jeered as we were driven by in chains. Still waiting in the selfsame corridor is the wench that once smiled at me with her husband, but she smiles not now but hoots with the rest. How misfortune contaminates the misfortunate. On stumbling across the foot of a beggar I was kicked back into place: to think that a man well-versed in Latin verbs may thus be used by blackamoors! I resolved to speak straight to the King, understanding him by rumour to be not a man impressed by importunate pleading and cowardly carriage, though my resolution weakened as singly my companions were taken before him and none seen again.

'God's pity, not another!' sighed the King as I was finally dragged before him. 'Is there truly no end to my labours?'

'Another traitor, sire,' said the Chief Intelligencer.

'Traitors, traitors,' said the King, 'so many traitors. In faith, at times I do believe there is not left one loyal man in my entire kingdom. Very well, then, get on with it, but briefly, I beg.'

In truth he appeared a very merry monarch, a stoutish fellow with lace at his wrists and a wig of curls that hanged to his shoulder, and a pleasing air of dissipation and good humoured weariness at the world. At his side was a comely wench, greatly younger than he, with fair fine bubbies well displayed, that I took to be his daughter and my spirits lifted at the sight of them, for I could not believe that two such could countenance viciousness or blatant injustice, and I happily discounted the smirking gaoler's report of the King's wanton cruelty.

Upon the Intelligencer detailing my mischiefs, to whit that I were liar, cheat, fraud, thief, personator, drunkard, tradeless idler and traitor, the King's girl remarked merrily that such a description fitted the Intelligencer himself, whereupon the King laughed mightily and patted her thigh with fatherly affection, and the Intelligencer himself scowled, remarking such jesting in court to be unseemly and that the recent treasons must be rooted out without ruth.

'Ah, treason, treason,' sighed the King, 'you speak so often of treason that my head akes and I perceive a distinct pain in the buttock. Have we not heard sufficiently of treason to fill a lifetime? God's mercy, man, I tire of treason. May you not enliven our days with wittier charges: incest, perhaps, or a man's cannibalism of his wife's mother?'

'Your father lost his head, sire,' muttered the Intelligencer.

'Aye, and since then many more, but I do not purpose to lose mine own.'

'Treachery and plot abound, my Lord,' urged the Intelligencer.

'Very well,' said the King wearily, 'I shall punish the fellow, if that is what you desire. What sentence do you ask?'

'Death by impalement, sire.'

'Death by impalement? Not again. In God's name, sir, you are a dull fellow. Death by impalement, death by impalement, day after day the same request, whatever the charge.'

'Perchance he has a stake in it,' quipped the wench.

'What? What?'

She patted his knee merrily. 'A stake, my Lord, a stake. Impalement.'

The King guffawed. 'Ah, Nellie, Nellie,' he cried. 'You are more to me than any. This business wearies me. What do we know of the prisoner?'

The Chief Intelligencer produced a document, and I saw it were the very same prepared for me by the Chancellor of the Exchequer and for which I myself had grievously paid and now might so grievously suffer, and, reading from it, reported to the King that I had quit this city many years hence by sea yet had recently returned upon the selfsame vessel, to lodge in the city without employment yet always enquiring as to my previous self.

The King regarded me with pity. ''Tis plain the fellow is insane,' he said.

'Your Majesty . . . ' said I, stricken with a sudden ingenious conceit whereby I might discover the stranger's abode and journey there.

'Silence!' cried the Intelligencer.

'Speak, madman,' said the King.

My voice faltered then, and my resolution, for I saw the enmity upon the Intelligencer's face, yet the King was willing and the lady's eyes twinkled merrily, so I ventured my request: that I be returned to my birthplace, where the insane are considered holy, henceforth never to trouble him further.

'And where is that?' enquired the King.

My dismay at such a question, since I knew not the answer, was instantly relieved by the Intelligencer, who studied the document for which I had so generously paid and announced: 'The villain hails from the hinterland, sire.'

'Why, we travel there ourselves on the morrow,' said the Lady, 'and I require another slave.'

'You would have this lunatic stripling?' said the King.

'Why not, sire? He will serve as well as another, and perchance we may sell him there at a profit, where lunatics are accounted holy.'

'Very well. The simpleton is sentenced to travel with us. Have him delivered to the slave quarters.'

'But sire,' beseeched the Intelligencer, 'the penalty for treason is death.'

Which remark occasioned the King much merriment, as he ventured that to be a slave to his Nellie was the very living death, as well he knew himself, and she chaffed him with great good humour. I knew not how to thank that wondrous gracious lady for this turn in my fortunes and could but admire my escape, for she had surely saved me from horrid death, and would carry me closer to the destination I sought, and I vowed then to be the veriest best slave she had ever possessed. Yet I said nothing, for fear of altering my Fate with a careless word, merely bowing low before being dragged thence, to join others in my position, thither to an enclosed yard still shackled and guarded on all sides, but blessed with air and sunlight, and my spirit lifted mightily at the prospect before me. And anon instruction from an eunuch in my duties, and a fine supper of chicken and oranges, for which in my condition I had little stomach, though ravenous, and soon lost it through sickness. But so to bed, mightily content.

23. Up betimes, and to my lady's chamber, where slavegirls attended her toilet and dressing, among them one or two most comely wenches but I with eyes only for my lady, who had saved me. What a merry scene was there, with her jesting and laughing as she did sport with her slavegirls and they answering her with such impudent sprankles I could only marvel that this were accounted slavery. Her beauty were not so much in her person as

in her character, and she greeted me with a cheerful quip about my resurrection from the dead, and instructed me to carry boxes and fineries to her waggon, which I did under heavy guard but with a light heart. The day was exceeding fine and I would fain give tongue in song for my deliverance and the beauty of the day, yet still accounted it best to play the humble servant, apprehensive yet of the horrors of the King's Intelligencer, who might surely even now drag me from my salvation toward some fearful fate.

Thence, from that damnable scrofulous town, which I did not regret one jot, at nine a-clock, a fine caravan of ox-wagons and horsemen riding and jolting bravely into the scrub and rock of the hinterland and beyond the dusty streets and thronging multitude, wherein methinks I briefly spied the lodging house slut, to whom I waved and called 'God Bwye' with much merriment. How strange is the human heart; for I surmised that I had never felt such contentment as in that slavery, and I rode upon the final waggon, still shackled, but mightily pleased at the freshness of the air and the fading vision of that town and the glittering cruelty of the ocean beyond.

Thence for many leagues beside marsh and mangrove swamp, beneath palm trees and beside thickets of acacia shrubs and elephant grass and banana plantations. Apes cry out and swing above our heads, free apes unknowing of captivity, at which I marvel, never having observed such apes before except in chains, yet I cloaked my wonderment for fear they might suspect I were not that I claimed to be, not in truth a stranger to such sights but a man returning to his natural home.

At night we camped upon an open plain beside a great river where scaly beasts, fearful to the tutored eye, reclined sinister beside the waters, and we slaves were unshackled, being advised that flight were exceeding unwise in these parts, considering the scaly monsters and other wild creatures of the night that would tear us apart should we venture beyond the safety of the fires. With my fellows I raised the lady's marquee and hung it with tapestries and builded for her before it a noble blaze, and by and by I were called to carry food and serve wine at a sumptuous table where she sat and jested with the King, touching him often in token of her daughterly affection. My heart warmed to see a father and daughter so, and I considered the man who would win her hand would count himself exceeding fortunate, for as a daughter treats with her father so too will she with her husband.

The feasting done, she repaired to her boudoir, I being summoned thither to carry hot water for her toilet. Two girls attended her, both naked above the waist and mighty comely both, yet even so my eyes were only for my lady, who bade me stay awhile with further water and thereupon divested herself of her apparel to step as the Almighty formed her into her bath. Her form being mighty fine, slim yet rounded, I wondered at her nakedness and blushed to see her so, and averted my eyes, she the first woman I had observed naked other than paid trollops.

On noticing my discomfiture she laughed merrily and cried: 'Look, girls, how he colours,' whereupon they twittered with mirth, occasioning in me an ever darker flush. 'Why,' said she, 'I do believe the boy to be a virgin,' at which they chaffed me greatly the more. 'Is he not a pretty boy?' she asked. 'Which one of you will learn him the ways of women?', and so they bantered, and I with twisted tongue not knowing how to reply. Betimes she relented, asking solicitously as to my welfare, before bidding me retire to my rest. I believe her to be the sweetest lady I ever met, and so fond of her father the King, who visited her to say goodnight and tarried long in fatherly affection for he had not departed her marquee before I slept. And so to bed, beside the fire, a trifle fearful of the monsters of the night.

24. Up very betimes, to carry water and food for my lady, and to dismantle her marquee and pack her boxes upon the waggons. The King were already up and in my lady's boudoir to wish her good day. What a fine example they serve for other fathers and daughters. He scarce quits her company even for sleep. The odours of the wilds at dawn are magical fresh and clean. Thence by waggon further towards the distant hills, a smudge upon the horizon, now blue at dawn, now green in the morning, now shimmering ochre in the midday heat, now purple and pink in the quick twilight. The waggons jolted and rolled across a marvellous mighty plain alive with darting deer, that the soldiers hunt, and mighty beasts like oxen with curled horns, and once an herd of monstrous elephant, the first sight of which trembled in my breast an admiration of the mighty works of God. The King and my lady rode in the van all day, though we halted for rest at noon, I bringing to her fruits and cheese, and we slaves brought up the rear, coated with warm dust raised by the earlier waggons but joyous to be free in the open air without chains. With great

contentment sundry slaves lifted voice in song, and presently I joined them, not knowing their melody but giving forth a hymn, at which none appeared offended, but the Captain of the Guard rode back to us to chide our impertience and threaten punishment. We fell silent on the instant. He is a surly fellow with arrogant mien and close-cropped hair, and a strict deportment as though his sides were braced with iron, methinks one of those puritans who abhor pleasure and speak incessantly of God yet know him not. A man less like the cavalier King could hardly be imagined, yet it may be so that a man so tolerant and pleasure-loving as the King needs have such stout scowlers about him to protect him.

We camped this night beside no river, but clear on the open plain, whereupon my lady needed no water and I was denied the sight of her at her toilet, a pleasure I had imagined all the day. And so, after a fine supper of venison, to bed, the King visiting my lady again and staying late in family discourse.

25. Up very betimes and abroad again toward the hills, that seem as ever distant, despite two days ride. A day much as before, though the caravan halted awhile as the King joined the soldiers in the hunt for venison. My lady smiled at me and asked after my contentment, and I told her truly that never had I felt more joy than in her service, as her slave. She touched my hand and thanked me graciously. Never have I seen so gentle sweet a soul, and so merry. Venison again for supper, and still camped on the open plain. And so to bed, the King in merry discourse with his daughter.

26. A commotion before dawn, a lion having entered the edge of the camp, despite the fires, and taken a poor slave. I shuddered to think that such might have been my own fate, had my lady's marquee not been raised in the very centre of the camp, beside the King's, and prayed for the poor wretch's soul. The soldiers went in chase of the beast, but failed to find it. In sorrow we moved on toward the hills, which now at last grow mightier with ever hour. Old Ironsides, as we have named the surly Captain of the Guard, is out of spirits and soundly whipped a slave who failed only by an instant to jump to his command. Yet every morning and eve he kneels before his marquee to pray. The contradictions of human nature are a great mystery.

Before nightfall we reached the woods at the foot of the hills and camped beside a pleasant stream, hanging nets above the camp to protect us from the mighty jungle cats that lurk in the trees. My lady demanded water again, so strong for cleanliness is she, having bathed not two nights hence, and I confess I accounted it to be bliss to stand again beside her tub, she utterly without apparel, as she splashed droplets upon her rare proud bubbies and sported and jested with her girls without shame or consciousness. I have learned now to look at her without offence or shame, and she cried: 'See, the boy grows bolder,' whereupon I flushed most furiously and they made merry at my expense, the slavegirls playfully threatening to strip my breeches from me to discover if there be any mysterious difference between myself and themselfs! I phrased a witty reply but by then it was too late to speak, and I cursed my awkwardness, wishing to make them merry, but the moment was gone. O that I were greater in years and experience. The soldiers have shot a monstrous large wild ox with horns a-curl, a fine supper, and not unlike beef. And so to bed, beside the fire, smaller for fear of setting the jungle alight, but warm enough, to dream lasciviously of my lady.

27. Up betimes, to greet the King as he emerged from his morning talk with my lady, and the freshness of dawn here is mighty different from that of the plains, being cooler, with the trickling stream, and the sunlight filtered by leaves, and a pleasant breeze. The going is harder now, uphill and into jungle with only a poor track cut, and we slaves needs push and pull the waggons with many a curse, the guards shouting and threatening their whips, though rarely, praise be, did they occasion to employ them, though twice I witnessed Old Ironsides strike a naked back. At times I trow he disapproves even of the King himself, whom I catch him regarding on occasion with sneering countenance, but such a man would fain find fault with a bishop, and what is there untoward in merriment and feasting and drinking, even if the King do take somewhat much in drink and appears familiar with the ladies? It is only his manner, and surely a more worthy tribute and thanksgiving to God for life than a tight-lipped countenance of disapproval. Also the King brings much pleasure to his daughter, for I hear them jest and laugh together often at night before he retires to his own marquee, and that alone must account him a goodly man in my eyes, for I would that so precious a lady be

filled with pleasure and contentment and bask in the fond affection of her father. I cannot but observe her to feel my heart leap, for never have I set eyes upon a lovelier, neither in form nor nature. There are rabbits in these hills, and we sup on their flesh. And so to bed, though not without unease, for one of the slavegirls, as we lie beside the fire, invited a kiss, and more, and comely though she be, and I not having toucher une femme la for many nights, yet I could think only of my lady, and made my excuse with much awkwardness, whereupon the slavegirl laughed merrily and without any offence. What may it mean? I am troubled.

28. *Lord's Day.* This day we lay long in the jungle, travelling not, it being Sunday and the King and my lady and the lords and ladies and soldiers joined in song and prayer, we slaves being considered heathen, though from our distance we could hear the raised mighty voice of Old Ironsides crying to the Lord and booming in hymn. Methinks he considers the Almighty to be a soldier as himself! Last night two slaves essayed to escape the camp and their bodies have been discovered torn and lifeless, half consumed by cats. I would never wish to flee even were there no cats, for I am not only in body but in spirit truly a slave to my lady, but others being not so fortunate, especially those owned by the soldiery, it is perhaps understandable for some. Though we travelled not, it were not a day of idleness, for the King demanded a banquet, and a performance of magic, at which Old Ironsides appeared most disapproving, and also a wrestling match between sundry slaves, myself included, though I were fortunate to be matched with a boy of lesser strength, which I vanquished, much to my lady's pleasure, for I wore her token. 'See my champion!' she cried, and the King laughed fondly at her pleasure and rewarded me with a gold piece, which I carry in my breeches beside my boules as a remembrance of her as much as for safety. A poor cold supper of ox and rabbit, there having been no hunting this day, but I retired mightily content in my lady's approval and the sound from her marquee of her merriment with the King. Vexed, though, yet again, this time by my lady's second slavegirl, who slided towards me beside the fire at a mighty late a-clock to request a kiss, whereupon I were greatly tempted but wished not to offend my lady, so declining again, at which she also gave a merry laugh and took no offence. I slept little, disturbed by the

125

lateness of the King's departure from my lady's boudoir.

29. Up betimes, to a day of the greatest joy I have known in all my days, for the King and half the soldiers, tiring of the slowness of our passage through the jungle, did go abroad before us on horseback, hunting, and vowing to meet us in two or three days at the crest of the hills, where they would prepare a camp, and my lady, pleading that she needed 'her champion' to protect her in the absence of the King, bade me ride beside her in her waggon, which occasioned much mirth and envy among my fellow slaves, who cried 'Give her one on my behalf' and such loud slogans, though one of what I knew not, accounting it wondrous good fortune to ride beside her. She and her slavegirls were in playful mood and jested and teased at my expense, remarking upon my strength and prowess as a wrestler, and comparing my physique with that of the apes we spied in the trees, and neither girl appeared offended by my earlier rejections of them, rather much amused and impressed by my chastity. At one spot in the jungle they observed coiled in a branch a serpent with which they also compared me with much chaffing and laughter, so that I came to believe their sport to be inspired not by ridicule but by affection, at which I was mightily content and was inspired once or twice to construct a witty reply, which much pleased my lady and them.

At noon the caravan were halted and after a dinner of fresh roast rabbit my lady despatched the girls to rest in their own waggon but bade me stay to protect her. I could scarce believe I were alone with the King's daughter. Within her waggon, draped with tapestries, she annointed herself with perfume and lay upon her couch patting the spot beside her, where I should sit, and questioned me with much seriousness as to my contentment and future ambitions and desires, whereupon I told her truly I wished for nothing than to serve her, all my days.

'To serve me?' she enquired with a merry gleam.

I were covered then with confusion and blushing, understanding too late the lewd import of my words, and made haste with much awkwardness to correct the impression, but she bade me be calm, laying her hand upon mine, with a fragrant odour that dizzied my senses.

'Come, boy, come,' said she gently. 'Do you know nothing of ladies and love?'

Indeed, said I hotly, I had made many a maiden, which untruth

126

I braved as best I could, having lain only with harlots, and she smiled sweetly and said she had thought as much, for I was a fine boy, and much desired by women, at which I blushed again and cursed my awkwardness.

'Why,' said she, 'even my slavegirls speak of your beauty and vigour, and marvel at the trusting eagerness in your eyes, yet believe you show no interest in them.'

'Because I love another,' said I, knowing not whence the words came.

'And is she comely?'

'She is the most rare lady I have ever seen,' I stammered. I were sweating mightily, for her touch and perfume bludgeoned my senses, and to my shame my yard were massive with longing, which I swore she must soon surely notice. The heat of the afternoon clung in sultry dampness to all, even my mind.

'As comely as I?'

I looked at her with thick passion and could find no answer, whereupon she laughed merrily and grasped my hand, coiling her fingers between mine own and saying: 'Why, boy, you are a goose, for I know whom you love. It is I, is it not?'

I could not reply, so dry was my throat with urgency, and also fear, for she were my mistress, and the King's daughter, and this were a dangerous game.

'You say you would serve me?' asked she.

I nodded dumbly, at which she laughed again. 'And so you shall, you silly boy.'

I cannot believe it yet, for there, upon her couch, within the minute, I did fazer ce que j'ai only dreamed avec her, my lovely lady, I her slave and bondsman for ever, avec grand tendresse et ecstasy, did I bastinado elle avec true amour, with a passion to reduce such sorry trollops as I had known before to mere painted dolls. I swore that never again should I touse les filles de joie, for the sorry joy they offer is as nothing to the honest passion of a woman for whom one would surrender the world, and I could barely credit the good fortune that had led me to this precious flower, as yet until my entry surely still undefiled and undeflowered, for at the first there were a moment of awkward adjustment which she hid and adjusted my yard in an instant, though no virgin blood, of which I had heard spoken. That I should lie first with the daughter of a King, and such an untouched daughter as surely truly loved me also, I could not believe, for when I told her of my love, again and again, and enquired of her whether she loved me also with equal passion she replied with much merriment, 'Indeed so, you silly boy, otherwise how should we be thus?' which gave me great content. Thence, after much sighing, to the front of the waggon and thither again through the jungle as the caravan struggled up the hill, with much mirth from the slavegirls, who seemed much excited with childish whispers.

And so to bed, though not to sleep, nay never, for the night were spent in love, for my lady bade me quit the fire and join her in her couch, and I vowed heaven to be a marquee set on a hillside in a tropical jungle, and told her so, whereupon she murdered my conversation with kisses and taught me joys I had never imagined should exist.

30. Up most very betimes, for my lady is rightly desirous of keeping our match privy unto only ourselves, and I understand full well that the time is not yet when we may tell the King, for fathers require to be gently broken to such matters. I worked dazed, on occasion insisting to myself that this were surely a dream, yet I knew from the blessed perfume still hanging upon my fingers that barely hours since I were lying with passion within my lady's marquee and within my lady. So befuddled were my thoughts and so confused my labours that I feared the guards might strike me with their whips, though curiously none even belaboured me with words, but several muttered unto each other and gave way to grunts and guffawing. I know not where I am nor what to do, only that I must return to my lady and lie with her again and so I did, at noon again, and in the evening, camped once more beside a stream, I attended her alone at her toilet, her slavegirls banished, pouring warm water over my lady's body and kissing her shoulders and lips and touching her bubbies, so fine and rare proud, until we were united in the tub, straining against the timbers with a passion I would never have believed to exist.

'I love you, I love you,' said I, many times, 'and I would marry you, my beloved, oh my love.'

'Silly boy!' said she with much merriment, and thus we continued in blissful jest and communion until just before dawn, when I crept once more from her marquee, to lie beside the fire as if there all night, vowing to tell the King before long of our troth and demanding my freedom and the hand of his daughter.

31. Up, ragged with weariness but suffused throughout with the warmth of love and the joy of a fresh new day and the prospect of my beloved, graceful and fragrant to ride before me all the day, nay, all my life should I win my dream. She bade me ride in the slave waggon at the rear, since today we should reach the crest of the hill and would meet with the King again, judging it unseemly to be seen with her male slave in close congress, which I understood right readily. I were greeted by my fellow slaves with much merriment and envious curiosity, they pressing for news of her and enquiring what she were like, whereupon I flushed scarlet, occasioning much mirth. 'So, you have indeed tupped the King's whore,' cried one, 'not the first to do so, nor certainly the last.'

King's whore? I did not credit my ears and turned to him, enjoining him to repeat himself.

'Is it any the different with the whore of a King?' asked he.

'Whore?' cried I. 'You speak of the King's daughter,' and struck him sundry savage blows, beating him to the floor of the waggon in a frenzy of fists and feet, while the others hooted with merriment, crying, 'Daughter, daughter, he thinks she is the King's daughter.'

I can scarce bear to tell the rest, but briefly. They restrained me, dragging me from my informant, and apprised me that my love, my beloved, that filthy bitch and strumpet, were not the King's daughter but his hired trollop, his courtesan, the mistress discovered selling oranges in the market place, whereupon I refused to believe them, striking out in all directions with the utmost ferocity until they brought to me one of her slavegirls, which confirmed it, touching my arm with pity and shaking her head. 'She has done it oft before,' said she gently, 'and will do so again, and always with virgin youths such as you, but none yet that knew her for what she truly is. For in her heart she despises the weakness of men, and speaks of a time to come when women shall rule the world and need men no more, not even for the procreation of children.'

'How can this be?' I wept. 'Such things are impossible. This is madness.' Yet I knew it finally to be true when we reached at last the crest of the hill and the King greeted her with a kiss and a fondling of buttock and breast that not even I could mistake for fatherly affection.

Torment, agony, rage, jealousy, fear – all coursed through me in instants, again and again in turn, and my fellows mocked and jested, crying, 'Daughter, daughter,' till I would hide my face and weep, for I had loved her, the first woman I had truly loved.

In the still, dark night I left the camp, while all around me slept, the King with her in her marquee, ah how blind I had been, and I stole a horse in silence and led it quietly away and then rode and rode across the plateau for hour upon hour, uncaring of any, even of the wild beasts, and wishing one of them to attack and devour me, and my face sore wet with tears.

(2)

I rode all night through the bush and across the plateau, my chains chinking with every hoofbeat, and crossed the border just after dawn. I dismounted with relief, stiff with riding but almost delirious at escaping the horrors and betrayals of the previous days. The guards would only now be discovering I had got away and if they followed me I had a lead of at least several hours and the border offered some protection. Even in these savage, lawless parts they would hesitate before raiding the domain of a local chieftain.

They would have beheaded me if I hadn't stolen the horse and escaped. The terror of those days still chilled my neck with nightmares of the axe. The bloody fools. They had thought I was a spy. The brutal paranoia of these coastal people was beyond belief. They were like vicious adolescents whose Independence had suddenly made them crazy. What did they have that anyone would want to spy on? Their ramshackle capital city resembled a seventeenth-century slum: a derelict harbour, a few shacks beside the sea, a telephone system that didn't work, a Ministry of Information which was so corrupt and inefficient it was the only place in the gossip-raddled place where you couldn't discover any information at all.

'Why are you wanting these informations about these persons?' the Ministry official had asked suspiciously when finally I managed to corner him after days of seeking an audience and asked him if he had a file on the stranger.

'I'm curious about him,' I said. 'My name is exactly the same as his. I would like to find out what sort of man he was.'

'He was not important.'

130

'Every man is important in his own way.'

'Aha!' said the official with cunning. 'You say these man was secretly important? You say perhaps he was a spy?'

'I said nothing of the sort. I only meant that he was probably important to someone – a wife, perhaps, or children, or his mother.'

'So these was an entire spy ring?'

'Look, forget it. I'll try the tax department. They must have some records.'

'These spy is making secret records also? These must be investigated. You also. Guard!'

'What the hell is going on?'

'You are arrest for suspicion of spying.'

'Don't be so bloody ridiculous.'

'Every evidence you make will now be taken down.'

'I don't believe this. I demand to see my ambassador.'

He had grinned crookedly. 'No ambassador here.'

'The consul, then.'

'No consul.'

'A lawyer. It's my right.'

He had stared at me coldly. 'You have no rights here, mister. We are the rulers now. The world is changed. No peoples here have rights, just only the President may God help him.'

I didn't doubt it. Half the population appeared to be in jail with no hope of ever coming to trial. I joined them. The place stank of urine and faeces and the prisoners either swore or shrieked through the bars as I was marched past them to my cell. The prison echoed all day and night with nightmarish howls and cries that made it sound like a lunatic asylum of 300 years ago, and it would take a Pepys properly to describe the brutal corruption of the place. I lay there for days, eating as little of the foul food as possible and becoming increasingly apprehensive that they might simply forget me and leave me to rot for the rest of my days. Life is still cheap in countries like this. I had not felt so helpless and bewildered since my teens, when the world outside had seemed equally irrational and ruled by vicious autocrats and there had seemed to be no alternative but to accept the tyranny of illogical rules you did not understand.

Eventually the interrogators arrived, the man to provide the alarming bullying muscle, the woman soft and sympathetic, the classic interrogation team of sweet and sour to numb my resistance. His questions were mindless and threatening. What was my grandmother's maiden name? Why was I not married? Where had I had the plastic surgery that had so changed my looks? He refused to believe that I was not the same man as the one he had on his files, the stranger, and twice he hit me.

'There is no need for that,' she said, and my eyes stung with gratitude even though I knew she was merely playing a role to soften me up.

'He needs to be beaten,' the bruiser growled. 'We should use the electricity.'

'There is no need for violence,' she had said.

'The man is a liar, and a spy. He will be tortured and then beheaded.'

'We do not know he is guilty.'

'Everyone is guilty. If he is not guilty he would not have been arrested.'

'The President will decide.'

'And then he will be beheaded.'

Once the man came with two others who beat the back of my legs with canes, and once she came on her own. She sat beside me on the hard little bed and took my hand. I nearly wept. After a while in prison even the smallest kindness can unman you.

'He is not a bad person,' she said softly. 'He too is frightened. We are all frightened here now. It is not like the old days. Today he is chief interrogator, but tomorrow he too might be in prison or shot. When he beats you it is only from fear that if he does not he too will be beaten.'

'Then there's no hope for me.' I confess my voice broke. I felt so helpless. The world was so unfair.

She squeezed my hand. 'There is always hope,' she said.

'But what can I do? I just don't know what to do.'

'You must tell me the truth. Everything.'

'I'm innocent, I swear it. Why should I want to spy?'

'I believe you, but we have to prove it. Here you are guilty until you prove your innocence.'

Like a Christian on Judgment Day, condemned already by an original sin committed before he was born.

'How can anyone prove his innocence?'

'You must tell me everything. I am your friend.' She locked her fingers in mine, and looked at me sorrowfully. 'Your name, for instance. It is not your real name, is it? And your passport. That is false?'

What was I to do? She seemed my only hope, the only possible ally in this hell of lunacy and terror. No one else even knew I was there. If she abandoned me I would be lost. I had not felt so impotent and dominated by any woman since my first love affair, when I worshipped a girl with that desperately serious tenderness and idealistic adolescent agony that leaves you blinded. She had jilted me quite casually, without kindness, and I had never again allowed myself to put any woman on a pedestal, or allowed myself again to be vulnerable in love. It had hurt too much, and I had come to suspect that women were stronger than men, not cleverer but more cunning, ruthless and predatory. Perhaps that too had weakened my marriage. Perhaps it would all have been different had I been less wary and more trusting with my wife and readier to take the risk of being wounded. Perhaps devotion and fidelity are possible without slavishness, and that a woman needs occasionally to be worshipped.

So I told her everything: about the stranger's grave, his name and birth certificate, the passport, my 'death', my compulsion to discover his roots. It all sounded most unlikely. Why is it that the truth so often sounds false? Now and then I hesitated, but she squeezed my fingers and murmured soft encouragement and I kept nothing back. She held my Fate in that little hand of hers. I was completely at her mercy. If she had ordered me to kiss her feet I would have done it. There was no alternative.

When I had finished she looked deep into my eyes, as if searching for my soul, and then nodded. 'You are telling the truth,' she said. 'I can tell.'

She betrayed me, of course. She jilted me just as brutally as my first love had done. I was no less blind or naïve than I had been then. When I came to court she stared at me contemptuously and played the tape she had recorded during my confession in the cell. It had been crudely edited but no one seemed to care. This was not a court of justice: it was a court of self-justification. The arrogant way she conducted herself made it plain that she, not the male bruiser, was the Chief Interrogator, and that she despised me for being white, being a man, being vulnerable and a loser. She would happily have cut my balls off and hung them above her bed.

The President, a stern, puritanical man with an expression of iron, nodded coldly as the story came out and each of my confessions added another confirmation of my guilt. It seemed that I was being tried for every crime that had ever been committed against his people. If I were the man *they* said I was, then I was guilty of treason. If I were the man *I* said I was, then I was guilty of spying. The penalty for both was death.

'The law demands that the prisoner is beheaded,' she said.

I stood to hear the verdict. It was lunatic. They found me guilty of treason *and* of spying. They seemed to believe I could be two men at once: both myself and the stranger. I was numb with fear and disbelief. It seemed I would have to die twice. What a desperate irony that my bid for freedom had led to slavery and imprisonment, that my born-again new life should now have led to an early savage death. There was a long argument in the court as to whether I should be executed for treason first or for spying. In my terror I heard little of it. I was surrounded by bestial madmen, but at least their bureaucratic lunacy gave me a brief breathing space. The President eventually suspended the two death sentences for a month while it was decided whether I should be beheaded first for treason or for spying, and he ordered me to be sent in the meantime to a labour camp inland. Shackled in chains, I jolted for several days by guarded ox-cart into the hinterland, but the night before we were due to reach the slave camp high in the hills the guards got drunk and I stole one of their horses and rode through the night for the border, towards the Equator, where only footpaths lead through the bush, flattened by centuries of native feet. I had no idea what sort of people lived in the unknown country beyond, but they could be no more frightening than those I fled. I was weak and defenceless and still in chains, alone and unarmed, surrounded by wild animals and bestial humans, but I felt both excited and afraid, like an apprehensive but optimistic youth standing on the challenging frontier of manhood.

6

(1)

The burning equatorial heat of day that shrivels men and crops and cattle all and bakes the very earth itself to dust did shimmer with mirages on the land when finally at noon I came to rest and rode alone into the meanest place, a village made of huts of wood and mud, round-shouldered huts with roofs of straw and twine, set in the roasted wilds of Barbary as though it were a tiny vessel tossed upon a lonely island in the sea a mighty distance from the sight or sound of any land or human habitation. Round about were fields of sorry crops, poor tokens of a desperate confidence in Nature and the kindliness of God, and thrown around the whole a poor stockade of feeble sticks to keep the beasts at bay, a barrier so humble that one cat alone would strike it down with giant paw. Two villagers awaited at the gate, a pair of men as thin as skeletons aroused no doubt to my arrival by the clouds of dust excited by my mount, whose pounding hooves across that desert plain had thus been advertising for an hour from distance great our imminent approach.

They spake a tongue I could not comprehend, but using gestures of a general kind they came to understand I needed rest and food and succour for my panting mount that had so stoutly carried me since dawn across that sparse and unforgiving land beneath the broiling sun whose golden eye had fixed us with so cruel and hot a glare that I would drink a yard of ale or more should I be given opportunity.

Presently they brought me to their chief, a fellow of such monstrous size and weight I reckoned he must surely have the post on grounds of girth alone, for only he, of all the male villagers at hand, was greater than some sickly starving child. Full round of face, and bearded, too, was he, and richly dressed in goodly flowing robes, and on his head a chieftain's hat of state, and

135

gathered round about within his hut six ladies whom I took to be his wives, of sundry ages from the very old (a crone of surely thirty summers gone) down to a pretty little wench who must not long have left her mother's tender care. And by their side some children, only three, a younger boy and elder sisters two, the younger with such smiling eyes and grace, yet shy withal and modest to a fault that when I gazed at her she looked away and blushed and hid her smile with a hand.

The Chief had been abroad and seen the world, or such of it as seemed the world to him, as maggots feeding on a lump of flesh will think it all they ever need to know, accounting it the very universe, and do not dream that close beyond their feast lies other flesh and other maggots too, and so to my good fortune he had learned to speak, albeit haltingly and slow, in accents barbarous and guttural, sufficient of my tongue to let us talk, for him to question me about my quest and I to answer him and ask for help.

'What urgent business brings you here?' quoth he, 'a boy of not yet sixteen summers gone, alone upon the unforgiving plain, with only steed for company, unarmed despite the threats and dangers of the wild?'

'I am a man,' said I.

'Yet beardless.'

'Hair alone makes not a man,' said I with heat. 'Indeed, some say that hairlessness portends a greater quantity of manliness, for was not even Caesar roundly bald, yet ladies and effeminates alike revel in longer tresses, locks and curls?'

He laughed with pleasure at my stormy speech, and tugged with humour at his beard as though to chide me jestingly for hinting that I reckoned my own manliness to be greater than his for being beardless.

'Hold, hold!' said he. 'Despite your tender years I see you have a temper that would match the fires of Hell if once allowed to rage unchecked. Come, let us cool it with a draught or two of ale, and food, and you may tell your history and hopes and whence you came, and where you go upon your careless quest.'

His younger daughter, tremulous but trim, with hesitating eyes and wary step, he urged to go and bring to me a gourd of native ale, a vicious bitter brew quite foul enough to force a rolling drunk to mend his ways and cry aloud for milk, but since they watched me close, the girl as well, I swallowed it without a pause for breath to prove to them my questioned manliness. Despite my mighty

136

thirst the bile rose in belly, breast and throat until my eyes pricked with disgust. The Chief called out for more, congratulating me upon my thirst. His daughter filled my gourd with ale again and gallantly I thanked her for her care.

'She understands you not,' her father said, 'your tongue to her is gibberish, and much to marvel at, as you and we are deaf to hearken to the chattering of apes.'

She brought me food as well, a dish of maize, poor pounded porridge but by now I guessed their food was of the meanest basic sort and meat a luxury for special days. Her father, as we ate, was much amused to hear me tell of why I passed their way. 'God's wounds!' he cried, 'Your task would daunt a man twice your age and strength and knowledge of the world.'

'Again you condescend,' said I with heat, 'and treat me like some snivelling brat whose lips have barely finished sucking at the teat. Would infant ride alone and weaponless all day across the unrelenting land? My years are few, I grant, but Time will soon resolve that small deficiency until in twenty years or less I too shall be as aged as yourself, and counted wise.'

'Stay, stay,' he cried, 'your anger is too quick that rises at the slightest small remark, rearing and spitting as the deadly snake suddenly aroused by careless step of him who had no wish to cause a hurt but merely did so by an accident.'

'Well!'

'Now you sulk.'

'Not so!'

'You do.'

'Not I.'

'No more contest the matter. You are tired. Rest here this night, and be assured your mount will faithfully be tended in our care, and on the morrow I shall send abroad spies and messengers on your behalf to ascertain the answer to your quest and find the information that you seek.'

Head buzzing from the unaccustomed ale, with step unsteady and uncertain gait, I followed where his daughter shyly led to show me to a hut they had prepared. I could compare her to a summer's day, and even so she would not understand. Sleep claimed me then and took me by the hand.

Ah, sleep, that lulls the soul and easeth pain, smoothing care and softening distress, sweetest oblivion like a mother's gentle fingers cool and soft against the brow, yet in that sleep the mind still resteth not, for dreams and images are conjured up, fevered fantasies absurd and true as though both Hell and Heaven ope'd their gates to let demented demons dance with saints and Reason flirt with gross insanity. Thus did I sleep and dream and toss and turn, as though remembering a life not lived, forgetting much and then inventing more, and seeing in my sleep a stranger's face enticing me to some strange distant shore.

The younger daughter woke me with the dawn, with bowl of maize and nervous modesty, flinching like the apprehensive colt unbroken yet to bridle, bit and rein. I took her task to be her father's way of gently schooling her to treat with men, and yet her nervousness was such that I too found myself exceeding shy alone with her, and though I would have bantered with her then could only wish a gruff good day, at which she started like a deer and then answered hurriedly in alien tongue. Her voice was as the music of the lute, her eyes were as lagoons, her lips as fruit, her hair as beauteous as filigree. To look on her alone were poesy.

That day the Chief sent messengers abroad, to north and south, to east and west, and all charged with commands to ascertain the place whence came the stranger, though they did believe that I were he myself and no imposter. 'How strange you do not know the place yourself,' the Chief declared.

'I left when only young,' said I, 'and cannot now remember whence I came.'

'Sold into slavery?'

'Aye, so.'

'And yet this be no massive tragedy. All men at times can be accounted slaves, for bondage is the common human lot, shackled as we be by circumstance, by parents, brothers, sisters, husbands, wives, by tasks and duties, fellow men and God, and you will come to learn in later years the strongest slavery of all is to thyself, for though men cry for freedom yet they forge great manacles and chains within their minds by which they choose their own imprisonments.'

'Not I.'

He laughed rumbustiously, a man sure in himself and certain of his fate, as strong and steady firm as fatherhood. 'Already you have made yourself a slave,' said he, 'for what but bondage is this quest of yours, already an obsession that binds you close in sure captivity?'

'I freely chose.'

'And so do all.'

'I need to know whence I came and how and why before I can embark with true content upon the journey of my life. 'Tis true, the secret of philosophy is this: a man's first duty is to know himself.'

'And will this knowledge alter what you are? Are you so frail that just a name and place may shape your soul and change your destiny?'

'Fie, sir,' said I with heat, 'now yet again you toy with me as though I were a child, and yet already, if I had a mind, I could be father to a dozen sons.'

'To father sons is no great victory, and simply done by weaklings, cowards, fools. To prove a worthy father, there's the test.'

I hated him and loved him all at once, confused by conflicts in my boyish breast, safe in his discipline and dignity yet also yearning to be proud and free.

For many days I tarried in that place, awaiting messengers to bring me news, urgent to make my way into the world yet also quite content to rest a while before the great adventure of my life. The Chief devised for me a cunning plan whereby I earned my victuals and keep by teaching English to his family, and learning them to ride, the daughters too trotting most sedately with shrill shrieks of girlish glee and fear and modesty. His younger daughter, fragile though she were, and still as shy as any butterfly, soon rode my mount as well as even I, with delicate but firm control and grace. Among the words I taught her there were some included merely for sheer devilment to hear her speak them with her silver tongue and gaze into her timid eyes the while: 'I love thee' and 'beloved' and 'my heart' and 'kiss me now, my sweet, or I would die', and there were music in her gentle voice and in the evening we would sometimes walk alone together o'er the silent plain, fingers entwined and hearts too full to speak, to sit beneath a gnarled and twisted tree or merely listen to the peace of God.

We did no more, for she were young and pure, but never have I loved a woman more.

He killed her mother on the fifteenth day. The Chief, the man that I had so revered, that god of strength and sturdy fatherhood, of power and philosophy, a rock to build upon or shelter close beneath, crumbled to dust before my very eyes, raving with anger, jealousy, and pride, damning his wife before the gathered tribe, accusing her of lying with another, crying of betrayal, treason, guilt. She pled her innocence on bended knees, begging for mercy and for God to show the truth of all she said, and spare her life. But he, ravaged with torment and suspicion, pronounced her guilt and sentenced her to death. To punish her the more he shrugged away the many years of marriage they had shared and sneered that for his part it were not love nor even lust that made him lie with her but merely cold political advantage and calculating hope of sturdy sons that she had failed so grievously to bear. The woman wept and begged and cried aloud in piteous tones to melt a monster's heart. Her child too, his daughter, my beloved, sobbed with such a grief that would have soothed the anger of Beelzebub himself, but he were adamant and mad with rage, a man beyond the reach of sanity.

I stood before him, trembling fearfully, yet, God wot how, my voice were strong and clear. 'I shall not countenance it, sir,' said I.

'What, thou?' said he with furious contempt. 'Thou impudent pup, be gone before I charge that thou shouldst also join her on the block.'

I stood my ground. 'I would remind thee, sir, of conversations that we shared anon, of observations thou accounted wise.'

'Silence!' he cried.

Yet I were brave with fear. 'Thou said all men can be accounted slaves and yet the greatest slavery of all is to thine own false self, since every man builds for himself his own imprisonment.'

'Guards!'

'Thine own bondage is false jealousy.'

'Seize him!'

'And see thy daughter's trembling fear. Dost thou forget thine earlier homily? *To prove a worthy father, there's the test.*"'

His guards restrained me, bracketing my limbs, and he

himself, in wounded pride and rage, struck sev'ral heavy blows upon my face, crying: 'Varlet! Thou shalt watch her pain,' and calling for the executioner, who, ignoring all her cries of pain and fear, instructed other guards to drag her close and hold her down, her head upon the block, and struck it off with one great savage blow, and held aloft her fearful staring head as my beloved fainted to the ground.

The Chief regarded me with cold contempt. 'And now,' said he, 'thou wouldst to follow her?'

Fear blossomed in my belly, and my limbs grew weak with horror at the awful sight. No courage now could save her from her fate, and impudence would now be foolishness.

'Nay, sire,' said I, in deepest cowardice.

'Her death were justice then?'

'Aye, sir, it were.'

'And thou repentest thy impertinence?'

'With all my heart,' said I, in trembling fear.

He laughed, and in that mocking ambuscade I first became a man, in honour bound to wreak revenge before that night were out. That night he served a banquet: chicken, figs, and fruits I never ate before, and ale, and sat me by his side and slapped my back and called me fellow, boy and blatherskite. More shabby wisdom came my way, and lies, and tawdry promises I once believed.

I stabbed him late that night, as he lay drunk, and cut his throat in worthy recompense, and took my mount and rode into the night, bidding farewell to none, not even she.

Cry 'murder' if you must, but this I swear: I killed him not for her nor yet for me, but only to release him from the care of knowing now his own hypocrisy. I loved him as a father, could not bear the knowledge of our shared indignity. All men must kill their fathers, that is clear, or else they never reach maturity.

(2)

It was dusk when I reached the native village tucked into the swiftly spreading shadow of a craggy mountain. Above me on the mountainside granite rocks, balanced in fantastic shapes, had looked for centuries as though they must surely topple over. They had been precariously there before Man and would be there long after. The chains had chafed raw patches on my wrists and the metal, chill with evening, stung my flesh, making me whimper. The small plots of semi-cultivated land around the squat thatched huts were sparse with shrivelled crops and weeds and a few scrawny chickens pecked optimistically in the dust among the refuse that littered the hard dry earth: empty cigarette packets, Coca-Cola bottles, rusting cans. From the thatch of the largest mud and wattle hut there protruded a TV aerial. Here, at least, the sixteenth century has discovered the twentieth.

A wizened old woman emerged from the hut, stared at me, and crossed herself hurriedly. That annoyed me, though I couldn't really blame her. My hair was matted with sweat and dust from the long ride, my face streaked with dirt, my shirt stained and stinking, and my chains rattled as I dismounted, stiff and throbbing in every muscle. I craved a long hot bath and there was not even a stream in sight. Why was everything against me? Swiftly a small, silent crowd of onlookers surrounded the old woman to witness my arrival. They were either very old or very young, and the children had swollen bellies. An entire generation seemed to be missing. They gazed at me with apathy.

'Good evening,' I said, and felt embarrassed by my ludicrous formality. My only excuse was that my emotions were in turmoil and my feelings unstable, and I had always hated being stared at. Why was everyone staring at me? Leave me alone. 'Greetings,' I said.

They nudged each other and jabbered. The crone shook her head. I felt unaccountably irritable. Why did nobody understand me?

'I need shelter for the night,' I said peevishly.

They gaped at me.

'Food,' I said, jabbing at my mouth and chewing. 'Drink,' I said, miming a gulp.

'Eh, eh!' cried the old woman, and disappeared into the hut, emerging a moment later with an ancient man wearing a pair of torn trousers, a tattered vest and a sun helmet which he wore as though it were a symbol of office.

'Ah!' murmured the crowd, almost as one. I guessed he must be the headman. It seemed politic to bow, though I felt ridiculous as I did so.

'Ahhh!' breathed the crowd.

'I need your help,' I said with what I hoped was a winning smile.

He pointed at my chains and frowned. I had expected them to

be mentioned sooner or later, and lies seemed safer than the truth. The truth had already nearly cost me my life. Why did no one ever believe me? Why was everyone against me?

'Bandits,' I said, and was embarrassed again by the shrillness of my voice. I pointed the way I had come. 'I was attacked by bad men who robbed me and chained me, but I escaped when they were drunk.'

He stared at me for a while, and then nodded. 'You welcome,' he said in passable English, and immediately I felt exhausted with relief at finding even such brief sorry sanctuary. He came forward and shook my clanking hand.

'Eh, eh, eh!' cried the old woman.

'Ahhh!' nodded the crowd.

'You stay one night?' He sounded like an hotel clerk.

'Please. If it's not too much trouble.' I disliked myself for sounding so ingratiating.

'No trouble. You tired.'

'I'm exhausted.' My voice was an irritating whine.

'Come. We give food, drink, you sleep.'

I held out my wrists. The chains jangled, the flesh chafed, and I winced. 'Can you get me out of these?' I said.

He considered them, frowning, and spoke to a small boy who ran off and returned with a small rusty chisel and a block of wood, with which the headman tried to batter at one of the chain links for ten minutes before giving up and shrugging. He had scratched the chain but barely dented it.

He pointed up the hill. 'Tomorrow you go up army camp,' he said. 'They do.'

For all his kindness I felt a surge of frustration. 'Surely you've got some bolt-cutters or something?' I snapped. 'Dear God, you've even got Coke and TV. Surely you must have some decent tools.'

He looked at me patiently. 'We poor people,' he said, and I was ashamed of my arrogant bad temper in the face of their simple decency.

'I'm sorry,' I said. 'Forgive me. I should not have spoken like that.'

He shrugged. 'You tired,' he said.

'It's just that I'll go crazy if I have to sleep with these on. How far is the army camp? Perhaps I could go up there tonight.'

He shook his head. 'Not far,' he said. 'One ten-minute on

143

horse. But . . . . '

'In that case I'll ride up there now,' I said.

He smiled for the first time, pityingly. 'I not advise.' He glanced at the sky. Already the fierce red tropical twilight was turning purple. 'One five-minute it dark,' he said. 'After dark they shoot you.'

I stared up the mountainside. I could see nothing: no tents, no huts, not even a radio mast. 'Surely not,' I said doubtfully.

'They fraid new revolution,' said the headman. 'All lock up at night, then shoot, no question.'

I hesitated. Was he having me on? The pain was excruciating, and these primitive people were probably just as apprehensive of spirits on the mountainside as of jittery army sentries, but I hadn't escaped beheading to be shot in the bush in the dark like a hyena. It was so bloody unfair.

A pretty teenage girl I had not noticed stepped forward from the back of the crowd.

'My grandfather is right,' she said in perfect English. 'You would be most unwise to approach the camp so late. The army is extremely nervous at the moment. There have been reports of counter-revolutionary guerrillas in the area, and after dark the soldiers shoot at anything that moves.'

Surprise left me tongue-tied. 'Your English is very good,' I stammered eventually, and hated my gaucheness and patronising tone.

She looked at me with amusement. 'You are much too kind, sir,' she said mockingly. 'But then I have been very fortunate. I was lucky enough to win a scholarship to the university and I have spent the past two years reading English Literature.'

'Forgive me,' I said again.

'Of course. And now you need food, drink and rest. My grandfather will organise that.'

'And my . . . ?'

She smiled. The flash of her teeth was like the moon coming out from behind a cloud. 'And I shall look after your horse,' she said. She seemed no more than sixteen or seventeen, but she might have been talking to a difficult child.

The night was surprisingly cold after the heat of the day and inside the headman's hut I shivered and started trembling uncontrollably, but I was shaken less by the cold than by fear and relief at escaping the horrors of captivity and a barbaric death sentence, and by apprehension that I was still not safe. What if my captors had followed me, tracking me with legendary skills across the dry bush? In two or three hours they might be here, or soon after dawn, and a poor mud wall would hardly protect me. Where were all the village's vigorous young men who might defend me with clubs and spears, perhaps a rifle or two? The old men and women and children who were left would probably stand and stare as they dragged me away. I was racked by helpless, lonely self-pity and could not control the shaking of my limbs as I slumped on the floor in a corner of the hut. Why me? What had I done to be hunted and persecuted? Why was the whole world against me? Why did everyone blame me for everything? Tears brimmed. Why was the world so bloody awful and unfair?

'Sssh!' she said. The girl. She was kneeling beside me and offering me a tin mug. 'Here. Drink this. It will calm your trembling.'

I sipped apprehensively. The stuff was foul – a sour brew of potent native ale that tasted of metal. I gagged.

'Drink it!' she snapped. 'Don't be such a baby. It will do you good.'

'I can't.'

'Of course you can.'

'I can't.'

'You can.'

'I can't. It's *disgusting*.'

Her eyes flashed. 'How dare you? My grandfather brewed it himself. Drink it!'

I closed my eyes, pretended my nose and taste-buds were out of order, and swigged the whole mugful. The bile erupted in my stomach and I fought to keep it down, and belched.

She grinned. 'That's more like it,' she said. 'And now I shall fetch you some more, and when you have had that you will be better.'

'No more,' I said, still shaking. 'Thank you, but I . . . . '

'Stop whining,' she said. 'I know what I'm doing. You're deeply shocked. You need it.'

Meekly I drank another mugful of the revolting stuff, and my stomach rebelled again but not so violently, and the trembling

145

diminished and eventually stopped.

'See?' she said.

I nodded. 'Thank you,' I muttered

She stood and looked down at me. Perhaps it was the effect of the beer, or relief after shock, or simply her kindness, but her certainty and strength seemed to offer some kind of protection although she was little more than a child. I too had once been sure and self-confident.

'The trouble with you Europeans is that you always think you know best,' she said.

'I'm sorry.'

'And would you please stop apologising?'

'I'm sorry.'

She looked at me with a wry affection that was tinged with contempt. 'You're still afraid, aren't you?' she said. 'I can tell by your eyes. You think those bandits are going to capture you again, and torture you, perhaps kill you. Forget it. Stop cringing. You're completely safe here.'

I nodded doubtfully.

'My grandfather is a powerful witch-doctor,' she said.

I looked away.

'He will put a spell around the village for tonight.'

I bit the inside of my cheek.

'No strangers will be able to enter the village. They will face an impenetrable barrier of fear that will force them to pass by.'

I coughed.

'That's another problem you Europeans are going to have to solve pretty quickly,' she said softly. 'You don't believe in anything any more. The tragedy of you Europeans is that you've lost your spirituality. You've shackled yourselves with materialism. You think my grandfather is just a primitive, superstitious senile old fool.'

'No, of course not, it's . . . .'

'He's the wisest man I've ever met,' she said harshly, 'and his magic works. Just because I've read a bit of Shakespeare and Dickens and Eliot it doesn't mean I've abandoned all faith. You have my word. You are completely safe tonight.'

'I'm . . . .'

'No you're not – you're not sorry at all,' she said, and was gone.

146

The third mug of beer was much more acceptable, the fourth almost palatable. The old woman brought me a bowl of cold maize porridge and stringy chicken that despite the chafing of the chains I gulped with as much pleasure as if I had been dining at Maxim's and someone else was picking up the bill. I began to feel light-headed and much more cheerful, and nearly laughed aloud when they decided it was time to watch the TV. The headman despatched the old woman outside to start a small electricity generator. Beyond the mud wall there were the sounds of cranking, grinding, clattering, high-pitched curses. I started giggling and had to pretend I was coughing as the old woman swore at the generator and struck it hard. It groaned and then settled to an unstable humming. A single naked lightbulb began to glow dimly, a one-bar electric fire started ticking as heat expanded the metal and the TV set flickered black and white with images from a different century. A sleek American diplomat was looking suitably concerned about famine in the Third World. A black politician was boasting about a new international airport. During the commercial break a nubile European woman with fingernails like claws gushed about the sheer impossibility of life without a computerised dishwasher. A dozen of the headman's family sat cross-legged on the pounded earth in front of the TV set and nodded wisely. I wanted to giggle again.

The teenage girl squatted gawkily beside me, her knees drawn up to her chin, her arms locked around her shins. In the gloom she looked more vulnerable, but alarmingly pretty. She made me feel absurdly shy and my throat seemed blocked and dry, and yet I knew that any feeling for her was not lust but tenderness. I must be growing old. Was this already my second childhood?

I cleared the tightness in my throat and forced myself to speak. 'How much of this rubbish do they understand?' I said thickly.

'Nearly all of it. They all speak English of a sort, but they're mostly too shy to use it with strangers. In villages like this, Independence hasn't changed their lives much. Materially they probably have even less now than when the colonialists were here. The only difference now is that they're exploited by a new ruling class that's black rather than white. Perhaps they have a little more pride: at least they're being exploited now by their own people. But their self-confidence is no greater. Twenty years ago they were treated like dirt by the whites, now they're treated like dirt by the army and the smooth civil servants who drop in once a year to shake their hands and then wipe them afterwards on their jackets.'

'You're a Marxist,' I said nervously.

She looked at me with pity. 'Of course,' she said. 'Maybe I wouldn't be if I were European, but this is my family. I love them very much. Why else would I spend some of my vacations here? Don't you love your family? You'd be Marxist too if that was your mother sitting there and your grandfather, or your own children.'

I looked at them. I thought of my mother sitting on hard earth in a mud hut. Yes, I would have carried a gun and murdered and burned to rescue her from that. My eyes pricked with ridiculously nostalgic tears. I too had once been not just rebellious but also idealistic. This girl was able to make me a boy again.

'They've been betrayed,' she said. 'The government has given each village a TV set and a generator, and the army hands out a few boxes of cigarettes and crates of Coke and Playboy magazines, but now they're even more dependent on their masters than they were under the colonialists. The crops keep failing, the children are hungry and look at the junk lying around the village. It's become a human rubbish dump. And all the promises that were made will never come true, not unless my generation does something about it. But we will. Don't worry – we will.'

'But you'll get arrested,' I stammered. 'You'll get yourself killed, or sent to prison for life.'

She shrugged with such elegant self-confidence. I wanted to touch her but didn't dare. 'The fear of death and unhappiness are two more absurd European obsessions,' she said.

I felt a surge of angry frustration at her ability to make me feel inferior, as though I were a child again and girls were sniggering at me behind my back. My own teenage children had had the same infuriating habit of discounting my years and undervaluing my experience. It was not that they were particularly offensive, simply that they made it coolly plain in the full strength of their adolescence that they considered my opinions old-fashioned and completely irrelevant. What was so annoying was their *certainty* that I was already redundant and my wisdom was merely middle-aged prejudice or tired compromise. In fact their polite condescension had been one of the reasons I had decided to change my life so drastically and be born again. Why hang around when even your own children consider you to be irrelevant? That would teach them. That would make them sorry. And yet hadn't I done precisely the same to my own father? In later years he had seemed to have little to teach me, to be a man from a different age. I had watched him grow old and weaken without compassion because youth is selfish about infirmity and wants the old to die. In my vigorous adolescence it had seemed that my father had fulfilled his function and it was time he moved on, and the end of my need for him seemed to make him shrivel and lose his pride. The young are not cruel, but they lack imagination. 'You'll understand one day,' my father had said to me, 'when you have a family of your own.' But I had thought he was a senile old fool and never had understood, not with my own children, not until now, and it had needed the child of another man from another time to teach me. My wife had known it, that a man must believe in himself whoever he is and whatever he has been. 'Why are you so afraid of growing old?' she had asked. 'What scares you so much?' I had never until now had the guts to face up to the answer: that I was appalled that I might be treated by the young with the same dismissive contempt that I had given the old when I was young myself. 'I loved being young,' my wife had said. 'I love being a wife, and a mother, and I shall love being a grandmother, and then old, and then dying. Why are you so afraid? Each age should be enjoyed and savoured. Each age is like a different new life, almost a reincarnation.' But I had despised her cosy acceptance of fate and rebelled against the inevitability of decay. Like a child myself I had cried silently: *Why me? Why should I get old so fast, and wrinkled, and tormented by twinges and aches and breathlessness, and despised by the sort of youth I once was myself?* And so I had destroyed my marriage as well as my father, and somewhere along the way I had mislaid myself.

The girl beside me stirred, moving her right ankle over her left. Some ignorant over-educated European woman on the screen was prattling on about test-tube babies and sperm banks and clinical mating for perfection. Apparently a team of rich Nobel Prizewinners had been paid even more money to wank into glass phials to provide neurotic women with master-race children, and she approved. 'Eventually men will become completely unnecessary,' she was saying, 'and once cloning has been perfected we could allow them to become extinct. My dream is of a world inhabited only by women, strong but compassionate. Only then will the human race be able to progress.' I wanted to smash her supercilious face in. The headman's family was nodding and pointing at the screen.

'You despise me, don't you?' I stammered.

The girl looked thoughtful. 'I need notice of that question,' she said.

I had never fallen in love with a mind, an idea, before. No, that's not quite true. When I had been about her age I had fallen in love with the idea of love itself, and at least by now I know that's a great mistake. I had mooned then over two or three girls with a sentimentality that was selfish narcissism rather than real affection.

The wizened old woman turned her face away from the TV and towards us with an angry expression. 'Shhh!' she said.

'Sorry,' said the girl.

I laughed, and then so did she.

I slept that night on a mat on the hard earth in the corner of a mud hut, with chains chafing my wrists, and did not stir until one of the headman's chickens came pecking around me soon after dawn. Had the old man cast a spell on me as well? It was more likely to be the beer. I woke with a throbbing head and a repulsive tongue but also an optimism I had not felt for too long. Perhaps this was precisely what I had yearned for when I had chosen to be born again: to experience again the raw, unstable emotions I had buried so long ago, the excitements and miseries of euphoria alternated with depression.

Despite the pain of the chains and my eagerness to be released from them, and the meagreness of the breakfast they served me – cold maize porridge again and some goat's cheese and a bottle of warm Coca-Cola – I lingered over the meal, loth to move on up the mountain just yet. Despite my hangover, despite the sharp clear honesty of the tropical daylight, she looked more beautiful than ever. I had never met a girl with teeth and eyes and character so clear. She wore a red ribbon in her curly hair. For her Marxist guerrillas? Or for me?

'They're very civilised up at the army camp,' she said. 'The colonel was a Rhodes scholar at Oxford and went on to Sandhurst and he could probably charm the pants off a white fascist lesbian. He'll treat you like royalty and quote Shakespeare if you like, and tell risqué jokes. But he's an absolute shit.' Her eyes went dull.

'It's charming plausible bastards like him that have betrayed this country. But we'll get him eventually. One day we'll get them all.'

I had always hated Marxists, and despised their blindness to the fact that no Communist society has ever resulted in greater equality and happiness for the people in whose name the revolution has been made. But here there seemed to be no choice. The only way these people would ever loosen their own chains would be by bloody insurrection.

'Are the guerrillas a real threat to them up there?' I asked.

She shrugged. 'Not yet, but they've got them worried. The camp is like a fortified castle, and they run it like a monastery.' She laughed bitterly. 'Which is pretty ironic when you consider the place was once an expensive boys-only boarding school under the colonialists. It was probably just like a monastery then, as well. Twenty years ago my grandfather worked up there in the school as a servant. A waiter! Small white children called him 'boy' and 'kaffir'. And now my brothers and cousins from the village are all incarcerated up there, press-ganged into the army, and the officers still sneer at them because they are peasants and call them 'boy' and 'baboon'. It's not all that different.'

I felt a tremor of excitement. The army camp was once a school? My stranger had come from these parts. Thirty years ago he might have spent his formative years up this very mountain.

'Does your grandfather remember many of the boys who were there then?' I asked.

She chuckled affectionately. 'Many of them? He remembers the whole blasted lot, every snivelling, snotty-nosed white kid who passed through there in forty years.'

I felt a curious sense of peace, of rightness. Instinctively I knew that the stranger had been here and that the old headman must remember him.

'It's amazing how nostalgic he is about those days,' she said. 'The whites treated his generation like dirt and yet he talks of the good old days as though it was a golden age.'

'For him it was. He was in the prime of his life.'

She looked sharply at me. 'It just underlines how much he has been betrayed by our present rulers,' she said. 'Even though he's old and weak now life should still be better for him than it was then. But it's not. He actually believes it's worse. Give him half a chance and he'll reminisce for hours about white children who have never given him a thought in decades and probably didn't ever know his real name. He's even kept some newspaper cuttings about a few of them: one who went on to become a politician, one who's an actor, another who's an author, and a boy who ran in the Olympics. They way he talks about them you'd think they were his own children instead of the children of fascists who used and exploited and despised him.'

'Maybe they weren't all bad,' I ventured hesitantly. 'After all, he'd hardly remember some of them with affection if they were all monsters.'

'They exploited him,' she said savagely. 'They didn't beat him or torture him but they tried to undermine his pride and culture and traditions. Oh, they were paternalistic enough. They gave him their cast-off clothes and a paper hat and cracker at Christmas. But they thought of him as no more than a pet dog.'

'Didn't they bring hospitals? Railways? Schools?'

'Only to suit their own purpose. If you keep a dog it might as well be healthy, intelligent and mobile.'

'I don't disagree with you,' I said, 'but there are usually two sides to any story.'

'I can't afford to believe that,' she said. 'If I did I would never be able to change anything. We can't afford to be decent and liberal any more.'

'Nice guys don't win?'

'They don't even try.' She stared at me with a teasing expression. I wondered whether it was possible to fall in love with a black child you had known less than a day. No. I didn't believe it. Once as a boy, but not now. 'Shall I tell you what happened to the last nice, kind, decent, liberal headmaster up there when it was still a school?' she said softly. 'The guerrillas came out of the bush one day and attacked it. The headmaster tried to reason with them. They raped the school matrons, the nurse, and the teachers' wives, in front of the boys. He still tried to reason with them, so they took half a dozen of the masters out onto the playing field and shot them one by one, in front of the boys. He brought out his Bible and tried to reason with them. They beheaded him.'

I was stunned. Had my stranger been there as a child when it had happened? Did it explain anything, perhaps his suicide years later? And surely she couldn't approve of such savagery, however much she hated what the Europeans had done to her people.

I imagined the boys lined up beside the soccer pitch in their school blazers with golden crests on the pockets and uplifting

Latin mottoes and the terror of watching Matron screaming as wild men mounted her on a clear sunny day and then old Stinks the science master and the others dragged towards the goal posts, and bloodstains on the turf. And then the Head, beheaded. And when the guerrillas had gone, the desolate silence of the place, ghosts in the library and echoes in the Hall where they once put on Shakespeare plays, and in the classrooms blackboards still chalked with vulgar fractions and cheeky slogans like *Watkins loves Mamselle*. And now no more Latin, no more French, no more sitting on the hard old bench. No more ragging on the stairs, no more crapping after prayers, no more horsemeat in the stew, it's end of term for me and you.

'Don't tell me you approve of what they did,' I said.

'Of course not,' she snapped. 'That's the whole point. The rational liberal was executed, but the leader of the gang is now in the Government.'

I had to know now. I couldn't delay any longer.

'I must ask your grandfather about a boy who may have been at the school about then,' I said. 'He might remember him.'

'Oh, he will,' she said, 'if he was ever there.'

We found the headman sitting under a tree wearing his sun helmet and watching the women working and singing in the meagre fields, bent low from the waists, their buttocks thrust at the sky. A mangy dog squatted beside him, panting in the heat, and now and then he flicked at the flies with a whisk.

I asked him if he remembered the stranger as a boy. He frowned and was silent for some time. We waited as he travelled back through the years, sorting through the cells of his memory, recalling names and young white faces and long forgotten triumphs and disasters. Occasionally he smiled.

'About twenty-five, thirty years ago,' I prompted.

He scowled, and we waited some more.

Eventually he nodded. My heart was beating unaccountably strongly. So the stranger was still alive at least somewhere, if only in one cell in the brain of an old black man in the tropical bush beneath a granite mountain.

The headman grinned, congratulating himself. His teeth were sharp and crooked but his pleasure blunt and straight. 'Small boy,' he said. 'Shy, afraid of big boys. Quiet. But clever. Oh yes, many brains. Always reading, writing. Actor, too, Shakespeare play often. And scholarship to big school. Headmaster give school holiday when he win scholarship. Yes! Head Boy also. You see up there.' He gestured towards the mountain. 'They keep old books. You find his name there, in books.'

The school records. Would the army really still have them? I felt an increasing excitement. If I could find the history of his childhood among the old school records I felt sure I would find some clue. Look for the child and you will discover the man. The Jesuits know.

'Ha!' The headman laughed. 'Yes! Very clever, but no good sports. Head Boy, but never in football team. Too small. Also very bad swimmer. Once almost drown.'

I shivered. Was somebody standing even now beside the stranger's grave? Or looking at my own? My old self had drowned too.

There was one more thing I had to know.

'Was he there when the . . . murders happened? When the Headmaster was killed?'

The headman looked at me sadly. There seemed to be guilt in his eyes. 'No,' he said quietly. 'Gone before. Gone scholarship.'

I felt a tweak of disappointment. I seemed to be no nearer an answer. The truth chided me for wanting a glib explanation, that the stranger had been scarred for life and driven to suicide by one terrible childhood trauma. But the truth is never that impure and simple.

'I must go now,' I said. 'I must go up the mountain.'

'The spirits protect you,' said the old man.

I had no money, and would not have risked offending him by offering him any. Whatever his granddaughter believed, the whites had never broken his pride. Even in his sun helmet he had dignity.

'You've been very kind,' I said.

'It is our custom,' he said.

I shook his hand. The chains jangled and the dog cringed.

'Go in peace, bwana,' he said.

'Bwana!' said the girl angrily, 'Jesus Christ!'

She took me to my horse. Standing beside it she looked so fragile and delicate it was difficult to believe her strength of character and opinions. She helped me mount, holding the horse while I struggled against the chains. From the vantage point of the saddle I thought she looked pathetically vulnerable. I wished I could protect her, and wondered how long she had to live before they arrested and raped and shot her too. The modern feudal barons who ran this fiefdom now could surely not afford to let her live. Or perhaps her beauty might just save her. Perhaps she would pawn her body to some powerful politician or general in exchange for protection. I felt a jab of jealousy, not merely physical but childishly at the thought that she would one day come to need someone who was not me.

'You'll be back in the twentieth century up there,' she said lightly. 'They're really terribly civilised, even though it really is just like a monastery, all puritan earnestness and dedication. They've got colour TV, videos, stereos. They even have washing machines and golf clubs. The only thing missing is women.'

'That seems very sensible of the army,' I joked feebly. 'A girl like you in a place like that could cause havoc.'

'And let loose the dogs of war.'

I was afraid for her.

'How old are you?' I said.

'Twenty, I think. They never registered my birth. Does it matter?'

It's not just policemen getting younger that remind you of the passing years: it's children turning out to be older than they look. Pat a boy on the head these days and you discover too late that he's already a father.

'I wish . . . .'

I hesitated.

'What?' she said. The red ribbon lay in her hair like a trickle of blood.

'I wish we had . . . .'

'Yes?'

'I'd have liked more time . . . .'

She smiled. 'Wouldn't we all?'

'I mean, more time to get to know each other better. Properly.'

'Yes.'

I had not felt so gauche since adolescence.

'I feel . . . .'

She patted the horse's neck. 'I know,' she said. 'But we'll meet again, somewhere. Somewhen. The ages are against us this time.'

Suddenly she loosed the red ribbon, and tied it firmly to the horse's bridle. 'Take this,' she said, 'to remind you.'

I rode up the mountainside like a medieval knight going into battle with his favour fluttering on the breeze. I didn't dare to look back. The chains were making my wrists bleed, but the ache in my throat was worse, and I had not even touched her once.

7

Noe more than a childe were I when first I entered ye monasterie to be prentic unto a pedant monk in loco parentis much given to learnyin and grately wise in astrologie and letters. Freshe of face were I, redcheekd and fayre, and much confused by separation from my dam for never had I been aparte from harthe and famyly and so atte first I wept much for manny days in grate bewilderment as a pup dragged too soone from its bitche. I wept for ye coldness of ye place, ye dirt, ye damp, ye thinness of ye gruel, ye echoing empty halls, ye odours of boyhoode ordure, ye foul words and proud boyhoode farting. I hadde with me a token of mine infancie, a softe pillowe embroydered by my dam, and this I clutched in sorrowe, wettyng it wyth teares, sitting aparte and small and startled as a kitten. In manhoode since have I revisitted ye monasterie and were amazed to discover it so small yet in childehoode it hadde towered about me grate and gray and colde and damp wyth corridors boomyng fearfull crys and jestyng of ye older prentices. It hadde seemed then a veritable dungeon, a torture chamber fashiond for mine own especial torment, and for manie months I were deepe in miserie. During ye passage of every nyte for severall weekes in slepe I wetted my bedde from nervousness and each morn were thrashed for doing soe by ye chamber monk, a fearsome felloe of gleamyng ey and sturdy arme who scornd et mockd mine unwittyng feebleness.

Fye boye, art thou a gurle? he sneerd, and soe ye older prentices tooke up ye cry, A gurle, a gurle! untill my teares flowd freshe again and free + my tormenters jeerd and calld, She weeps! See the maidens teares! I wolde have fled that place had I ye courage but I were puny and ye land around about ye monasterie were hostile with warryng bandits and wilde beastes, and feare preventd mee.

Tis sed such suden threats in childehoode do mould or brake ye future Man yet this I doute for in my case I trow nor one nor other came to pass for I were bowd notte nor hardend but rather did but endure and reckon ye days and weekes and yeares. Ye threats and jeers of ye other prentices causd me to become wary and secretif, taking refuge in silense and carefull warchfullnesse & voweing to give noe offense. I considerd wyth grate care before I spake and sometimes stammerd soe that anon my gentleness arousd compassion in ye breste of one of ye oldest prentices, a boye of onlie twelf yeares butt alredy given to scrapyng his chinn and cheekes wyth pumice. Upon one eve he came upon me in ye chamber by ye chapel where others were tauntyng me and threatenyng to remove my breeches and painte my tiny privates withe some noxious mixture and hee being senior to them alle et set in a position of power over us he bad them begone and they obeyd, as fearfull of his power as I of them.

Come, childe, sed he in a voise thatte boomd and squeakd alternately with pubertie, why dust thou take their torments soe without complaynte? Strike back, for then they wolde respecte thy spirit and leaf off their persecution.

In shame I wepte agen.

Art thou a coward? askd hee.

I nodded my assent and he to my surprise did onlie larf and rest his hande upon my shoulder. Come then little Coward, sed he, I shall protect thee and learn thee braverie for it is onlie thy youth and smallnesse of stature that preventeth thee, and indeed he tooke me into his care, appointyng me his serf and learnyng mee each day ye arts of combatt. My tormentors, seeyng ye favour in wych he helde me, still jeerd and calld me gurle and weaklyng butt dared not attack me further for fear of his wrothe, and soe as ye monthes passd my protector, may ye Lord blesse him, prepard me for ye daye when he would leave ye monasterie and I would needs defend myself alone without his care. I came to love him in my boyysh fashion and he to take a gruff delyte in my softe childishnesse and oft times wolde fondle me in ye privacie of is chamber wych did confuse me yet wych did give him much plaisir.

My feeble stature and my cowardise conspired against my successe in ye prentices games, and I were never grately accomplished nor in fleetnesse of foote nor archery. Yette in learnyng I made swift progresse, pleasyng my monkish pedant master oft wyth my egernesse and growyng connaisance of Greke and Lattin and my pleasure even in numbers and asstrologie, which tidynesses much appeald too me. I gorged my hunger for learnyng as iff it myte tame ye wilde unreason of ye worlde and gif to lyfe some forme and meanyng.

Wee shalle make a scolar of thee yet, mie boye, sed he, and soe I believd, for learnyng were much to my taste and I found a pryde + refuge in bookes et knowyng more than others that lessend for me my cowardise tho stille my tormentors, among them ye biggest and ye dullest wittd, would crie gurle, and worme, and pedants pette soe that I vowed eventual revenj if not upon them in their own persons then anon upon ye verie worlde itselve from wych I promised myselve acclaim and fortune in God's own tyme.

Dullwittd tho they were their crie of pedants pette were justyfyd for my master tooke much plaisir in my progresse holding me uppe before ye others as an example of industrie and selectyng me for choise assynmentes. In chapel from a tender age hee orderd mee to syng wyth ye quire and to rede from ye Testaments wych I didde wyth a clere and pleasyng voise, wyth nor stammer nor stumble & in the revells I oft playd ye Abbott or ye Lord of Misrule, fyndyng in their dysguises a freedom of act I colde nott indulj in mine owne small lyfe. My pedant monke urjd me to wryte verses and to illumynate them and oft atte eventyde after vespers he wolde lerne me ye lute in ye privacie of his owne cell where we wolde raise our voises in song, he wyth soreing tenor, I trebble, in harmonie. He also I came to love, mine owne especial pedant, for he learnd me more than any other in alle my lyfe, a parfit gentil manne of grate aje, being certes ten and twenty yeares, who learnd me love of wordes and hate of harshnesse, seeyng mayhap in me a shadowe of his owne gentilitie. I vow he were the gratest manne I ever new nor never will, yet no more than monk and pedant, such is the worldes rewards, yet he content in his dutie and care of the young and in his own unheralded sygnyfycanse. I trow he also bore me love wyth courtlie gallantrie, he being wythout wyfe to bere him sonnes soe that I became for him a sonne, notwythstandyng that he compared oure affection wyth that of Arthur for Sir Lancelotte, wych pleasd me.

Yett there were a pryce to paye for his approvall for he were much envyd and dislykd by ye Abbott, a manne of much lesser learnyng and grate coarsenesse of minde and soule tho sed to be powerfully versed in witchcraft, who were jealous of my pedant and his devotion and punishd me whenever ye chanse arose, beatyng me anon for failure. I believe my pedant tooke my parte wyth the Abott in much heate on occasion to defend mee but such intrest onlie goaded him to greater furys and revenj soe that once I were beatn thryce in a syngle day, for wych trialls I were anon exceedyng gratefull synce ye site of my bruses silensed wyth awe even my tormentors, for whom paine were an indycatyon of fortytude.

Soe there I grewe as ye yeares passd, sufferyng both joye and hardshipps, pleasure and sorrows. My stature remaind smaller than moste soe that I needs must develop a certain agile wyt and cunnyng to deter my persecutors and tho I were badly beatn by them the very daie my protector left ye monasterie to make his own waye in ye worlde I did stryke back as he hadde taut and gave some account of myself before I were heavyly bloodyd and carryd to the dispensarie there to lye for severall days, where myne own fond pedant came bye and bye to sitte wyth mee.

Ye worlde is full of such tryls, said he comfortyng, and thou wilt learne that many menne will hate thee and envie and scheme agaynst thee for no greater sinne than that thou art not as thay. Yet noe this, boye: however they and ye worlde assault thee they can never bruse thy soul, soe long as thou keepest it pure and true to thyself. Evil menne haf never yet devisd a scheme to stele a pure soul, nay, not Satan himself, not even sholde they put thy flesh to death. For ye sole that is strong and clene is as a quiet sanctuarie in a castle wyth impregnyble walls and mote and drawbrij, and a sole that is filld wyth a love of learnyng can never be stormd, but remayns as stille and strong as a librarie in ye midst of Babel.

Even now I noe notte how true he spake, for I have sinse encountered pedants et scolars whose cold aloof remotenesse chilleth ye blood, yet in my ignoranse and love of him I accepted his teachyng and builded a barrier between myself and ye worlde and a rampart about my mynd soe that none myte invade it, nor manne nor womanne, nor ecstasie nor grief, soe that when I wed I were pleasd rather than happie and when my dam dyed I wepd much but felt little grefe. It hath givn me a protection from lyfe that hath servd its purpose for never agayn have I been brutally assaultd by fere or miserie. Even my prentice persecutors at ye monasterie desistd then, content to have beatn mee soe, and for me to have givn them some weke account of myselve and puzzld by my newe tranquillitie.

My new demeanour servd me well as my older tormentors in turn quitt ye monasterie to join ye worlde and as ye yeares passd I too rose to a position of power over younger prentices. Ye pedants prevaild upon ye Abbot, wyth much grumblyng, to appoynt me Chefe Prentice in my finall yere at ye monasterie and my name were engryvd for enternitie in ye chapel record. By som straynj turn that plase that had givn me such feare and miserie were now as a gentil haven from ye worlde for beyond ye walls of ye monasterie were fearfull battels rajing, barons and mersenarys sette agaynst each other, sitys burnd, churchs sackd, dams ravajd, babes slaughtrd. My scolarshippe now become soe grate my fayvryt pedant beggd me to renounse ye worlde and staye wyth hym safe in a cell of mine own and shielded from ye plagues and wars that rajed beyond ye walls, but tho I were temptd by so tranquill a proposition I dreamd of wenches and dyce and bear-baytyng and falcons and hawks, of tapestrys and profane music, and new that for me a lyffe dedycatyd to monkish learnyng were a betrayall.

I must depart, quoth I, in tyme to take my plase in ye worlde and rayd its plaisirs. I be notte as godly as thou nor tranquill.

But thou art a scolar, sed hee.

Nay, nay, quoth I, merely blessed wyth a small talent for vers and memorie and cunnyng. Ye true measure of thy teachyng hath bene to lerne me to obey mine own nature and be true to mine own self and noe longer to fear ye worlde nor seke sanctuarie from lyfe. There be tyme enow for that in ye grave.

What wilt thou do? he enquird wyth sorroe.

Why, sir, I jested, I shall sell myself to some grate lord to plaie amanuensis and live in soft bondij and I shall wryte verses and wed and sire sonnes and win acclaym and ryches.

Then I have fayled, sed hee. Unto what end wolde you do alle this, my sonne?

Unto Death, sed I, noeyng notte wyth what swift prescyence I spake, for that verrie nyte a drunken rabble armie brake into ye monasterie blasfemyng and destroyng ye holie relicks et treasures, befoulyng ye chapell, ravishyng ye youngest prentices. Here be a pritty gurle! cryd one hairy soldier of an especiall softe childe and his brutysh felloe sots took up ye crie A gurle! A gurle! and one called, She weeps! See ye maydens teares! Ye monks huddld close in fear and impotense doing nought except for mine own especiall pedant who feeblie venturd to reason wyth ye brutes and were slayn for his paines wyth suddn carelesse horror, his aged gray head contaynyng soe much wysdom struck from his shoulders wyth a staynd sword as tho it were noe more than a dandylyon. In that terror and ye smell of drunkn swete I were a childe agen hydyng agen in horror at ye worlde, weepyng wyth feare and grefe, tremblyng and bewyldered wyth damp about ye breeches. In my harte I cryed out for my dam as ye soldiers swore et buggerd et grunted et fartd and in my mynd there arose an hellysh visyon of ye future of Mankinde: of a worlde enslavd by creatures intelligent yet ruthlesse and inhuman wyth mynds of cold clere reason yet bodys of nor fleshe nor bloode and souls of metall.

Privyly I stumbld awai from my childhoode intoe ye chillie nyte fleeyng on foote across ye harsh lande lyke an huntd beste wyth flaymes in a lyne across ye skys and prayers for ye glorious sole of mine own especiall pedant.

REQUIESCAT IN PACE.
DOMINUS ILLUMINATIO MEA.
Amen.

(2)

The army's training camp was perched on the top of the mountain like a medieval castle and it looked almost as impregnable. There were no turrets or drawbridge or portcullis but four tall watchtowers stood at each corner, armed with machine guns and searchlights and connected by vicious rolls of barbed wire coiled in triplicate behind a ditch six feet deep that encircled the whole site, except for the only entrance where a high double gate was guarded by a very black officer and half-a-dozen tough-looking soldiers. As I rode towards them with chains clanking at my wrists the officer gave a hoarse command and six rifles pointed smartly towards me. Out of the corner of my eye I saw machine guns in both the nearest watchtowers swivel towards me. She had been right. I was very glad I had not attempted to arrive at night.

'Halt!' cried the officer.

I was still at least a hundred yards away but I wasn't going to argue.

'Who goes there?'

Either he had been to Sandhurst too or he had read all the right war novels. So had I. 'Friend,' I called. Did anyone ever say 'foe'?

'Dismount!'

I did. The chains rattled loudly in the bright clear silence of the mountain air, echoing across the valley.

'No sudden movements!' shouted the officer. 'Or we shoot!'

I stood without daring to tremble.

'Why are you in chains?'

'I was captured by . . . .'

'Speak up, man! We can't hear!'

I raised my voice. 'I was captured by bandits,' I yelled. 'They were going to kill me but they got drunk first and I escaped at night.'

'Where?'

'Towards the coast. A day's ride away.'

He pondered a moment. 'What is your name?' he shouted.

I told him and then realised that in my apprehension I had given my old name and not the name I had taken from the stranger. The weapons still gaped at me, eight metal beasts with sixteen hollow eyes. I prayed that none of the soldiers was as nervous as I.

'Age?'

For a moment I hesitated. For some reason I simply could not remember.

'Age!' he bellowed.

Then I remembered.

'Address?'

I gave him my old one. This time it seemed safer to tell the truth. For all I knew they had computers in the place that could check within seconds.

'Occupation?'

I told him.

'What are you doing here, then?' he demanded.

'I'm on holiday,' I said. 'A sort of sabbatical.'

'There are no beaches or brothels here, man,' he boomed, with a trace of amusement.

'Not that sort of holiday,' I said.

'What's your business here?'

I was getting fed up with all this shouting but it didn't seem wise to display any irritation. 'I need to be released from these chains,' I called. 'They tried to free me in the village down in the valley but they couldn't.'

'This isn't a blacksmith's,' he shouted. 'Ride on by!'

She had said they were civilised up here. Ride on by? Where the hell to? In the beating sunlight the chains were burning the raw flesh on my wrists.

'I'm in a lot of pain,' I shouted. There was an annoying whine in my voice. 'The chains are making my wrists bleed.'

'What do you think this is? An out-patients' department? The Red Cross? Ride on by. Follow the road north. There's a town twenty miles away. You'll get help there.'

'Twenty miles?' I was definitely whining now. 'I'll never get that far with these chains on my wrists.'

'I said ride on!'

'I'm also looking for someone.'

'And you've found someone, man. Me. Now ride on! This isn't a missing persons' bureau, either.'

'I was told the colonel . . . .'

'You know the colonel?'

I hesitated. Was it a chance? I wasn't going to risk it. When eight guns are grinning at you the truth seems the best policy. 'No,' I said.

'Then ride on! That is an order!'

I nearly wept with frustration. The sun by now was high and hot, my wrists stabbing with pain, and the prospect of another twenty-mile ride through the bush unarmed and manacled was appalling.

'This is ridiculous,' I wailed. 'Look, I'm unarmed. Hurt. I'm not dangerous. Why not search me? I only . . . .'

He bellowed an order and to my horror there was a fusillade of bullets on each side of me, missing me only by a couple of feet, raising clouds of dust and ricocheting off granite rocks. The horse reared in terror, wrenched the rein out of my hand and it took two terrified steps, screaming, before collapsing on the ground.

'Christ Almighty!' roared the officer. 'You stupid fucking bastards. Some stupid fucker has killed the fucking horse!'

They searched me roughly and marched me through the gate towards the sprawl of long·low buildings beyond the parade ground, where hundreds of soldiers were drilling and being put through an obstacle course. Two rifles kept poking uncomfortably at my ribs and the officer strode in front, his baton firmly gripped between elbow and body. Except for the goalposts on the playing fields you would never have guessed that this had once been an exclusive boarding school. Barbed wire and sandbags guarded buildings that had once been classrooms and what had probably once been flower beds were planted with vegetables. The whole place was ferociously tidy, the stones beside the paths and roadways immaculately painted white, the national flag lying limp at the top of a pole that had probably once borne the school's own badge and motto. Armoured cars and jeeps were parked neatly in front of a building that was probably once the school hall, and beyond the chapel, which still carried a cross on the roof, there stood a helicopter. The colonel's office was guarded by two of the biggest men I have ever seen, both armed with grenades and bayonets. I trembled to think of the girl in the village below and her hopeless dreams of yet another revolution. She and her friends had no chance against men like these.

'Halt! Wait!'

The officer knocked on the colonel's heavy wooden door and paused, nervously stroking his hair with his hands.

'Come!' called a muffled, cultured voice from the other side of the door and the officer marched smartly in. 'Sir!' he yapped. 'Begging your pardon, sir!'

'Very well, captain, what is it?'

'An intruder, sir. A European . . . .'

The door closed behind him, muffling the conversation so that I heard no more than a low buzz of voices. The soldiers each side of the door stared coldly at me with baleful eyes, their bayonets gleaming in the cool gloom, and two rifles were still pressed into my back from behind. I hoped to God none of them sneezed. *The colonel is civilised*, she had said; *he'll welcome you like royalty; he could charm the pants off a lesbian.* Perhaps he was less amenable with men.

The door opened. The captain was standing to attention. 'Enter, prisoner!' he yapped.

I went forward, trying to control the jangling of the chains.

'The intruder, sir!' snapped the captain.

The colonel looked up from behind his desk, a slim fit-looking man in camouflage battledress and appearing far too young for such a responsible job. It's not just policemen and children whose ages are confusing: it's soldiers too.

165

'Forward, prisoner! Halt! Attention!'

I stood before the desk.

'Thank you, captain,' said the colonel. He looked at me, and seemed mildly amused.

'Sir!'

'Very well, captain. That'll be all.'

'Sir?'

'That'll be all.'

'But sir!'

'Yes?'

'The prisoner, sir.'

The colonel smiled. At least the man seemed to have a sense of humour. 'I doubt whether he will try to attack me,' he said. 'You may have noticed that he is manacled, captain. He is also unarmed.'

'Sir!'

'So that'll be all, captain. You may go.'

'Sir!'

The captain saluted, turned smartly and marched out. The door closed behind him with a loud thud.

'Dear God,' sighed the colonel. 'Hollywood has a lot to answer for. Relax, my dear fellow. Take a pew. I expect you could do with a stiff drink. Sherry? Scotch? Gin?'

I started laughing, a touch hysterically.

I sank into a large leather sofa and he poured me a very large scotch from a cut-glass decanter and handed me a chunky tumbler engraved with a regimental badge. His movements were smooth and languid and yet they seemed merely to disguise an energetic alertness that simmered beneath the easy, relaxed manner. Sandhurst had done its job well. I only hoped he had made the right decision and joined the right side.

'Cheers,' he said. 'You must be gasping.'

'Aren't you having one too?'

'No, but that's no need for you to feel guilty. I can't drink. I'm an alcoholic. So the next best thing is watching someone else destroying his liver.'

I took a long slow mouthful. It was superb, one of the more expensive malts, and even the chains fell silent as though with respect. The warmth flooded my stomach and veins with well-being and relief. She had been right. This was a world as different from that of her village as the whisky itself would not recogise their native ale as being even a distant relation. The colonel's desk was broad and polished and had three telephones, his office was covered on one wall with maps and on the other three with bookshelves from floor to ceiling. One window overlooked the parade ground and the valley and the hazy horizon towards the coast, the other faced inland towards distant and higher purple mountains with their peaks hidden in cloud. A teleprinter stood silent in one corner, a huge TV set, radio and computer in another. The colonel's office was an oasis of civilised sanity in a desert of brutal ignorance for miles around. He and the village headman just down the mountain had nothing in common except their colour and perhaps a similar feudal dignity. Both would have thrived as medieval barons.

The colonel sat on the edge of his desk, swinging a leg and looking critically at me. 'Those wrists of yours don't look too clever,' he said. 'We've got a chap here who's marvellous at picking locks, and I'll get him in as soon as we're done and then we'll have one of the medics to look at you. You don't want to take any chances and risk infection. There are some pretty nasty bugs around in these parts, but don't worry – we've got plenty of the right drugs and things. You'll be fine.'

My eyelids pricked with gratitude and I might have embarrassed us both by weeping with sheer relief after the horrors of the past few days had I not taken another swig of whisky. His strength and decency marked him out as a man to be admired. He reminded me of someone, but I couldn't remember who it was.

'You've been through hell, haven't you?' he said. 'Want to tell me about it?'

I told him the absolute truth, right from the start, and I had no qualms at all. He was nothing like the woman interrogator down at the coast, and I simply did not believe that he would need to betray me. Why should he? His position here was so strong that he could afford to show mercy. It is weakness and fear that breed brutality. He listened in complete silence, merely nodding now and then or shaking his head, except when I told him about my arrest and death sentence down at the coast. 'Savages,' he said. 'They're all savages down there. They simply don't know the meaning of freedom and independence.' Once he topped up my whisky, and as I reached the end of the story I felt cleansed. A burden was lifted. Perhaps religious people experience the same comfort and gratitude from going to confession.

He thought for some time when I had finished, but the silence between us was warm and companionable rather than tense or threatening. For the first time in days I felt completely relaxed. Even my wrists seemed now only to smart, as though they knew that soon he would make them better. I had nothing to worry about here in this shelter, this sanctuary, and I had no decisions to make. He would make all my decisions for me, and the lifting of that responsibility and the whisky made me feel cheerful and carefree. For a few hours at least, maybe for a few days, I could let go of my life. I was no longer required to be in control of it, and the sensation was glorious. I began to understand why long-term prisoners hanker to return to jail. Not all of us are strong enough for complete freedom. Freedom is a messy business, untidy, unsure, and many of the most contented people are those in some sort of bondage: children, monks, soldiers, recidivists, women with dominant men. The silence of the colonel's study was the mellow calm of the cloister or the nursery.

'I think you're one of the bravest men I've ever met,' said the colonel eventually.

'Me? Brave?'

'Absolutely, old chap.'

I laughed. 'I'm afraid of heights, and closed spaces, and if I ever found myself in a battle I'd be paralysed by terror.'

'Nonsense,' he said. 'Everyone knows physical fear, but you'd be amazed at how people react in battle. It's often the cowards who fight the bravest because they're terrified of being thought cowards. But to gamble with your whole life in middle age, to give up your comfort and security and habits and prospects, to throw everything away and change your life – that's courage of a very different order. Most of my men want to go back to their wives and families, not leave them. You're either insane or extraordinarily brave, and I don't think you're insane. If I had an army of men like you I could conquer the world.'

I felt already that I knew him well enough to joke, even about his colour.

'A black Napoleon?' I chuckled.

He looked at me sternly, and then grinned. 'Maybe,' he said. 'Or perhaps a technological Shaka, king of the Zulus.'

168

He had style, strength, humour and decency. Who was it that he reminded me of? And why had such a man been given command of such a remote camp? Was it because the place was really so sensitive and important to his government? Or because they feared him and needed him out of the way? A man of his calibre at loose in the capital would have terrified the politicians. He was a natural leader, a modern headman. No wonder my teenage girl down in the valley feared him so much. In different circumstances she would have worshipped him.

He sat in the swivel chair behind his desk, picked up the green telephone, and ordered one of his soldiers to report to him.

'The locksmith,' he said to me. 'He'll have you out of those things in a jiffy. He was a bank robber in civvy street. Very useful chap. We get all sorts in the army. One of my blokes used to like dressing up in women's clothes, but he's an absolute whizz when it comes to make-up, disguises and camouflage. A bit temperamental, but a bit of a genius. Can't let him dress up as a lady here, of course. Could cause all sorts of problems. Other chaps a bit sex-starved. But I make sure he gets lots of leave. Wouldn't like him to have a nervous breakdown.'

The ex-bank robber appeared, looking as nervous as if he were trying to break into Fort Knox. He produced an implement from a bag and had me free in twenty seconds. The manacles fell to the polished floor with a dull, beaten clunk. I stretched my arms wide, flexing the muscles and wrists, and held them there as though I were about to be crucified. Some freedoms are well worth having.

'God, that's marvellous,' I said. 'Thank you.'

The soldier saluted smartly and left.

'Did he manage to pick your pocket?' asked the colonel. 'He does sometimes, just to keep his hand in. We have to make him give things back.'

I smiled. 'I've only got an old handkerchief on me,' I said. 'The guards at the coast stole everything else.'

He shook his head irritably. 'I don't understand those savages down at the coast,' he said. 'They don't seem to understand that freedom requires discipline, self-control and a strong sense of duty. Rousseau was wrong: in fact Man is born in chains but everywhere nowadays is far too free. We need less self-indulgent freedom and anarchy and more restraint. Those barbarians down at the coast seem to think they're still living in the Middle Ages, and what's so annoying is that they give the rest of us a bad name.

Because of backward idiots like them the world is beginning to think we're all vicious, incompetent and corrupt. We're going to have to sort them out one day. Send in a few tanks, perhaps. Can't have them queering our pitch all the time with their thoughtless brutality.'

I felt exultant with a prospect of revenge. I thought of him rolling down to the coast at the head of a conquering army and meting out justice to my tormentors there.

'When you get there,' I said, 'don't forget the judges and the Chief Interrogator.'

He smiled bleakly. 'They're always the first to be shot,' he said. 'And now, old chap, I'm going to have to get on with some other things, but I'll see you at lunch in Hall and in the meantime I'll get the captain to pop over to the san with you to get the medics to look at your wrists, and then you could probably do with a decent kip. We've got a spare VIP suite you could use for a day or two while you look through the old school records to see if you can find any trace of this chap of yours who was here.'

'You've still got them?' I said, amazed.

He looked serious. 'I thought it only right,' he said. 'The guerrilla massacre was disgraceful, just the sort of pointless brutality you'd expect from those barbarians down at the coast. So we've kept all the school records, books, trophies and honours boards in the library as a sort of museum, a token of regret and repentance. It's not just sentimentality. It's a constant reminder to the men that we will no longer tolerate medieval brutality in the twentieth century. I'll tell the library orderly to let you see whatever you want, and you're welcome to stay as long as you need.'

This man was a miracle. In Ancient Rome they would have made him a god, and I would have voted for him. And still I couldn't remember who it was that he seemed to resemble so strongly.

'Till lunch, old chap,' he said, 'and I'm sorry about your reception here, and the horse. We'll have to find out who was responsible for that and make sure he's never so stupid again.'

'No, please don't . . . .'

He smiled. 'My dear chap, the culprit expects it. He needs it. He must be punished. You can't run a place like this without firm discipline. Humanity is vital, but discipline comes first. The whole world needs more of them both, but discipline and duty are

170

paramount.' At that moment I would have done anything at all that he asked.

I stayed at the camp for three days and nights and wallowed in the luxury of having others to take care of every need. It was like being back at school again but without the frustrations and torments of childhood. Shrill bells rang to tell me when to get up in the morning, when to attend meals, when to go to bed, and although there was no need for me to obey them I took pleasure in accepting the routine and willingly binding myself to the soldiers' timetable. It is not only soldiers, children or monks who derive an odd comfort from a firm routine and regulations: as the colonel had said, almost all of us have a deep subconscious need for restrictions and a sense of duty and discipline and would become restless and uneasy in conditions of complete freedom and anarchy. Look at the sorry mess the very rich and completely free so often make of their lives.

The soldiers slept in the old school dormitories and queued in silent lines for meals. They gathered in the Hall every morning and the chapel each night. Each day they studied English, geography, law, politics and military tactics in the old classrooms, with a midday break for milk and buns, and each afternoon they played football on the school playing fields or had shooting practice where once small boys had built hideouts and hunted each other with catapults, or they went swimming in the pool. At night there were film shows and club activities, and Lights Out at ten o'clock. I felt warm and secure in this cocoon, safely protected from the random madness and brutality of the real world outside, and it was strangely reassuring to live for a while in a society without women. The school sanatorium was still used as the camp's sick-bay, and the smell of ammonia and starch conjured up the ghost of the school Matron who must have once run it: unmarried, nun-like, probably ugly, almost masculine, brisk and no-nonsense in crisp white uniform but gruffly loving towards her small charges, worried each term by the usual childhood plagues of mumps, measles, jaundice, chicken pox. I hoped her ghost was not alarmed by the small black major who ran her little empire now, for she too had been raped and slaughtered during the guerrillas' massacre so long ago.

Did the spirits of their terrified victims still haunt the school quad where the invaders had corraled them, or the football pitch where the headmaster and his staff had been killed? In the early evening, as the tropical sun died swiftly in a blaze of garish changing colour, I sensed in the heavy silence of the corridors a presence of unseen shadows and unheard screams, and I shivered with the chill feeling of fading ancient memories and the damp monastic must of the chapel at night. Behind it was a mass grave where the guerrillas had dumped the bodies. It was marked now by a simple white stone engraved with more than a dozen names and the line 'Requiescat in Pace'. I stood before it one evening with bowed head and prayed that they were indeed at peace, that it was only my imagination that sensed them flitting with horror and bewilderment through classrooms and dormitories filled with men of a colour always to haunt them in their restless eternities. Can the dead be haunted by the living? Are there ghosts from the future as well as from the past? I remembered the story of the man who had suddenly come upon the ghosts of four young soldiers in First World War uniforms, standing singing silently around a piano in a country house. One of the ghosts had looked up, seen him, and pointed. The other three had stared at him. 'A ghost?' said one of the ghosts loudly. 'I don't see anything.'

By contrast the old school library was calm and snug, as though somehow it knew how privileged it was to be the last quiet refuge in a noisy military camp which itself was a sanctuary from the surrounding desert of ignorance and barbarity. There for three days I rediscovered the discipline of study that had given me so much pleasure as a child, the hunger for learning and knowledge, the need to make some sort of sense of the baffling inconsistences of the world. Among the military biographies and studies of warfare and tactics they had kept many of the old school library books: *Swallows and Amazons*, Biggles, *The Wind in the Willows*. I could not resist wasting a few hours turning their grubby pages at random and was overwhelmed by nostalgia for my own youth and an almost physical whiff of liquorice sticks and sherbert, linseed oil, blackboard chalk. I have never been one of those who pine for the past and believe that your schooldays are the happiest days of your life, but there in the library for half a day or so I remembered with sweet pain the best of those days when I had still been too naïve and innocent to be untrue to myself and had lived without guile or pretence like a small animal, often helpless and bewildered, even frightened, but always honest. Why is it that as we grow older we strive to be other than we are and begin to wear increasingly uncomfortable masks and play increasingly unlikely parts? I had lied too often not only to friends and colleagues, people I hoped to impress, but to my wife as well, and my children, and even to myself. I had tormented myself with trying always to be decent, successful, nice, bland, and I had eroded my marriage by expecting too much from myself as well as from everyone else. Even my decision to change my life and be born again had been based on a lie: I knew now that I was unfitted for this sort of 'freedom' I had chosen, and that I had deceived myself by thinking that I might ever be. I had fooled myself then into thinking I had been hiding from the world, and in fact I had been hiding only from myself.

I saw the stranger's name almost immediately. On one wall of the library there hung the old school honours boards, long slabs of darkened polished wood glittering with gold lettering record-ing the names and years of long forgotten little boys and appropriately shaped like tombstones. One of them listed the names of Head Boys, another those who had won scholarships, and his was on them both, fading now after thirty years. I felt a shiver of recognition, almost of pride, and then a deep melanch-oly to remember that his name was also engraved on a tombstone thousands of miles away across the sea.

For two more days in the library, watched by a frowning black orderly and a loud notice yelling SILENCE, I thumbed through copies of old school magazines, reports, records, newspaper cuttings, that had survived the barbarians' invasion even though their authors and subjects and way of life had failed to survive. There is an immortality in words and paper, and a powerful affirmation of human achievement and dignity in listening to the silent voices of men long dead. I was strongly conscious then of the truth that Man is not a fallen angel, as the priests and monks would have us believe, but a risen ape whose strivings and occasional triumphs are truly awesome against the background of his animal nature and ancestry. The priests spread despair and helplessness with their guilt-infected, Death-worshipping in-sistence that Man is a feeble, sinful angel cast out from the Garden of Eden and foredoomed to failure. I preferred to believe that because Man is in fact no more than an ape the world should glow with pride at the greatness of which the ape Man is occasionally capable, and the pinnacles the beast can reach.

The details of the stranger's childhood history do not matter: not the subjects in which he excelled, not his own small triumphs, nor his defeats. What mattered to me was the confirmation of his existence and the evidence of the similarities between us. I felt very close to him in that quiet little library. Had he handled some of these very books and magazines? Instinctively I knew the answer was yes. He had sat in this place, and walked these corridors, and dreamed of seeing his name upon these honours boards. These walls and hills had moulded him, but the secret of his tragedy did not lie here, I knew.

'I've discovered where he lived,' I told the colonel on the third day. 'His home was only a few miles away, up in the mountains.'

'And you must go to it.'

'Yes. I need to see it, and take him back to it. Then we can both rest.'

He didn't even blink. He understood.

'And then,' I said, 'I shall return where I belong, with my wife and children.'

'And face the music? They'll send you to jail.'

'Yes.'

'And she'll probably divorce you. Then you really will have nothing left.'

'Yes.'

He stared at me. 'You're even braver than I thought,' he said.

'I'm brave enough now to accept my own nature, my own cowardice.'

'No man can be braver,' he said. 'But there's one risk you don't have to take. You'll need transport, and protection. The guerrillas control the mountains, but you'll be okay if I send you in a convoy with an escort and a couple of armoured cars. I could spare a couple this afternoon, if you like.'

'You're very kind.'

'Not kind,' he said. 'I'm repaying an old debt.'

I knew now who he reminded me of. My own headmaster had been a man of quiet strength and honour, and I think I had loved him more truthfully and honestly than I have ever loved any woman. He had always aroused in me a knowledge of the possibility of achievement, whereas women had always aroused a fear of failure and an uneasy threat of suppressed violence. It had been he who had first taught me as a boy of the possibility that

174

greatness may lie in men of small apparent accomplishment or worldly recognition. When I came to leave his school he told me he had failed to teach me only one thing: that humility is a vital virtue and that no man can ever be great until he learns properly how to apologise, and it had taken me more than thirty more years to begin to learn.

The guerrillas attacked the convoy when we were ten miles or so from the school and climbing a track into the mountains towards the cloud-line around their peaks.

The first armoured car was blown off the track by a huge landmine explosion and it was obvious that no one would emerge from that alive. The second car – my own – was bombarded with howitzers and grenades and swerved off the track into the bush before crashing into a tree. As we struggled to climb free the first man out was shot through the head, the second cut in half by machine-gun bullets. The third soldier and I looked at each other. 'If I fight they will kill us both,' he said. 'If I surrender they will kill just me. You are safe. They do not kill white men now.'

'Then we'll fight,' I said. 'Give me a rifle.'

The colonel was wrong. Cowards are not brave in battle. I was terrified.

The soldier shook his head, shouted in a local dialect, was answered from outside, and climbed from the car without his weapons and with his hands high. I waited for the sound of his end, but there was silence, and then a guttural voice calling to me.

'White man! You come! You safe!'

I held both hands high and emerged from the armoured car. There were at least twenty guerrillas. Was my girl among them? Of course not. None of them wore a ribbon in his hair. Three of them were roughly tying the hands of the only surviving member of my escort, but the others were immobile and expressionless, living robots, mechanical men of flesh and blood but souls made out of metal. They would not understand compassion. I stood with my hands up. The guerrilla leader motioned two of his robots forward. Their hands were all over me, searching with sharp mechanical efficiency. They found nothing.

'Why you here?' said their leader. His eyes were streaked with yellow and in my fear he seemed more like a gorilla than a guerrilla. My throat was dry. I tried to swallow, but there was no saliva.

'I'm a tourist,' I said.

He looked at me as if I were mad. 'Tourist? No tourist here five, ten year. Where you go?'

My life seemed to depend on whatever I said in the next thirty seconds.

'A friend of mine used to live up this mountain many years ago,' I said. 'He was born here, he was a child here, but now he has died in my country, a long way away. He killed himself, so his spirit is not free. So I bring his spirit back, to his home, so he can rest. Then I will go home too.'

The guerrilla leader stared at me. My pilgrimage was the sort of medieval quest one of his own people might once have undertaken, perhaps still would, but I could see the disbelief in his eyes. *The tragedy of you Europeans is that you've lost your spirituality*, she had said, my girl with the red ribbon. Did he believe that too? Did he also despise us, and refuse to accept that a white man could possibly return to a dangerous area on a mystical mission like mine? If he didn't believe me, I was dead.

I forced myself to speak. I was leading my own defence on a capital charge. 'The army killed my horse,' I said, 'because at first they thought I was an enemy. Then they gave me protection, these soldiers, to take me to my friend's home.'

'Where this friend home?'

I pointed up the road. 'It's called Travellers' Rest,' I said.

He nodded. 'I know, I seen.' He hesitated, and lit a cigarette.

'You like army?' He was almost conversational, as though chatting at a cocktail party. It would be so easy to say no, to accuse the colonel and my comforters of injustice and brutality, and to win a tawdry approval. The last of my escorts, his hands tied behind his back, was looking at me. There was no expression at all in his eyes.

'Yes,' I said. 'The army's been very good to me. They killed my horse, but then they took me into their camp, and fed me, and looked after me.'

I looked up beyond the branches. The sun was so high and hot the sky was not blue but a sort of washed-out off-white. I was very afraid of the pain of dying, but it would probably be over quickly, and I was grateful. I had had a much better life, and a longer one, than 90 per cent of every risen ape who has ever been born since

the beginning of time. In the long history of Man so very few have
even reached 40, let alone lived in comfort and security and still
been free enough to choose to reject them. Most of us forget just
how bloody lucky we have been.

The guerrilla leader made up his mind. He nodded. 'You go,'
he said.

'Go?'

'You free. Go.'

'Free?'

'So! You speak true. If you are said you not like army, you be
lie, we kill you. But you speak true. I see true in you eyes. They
soft, like monkey. So you go.'

'Go where?'

He shrugged. 'Up for friend, down for army, you go where you
like. You free.'

I gestured towards the tied soldier, who had probably saved my
life. 'And him?'

'We kill. Now.'

'No,' I said. Could I save another life as well? Was I asking too
much? I had to try. 'I beg you,' I said. 'He saved my life. He is a
brave man.'

The guerrilla leader flicked his cigarette stub into the dust at
his feet, and stepped on it. Beneath his boot an ant was probably
dying without knowing why. Perhaps God is just a massive cosmic
boot.

'We not want brave mans in this shit Government army,' he
said.

'Then keep him prisoner,' I said. 'When you win your war
you'll have him on your side. You'll need brave men then.'

'No prisoner. No food for prisoner, no guard.' He spoke almost
gently. 'You go, white man. This not you fight. You lose you fight
already.'

It is not good to be treated with contempt and to be considered
worthless and irrelevant, but then he and his forefathers knew
that already.

'He understand, this soldier. He know he have to die.' The
guerrilla leader laughed. 'Maybe he come back again soon as
baboon, or white man.'

I looked at my saviour, the condemned captive, for reassur-
ance. He gestured with his head for me to walk on up the
mountain track. Like so few of us he accepted that we are all

condemned, only he was going to die a little sooner than the rest of us. I wanted to thank him, but didn't know how.

I turned and walked away, past the two bodies beside the armoured car, past the wreck of the first armoured car with its shattered corpses inside. I was free and yet captive. Helplessness is so difficult to accept. In childhood we understand it, but we come to forget.

From behind me there came the sound of a single shot. I didn't look back. I didn't need to, and I know now that looking back is always a mistake.

8

(1)

1. And it came to pass in those days that a child moved weeping across the land without father nor mother, which were slain by bandits. For the tribes had risen in revolt and taken up arms the one against the other, and great was the slaughter and sorrow thereof and rending of clothes and gnashing of teeth.

2. So feeble were the child in its woe and hunger that it crawled upon its four limbs, and lay upon its belly, like unto a beast of the field, wailing for suck.

3. The beasts themselves marvelled at such a sight, and the apes made great chatter at this mystery whereby a son of man should crawl again upon the earth as lowly as a serpent.

4. Lo, they cried, the son of man is reduced and weak and lords it no more over the earth. Is it not right that we, who also go upon two legs, should inherit the kingdom of man?

5. And the apes advanced upon the child, intending to beat it and stone it to death, but the child in its feebleness saw not apes but cried out in despairing hope as bitter as aloes, Father, Mother, and the apes fell back in wonder and were sore afraid.

6. Now there was among them a she-ape of great years and wisdom who counselled them closely, saying, O brothers, O sisters, hear me:

7. For whosoever calleth me Mother is truly my child, and whosoever harmeth my child must first reckon with me. And she gathered the child to her breast and gave it succour, soothing its

cries and tempting it with wild fruits and nuts and sweet waters.

8. Now among the apes there were those much given to disputation, that asked, How can it be that an ape may be mother unto a son of man?

9. And among the apes there were those much given to reason, that asked, How can it be that the child also cried unto her, Father, yet she be no male?

10. And among the apes there were those much given to levity, that cried, Lo, the child is surely of the same kin as she, for both are passing ugly.

11. And among the apes there were those much given to envy, that cried, Why should she alone have a child that is hairless?

12. And among the apes there were those much given to sloth, that asked, What doth it matter?

13. And among the apes there were those much given to violence, that said: Kill them both.

14. So the she-ape fled in the night with the child, notwithstanding the greatness of her age nor the weakness of the child nor its lack of years, and they journeyed slow across the land, hiding by day, crawling by night, hunted by apes.

15. And there were abroad in the land in those days preachers that spake fine words and wrung their hands and did nothing.

16. And it came to pass in the fullness of time that the child and the she-ape reached the place where the child's father and mother had been slain by bandits, but the child knew it not, for its eyes failed dim unto darkness, and it cried again, Mother, Father, and the she-ape comforted the child though being herself weary unto death.

17. Birds of prey perched, abiding their time, knowing. For there were no life there, only desolation, charred corpses, smouldering timbers, blackened earth crusted with blood, and

the she-ape carried no memory.

18. In time they fell into a deep slumber and there chanced that way hunters, whether apes or men or gods it is not written, and they took a mighty anger to see an ape with a son of man, and they killed them both, which is why that place henceforth has been named Olduvai, the place of the ape-man.

19. But verily it is written: both she-ape and child still live, for we know their history, and the hunters destroy in vain, and the birds of prey will tarry until eternity, for wheresover there is remembrance, there can be no death.
Amen.

(2)

I trod on the snake in the mist of the jungle, just above the cloud-line, near the top of the mountain.

Fangs in my leg, vicious pain. I saw the eyes. There was no hate in them, just surprise and fear, and a strange, entrancing beauty. The snake was only fulfilling its destiny.

I can't write. The pain is horrid. It burns. I feel like a baby and also like a very old man. My eyes are getting dim. I sucked the snake-bite but it hasn't helped. The lights are going out. Ah, mother, mama. Help me, mummy. It's so sore. Make it better.

I've dragged myself into the stranger's house. It's a rambling ruin with broken windows, cool once with verandahs and breezes but now gloomy with overgrown vines and creepers in the drawing room and tropical weeds sprouting monstrous from the walls. I can see the sky. The roof has fallen in. The quiet is like Sunday afternoon.

There was music here once, and laughter, and clinking glasses. A baby grand piano stands rotting in one corner, with mushrooms growing on it. Mummy used to play the piano, and we used to sing. I was safe then. She smelled so good, and her smile made me warm in my tummy. Her eyes were green. She used to call me her little monkey. She told me the secret of life was to love myself, and then I would love other people and love the world. I never learned. How can you love yourself when you're someone like me?

Mama, help me. I've wet myself now, and yet I feel old and tired and ready to die. There are animal droppings on the faded old carpet. Two huge insects are mating on the mouldy sofa. They have lovely green stripes down their backs. Once the whole world was like this, just insects and plants and no people. Perhaps one day it'll be like that again.

They read a lot, too. It was cosy when they read, Daddy with his pipe, Mummy with her funny glasses on the end of her nose. I used to curl up next to her, smelling her warm. The world lasted for ever, then.

There are books here, too, lots. I can't see their titles. Have they got *Nineteen Eighty-Four*, Chandler, Pepys, Shakespeare, the Bible? I think they probably have, because I seem to know this place. It's like coming home, and I can hear voices that have been dead for years. I'm coming, Mummy. Reading made Mummy very wise. She told me how lucky I was to be born, to breathe, to smell, to see the dawn and the sunset. She said that billions and zillions of people who might have been born never were. I wish I had listened to her. There are framed photographs on the shelves, but the faces are blurred, and delicate Royal Doulton figures smashed by small animals in the night, and a silent clock on the mantelpiece that says 2.22 or 3.33 or 4.44. I knew a place like this once, and I've dreamed of it ever since. And the stranger is happy to be home. He's somewhere here, I know, and I know now too why he killed himself because at the far end of the room there are two human skeletons lying on the floor, their bones picked clean by rats. Their skulls are smashed.

I'm so tired, and old. My bones ache. I want to go to sleep, Mummy. But I'm so thirsty. Can I have a drink before I go to sleep?

There's water in front of the house like a dark lagoon. I will go and drink and then go to sleep. I can see the water beyond the front verandah. It's frightening but also exciting. Its eye is green like a woman I once loved too long ago.

My leg is swollen so big now I can't walk. If only I had a walking stick or a wheelchair. I'll have to drag myself to the dark lagoon. Maybe the water will kill the poison in me. Naughty snake! I should've smacked it.

Maybe I'll find a boat on the lagoon. I seem to remember something about a boat the last time I died, and there was water when I was born.

9

The waters are quiet and warm. He floats just beneath the surface, his knees drawn up to his head, his arms crossed. He is blind, dumb, wet, helpless, but so he was before. Primeval sounds penetrate from somewhere beyond the waters, distant murmuring, rumblings. They seem to hint that something momentous is about to happen. He can only wait and drift like sea-wrack. Shadows flicker in the ooze, like fish or memories or premonitions. Perhaps it is all over, or perhaps it is only just about to begin.

He smiles.